SCREAMING BEAUTY

"Just as spellbinding as the first… and then some! Five stars and two thumbs, way up!"

One Guy's Guide

"I have been looking forward to this book and the author didn't disappoint… If you like fairy tales with a twist, this series is for you!"

The Literary Vixen

"This is probably the best fantasy book you're going to read this year, let alone in your lifetime. 1000/10 recommendation."

AnnaJ, reviewer

TALES FROM THE
POISONED APPLE
BOOK TWO

SCOTT MOONEY

OWL HOLLOW PRESS

Owl Hollow Press, LLC, Springville, UT 84663

Screaming Beauty: Tales from the Poisoned Apple Book Two
Second Edition
Copyright © 2022 by Scott Mooney

First Edition — 2020 by Bleeding Ink Publishing

Library of Congress Cataloging-in-Publication Data
Screaming Beauty / S. Mooney — Second edition.

Summary:
When a malevolent curse invades the dreams of the sleeping princesses across the Apple, spreading nightmares and violence throughout the city, Briar and her friends must journey to the penthouses of the Upper East Side to wake the princesses and save the Poisoned Apple.

ISBN 978-1-945654-94-7 (paperback)
ISBN 978-1-945654-95-4 (e-book)

For Grace Jacobs,
Whose beauty never screamed,
but instead called us into our own.

ONCE UPON A HAPPY HOUR...

I was at a horrible cocktail lounge in the Financial District, trying to keep my eyes from drooping. The sweaty investment banker in front of me had been droning on about himself for the last ten minutes, and my patience was thinner than the wispy moustache clinging to his upper lip. He'd told me his name, but honestly his voice was so monotone my brain had barely even registered it—Thurston? Thaddeus? Something like that.

"—because the thing about these older firms is, they don't have a grasp of the intricacies of the truly burgeoning growth sectors. Do you know much about the Asian markets?" Tristan paused to take a breath to fuel his next diatribe, rather than to listen to anything I had to say.

"I love Asian markets. Only place you can get legit kimchi," I said, finishing the last sip of the old fashioned that had cost half as much as my mattress. Thompson had offered to pay for it, but accepting *anything* from him wouldn't have been worth it. "Now, if you'll excuse me."

I practically ran away from poor, boring Thurgood and scanned the busy, multi-level bar for my friends. It was all sharp corners and lacquered wood, and whatever chic aesthetic they were going for apparently didn't include hand rails, so I stepped slowly as I took a staircase down to the main floor.

It didn't help that Jacqui had made me wear a ridiculous electric blue pantsuit we'd found in a Bushwick thrift store. It hitched up when I walked and got me more than one wide-eyed look from the assorted consultants and traders around me. On the plus side, it had badass shoulder pads.

I finally spotted my two best friends / housemates at the corner of the bar, going shot for shot with a pair of spindly guys in ill-fitting suits. I gestured to them frantically, and they extricated themselves from their company with a fit of giggles.

"Briaaaaar!" Jacqui squealed, her normally graceful gait turning into a tipsy clomp. "This is so ridiculous! Can you believe those two drunk twenty-three-year-olds manage a hedge fund worth four million dollars? The economy is *so* messed up." She let out another giggle and swayed a bit on her heels. Somehow, even drunk, Princess Jacquinetta D'Lucien Ardor's regal bearing was not diminished, and she looked completely at home in her blazer and blouse amongst New York's jet set. "Also, what's a NASDAQ?"

"No one knows," Alice said with an air of fake solemnity. She'd gone for a green-checkered dress that was slightly too fashionable for this cultural void of a drinking establishment, and her choppy black hair would never have been approved by corporate HR. She took a quick nip out of the flask she'd hidden in her owl-shaped purse.

We'd been planning this night for a few weeks, to celebrate Jacqui's first night out now that her curse had been removed. She had this fascination with businesspeople and she desperately wanted to observe them in their natural habitat, like drunk anthropologists. A few thrift stores later, we were barely passing as acceptable members of capitalist society.

A princess, a maid, and a Free Spell walk into a bar…

"You guys wanna go to the Woodsman's Log for trivia?" I asked hopefully. Being around this much money was making me twitchy. "First round is on me."

Thankfully, Jacqui shrugged in agreement. "Yeah, I think I figured out all this investment stuff anyways. Buy low, smell high. *We get it*." She flipped her long, wavy blonde hair over one shoulder dismissively.

"Sweet," I said, already feeling better. "You know, we're sort of by Battery Park. They opened a new Door there a few weeks ago…" I let my voice dangle.

Alice grinned indulgently. My friends know how obsessed I am with trying out new ways to get around the city. "Fine. But only because I feel sorry for you in that pant suit. You look like Smurf Hillary Clinton."

"I'm taking that as a compliment. Onwards!"

I slammed the doors to the street open with relish and let the cool September air whisk away any lingering stench of day trad- ers and dividends. The wet breeze off the river led us a few blocks south to Battery Park; framed by the old stone buildings of downtown on one side and the water of the Hudson River on the other, the open space felt like we were finally escaping the tightened fist of Manhattan. The park was still crowded in the light of the setting sun, but everyone was enjoying the good weather too much to give me side-eye for my ridiculous outfit. We split off from a crowd of commuters trying to make the next ferry to Staten Island and walked next to the railings by the edge of the water.

The path we were following was dotted with whimsical statues of cartoonish cats and little men in top hats. Alice drifted to a standstill, pausing to look out over the water at the Statue of Liberty, distant but still magnificent. "You know, when I was younger, back in North Dakota… that cocktail bar would've been my dream. Rich people, fancy clothes, strong drinks…" She looked over at me and smiled. "It's funny how that's all there is for some people. That's their happily ever after."

I returned her grin. "I think I prefer ours."

"Hell yeah. Magic beats money any day of the week."

Jacqui turned to face us from farther down the path. "Are you bitches coming or not?"

I snorted and waggled my eyebrows at Alice. "Our fair princess calls. C'mon."

A little way down the path, a series of huge log posts stuck vertically out of the water, some holdovers from the time this was all a harbor and Alexander Hamilton was still alive and rapping. I counted three posts in and then motioned at my friends to stop. Tilting my head, I used the posts to perfectly frame a row of buildings across the water.

"Whatcha doin'?" Jacqui muttered.

I nodded in the direction of the view. "Look closer."

She squinted for a moment, then her eyes widened as she broke into a goofy smile. Instead of seeing the line of New Jersey office blocks and construction sites reflected in the water, there was a shimmering image of thatched-roof cottages, ramshackle witches' towers, and a looming castle of white stone. A passing boat broke the surface of the river into ripples, adding to the otherworldly beauty of the sight.

The vistas of the Poisoned Apple never disappoint.

As I stared, I noticed the railing in front of us was different from those around it. The sheen on the metal was slightly off, like it had been doused in petroleum. What looked like random scratches or engraved initials, on closer inspection, formed into the grooves of looping sigils and complex runes. I walked closer, feeling the thrum of the magic inside the gate start to drown out the bustle of the people in the park behind us. Soon, the light and noise of Battery Park began to dim, as if we were in a giant celestial spotlight, separating us from the everyday world of the Manhattan evening.

"Well, they're certainly pulling out all the stops for this new Door," Jacqui said, sniffing the air. Every so often, she still pulled out a mannerism that was a holdover from the year she'd spent cursed to live in a cat's body. One nibble from a cursed muffin basket, delivered with my name on it, and she'd had her whole life put on hold.

But she was right. The amount of power it took to mask our disappearance from the middle of Battery Park was much more than your average spell. I guess even the magic in the Financial District is swanky. No doubt some well-connected fey had pulled strings to make this happen.

The gate opened of its own accord when we got close enough, leading to a set of stairs on the other side that definitely weren't there thirty seconds ago. The smooth stone steps were wide enough for all three of us to spread out on, leading us straight down into the choppy waters of the river.

"…are we supposed to *swim* to the Apple?" Jacqui said, her Royal haughtiness somewhat lessened when she ended the sentence with a whiskey burp.

"There must be a trick. They wouldn't expect—no one would use a Door that required a dip in the Hudson."

Alice shrugged, and Jacqui looked unimpressed.

Well, this was *my* idea.

I climbed down the next few steps and paused on the step above the water. I was wearing black ballet flats—I'm tall enough that heels make me go from being impressively statuesque to crashing through Tokyo skyscrapers. The water sloshed around beneath me, an oily residue on the surface that definitely didn't look magical.

Sometimes you gotta just close your eyes and kiss the frog.

I gasped as my foot hit the water, only it wasn't water. Not exactly. I felt all the pressure I was expecting, of sloshing liquid pressing up against my bare ankles. But it wasn't cold, it wasn't wet, it was just… substance. The waves pushed up and down my ankle, but when they retreated, my skin was as dry as before.

"Guys," I said, "you've got to try this." I took the next stair down, and another. To my eyes, it seemed like I was waist-deep in the latrine that we call the Hudson. But to my other senses, it just felt like a slightly warm mass was surrounding me. Supporting me, even.

The steps ended when I was about armpit deep in the dry liquid of the spell. The dusky lights of Manhattan danced in the distance, dimmed by the magic surrounding us, and waves from the now-departing Staten Island Ferry nearly knocked me off balance. There were another few yards of solid concrete, and then my feet found an edge. Beyond the platform was just… nothing, and I could feel a slight current in the water, pulling me down.

Alice giggled as she came up next to me, her dress swirling around her body as she moved, weightless in the water. "This is like the world's best ball pit," she said over the crash of the current.

"What do we do next?" Jacqui asked, her drunken exuberance dulled by the sublime strangeness of the situation.

I looked around. There was only one way to go.

"I think we take a deep breath and make the jump," I said.

Alice and Jacqui looked at each other and shrugged. Alice might have rolled her eyes. I gave them a mock salute and stepped off the edge, like a paratrooper in a blueberry-colored pantsuit.

As soon as the water covered my ears, everything went silent. The yellow glow of the skyline glimmered above me, the current pulling me gently downward. For a second, I felt my brain panic as the light began to dim and the darkness rushed up around me. A deep void stretched beneath my feet, the air pressing against the inside of my chest. But just as the pressure felt like too much, the strange, warm non-water around me seeped its way into my nose. It smelled like freshly cut grass and growing vines, and soon the soothing feeling filled my lungs. I gave a deep gasp of breathable non-air just as the water below me started to glow with blue light. The current didn't seem to be pushing me downward anymore, and I felt weightless in the light, womb-like pressure of magic encasing me.

Jacqui and Alice floated down to join me, their clothes drifting around them like some high fashion photoshoot. Soon, a part of the light in front of us formed into a hazy, indistinct archway of blue. We floated closer to it, or it floated closer to us, and soon it became another concrete walkway, identical to the one we'd left atop the Hudson, jutting out from a stone arch filled with shimmering blue light. My feet alit onto the concrete, and as I stepped forward, a faint, gurgling sound began to fill the silence. Growing louder, the noise become a rush of falling water, and I looked through the archway. What before looked like some CGI nonsense was now recognizable as blue daylight, filtering through a waterfall.

Only we were on the inside of the waterfall.

The three of us stepped through, the pressure feeling like a strange massage as we passed into the daylight. We were emerging from a water feature in a large stone fountain. Lily pads floated in the still water beneath our feet, and around us was a small courtyard, with a few benches and shrubs. Just to the left of the steps leading out of the fountain was a thick wooden perch, supporting a raven about the size of a Cocker Spaniel. He didn't deign to look up from the copy of *Neuromancer* he was reading.

"Welcome to the Poisoned Apple, where every journey begins with a single wish," he deadpanned. "Please enjoy your stay."

"Uh, thanks. We're locals," I said, shifting in my pantsuit. I was still completely dry, but I had definitely gotten a wedgie during that interdimensional voyage.

The raven coughed and looked down pointedly. A mason jar with a few coins sat next to a folded scrap of parchment, on which "Tips" had been scrawled out in talon marks. I sighed and threw him a dollar as we left the fountain and made our way out of the courtyard onto the streets of the Poisoned Apple.

EVERY CITY IS FULL of stories. That's what draws us to them. We thrill to know that just down the block, a young man is getting a text message that will irrevocably change his life. That in the apartment below us, under the soft strains of a Spanish guitar, a woman is saying "I love you" for the first time. That the young singer on the subway car next to us is in over their head, at a loss for what to do, and wouldn't change a thing. Put anything in front of the backdrop of brownstones and skyscrapers and it automatically becomes fascinating.

The Poisoned Apple is a city *made* of stories.

A trio of naga in glittering saris slithered past us, their warm laughter mixing with the sound of the cobblestones on their scales. A man in a leather jacket and a worn jester hat stood at the entrance to a skinny alleyway between two shops, his expression an invitation to some secret pleasure one couldn't indulge in out in the open. Above, a fluffy white griffin pulled a banner advertising carriage tires through the cerulean sky, weaving in and out of the towers and chimneys around us.

We were in Tuffet Town, one of the posher districts of the city, right outside the walls of Castle Fortnight. A few Royals even deigned to walk among us, leisurely making their way to the glitzy boutiques and day spas this area was known for. The winding cobblestone street was remarkably spic and span, and not a speck of graffiti could be found on the trendy shops we made our way past.

"I'm sending out a mass mirror," Alice said as we walked, her attention completely enraptured by the small, hand-held compact in front of her. "Who should I invite to trivia? Rick and Tarris, for sure, then…" She gave me an impish grin. "Cade or Antoine?"

I groaned. Over the summer, my roommates had gotten obsessed with manufacturing some dramatic love triangle to make my life hell. On one side, Knight Bachelor and annoying do-gooder Antoine DuCarr. On the other, rugged Red Hood scout and our fourth roommate, Cade Arden. In the center, me, Briar Pryce, wishing I had different friends.

"Antoine is great with any heraldry questions. He's a real asset to the team," Jacqui said, her voice dripping subtext.

"But they always have a sports category, and Cade knows jousting stats for the past thirty years—" Alice said.

"Invite them both," I said, turning to give them my most gorgon-y stare. "Because we are friends. I would enjoy hanging out with either of my *friends*."

They exchanged a look, and Alice went back to her mirror. As I turned and stalked off, I swear her cough sounded like "#TeamCade."

"It's not as subtle when you say the hashtag," I called over my shoulder.

The Woodsman's Log was a squat, multi-storied Tudor building that had expanded over the years and taken over the nearby businesses, creating a network of dingy basements, open-air balconies, shadowy private rooms, and mahogany-laden lounges. The ceilings were low, the drinks were cheap, and the floor was a level of stickiness rarely found outside of basilisks' nests and teenage boys' bedrooms. The bar wasn't a dive as much as a plunge.

I loved it.

Leaning against the balustrade of the Woodsman's wraparound porch were two of my favorite people in the Apple. Tarris Grimmour was underdressed for a Prince: his grey trenchcoat and periwinkle shirt were immaculate, but he had enough buttons undone to look more trendy than traditional. His blue eyes sparkled at something his boyfriend Rick was saying as they waited. Rick was a few years younger than me, but his boisterous enthusiasm marked him as someone who'd only recently moved to the Apple. He wore a cute green sweater vest that looked like it was finely spun bugbear hair and he had a sleek magic mirror clutched in his hand like it was precious treasure.

Tarris and I had met when his father, Count Grimmour, hired me to find Rick, who'd been kidnapped by none other than—*spoilers*—Tarris's sister Miranda. After I figured that out, shit hit the fantasy, a civil war almost broke out in the Apple, and a castle tower freakin' *fought itself.* So even though I'd just met them six months previously, it felt like we went way back.

Alice called out a greeting to the boys, and we did a round robin of hugs.

"You're dressed way too nice for trivia at the Log," I said, admiring Tarris's sleek Oxford shoes with faint glowing runes stitched into the leather.

"We already had plans when we got your message," Tarris said.

"We're going to a sidhe cabaret in SoLArca," Rick said, barely able to contain his excitement.

"But we wanted to swing by to say hi," Tarris said, smiling at his partner's enthusiasm, "and I was hoping I could borrow you for a second, Briar."

"Sure," I said as he led me away from the others. Rick began gushing about the revue act they were going to see, and it seemed like no one noticed as Tarris drew me aside, a serious expression overtaking his pale features.

"Any updates? Have you been able to dig up any leads on them?" he asked quietly.

He didn't need to explain who he was talking about. Miranda's plot against her brother was part of a larger plan she'd hatched to bring down the Multiarchy of Royals who ruled the Poisoned Apple. But she didn't organize it alone—she'd been helped by a mysterious group she referred to as the Arsenic Queens, who'd provided her serious magical backup. They were also the ones who'd turned Jacqui into a cat in an attempt to get at me.

The problem was, no one had ever heard of them.

I shook my head. "I've tried. I've followed up with every delivery service in the Apple, and none of them have records of the spells they sent to curse Jacqui or kidnap Rick."

Tarris groaned. "I've been going through all the Royal records I can get my hands on, trying to find any mention of them, or suspicious funds being diverted from the Multiarchy's coffers. But so far, nothing." He huffed and kicked his shiny shoes angrily at the ground. I could understand how frustrating the bureaucracy of Royal records might be; once up a time, there was just one King who ruled the Apple, but now there were dozens and dozens of Noble houses, sultanates, and duchies all jockeying for power. But for tradition's sake, we called all of the young people with Royal blood princes and princesses, just like in the Old Stories.

"Hey," I said soothingly, "it's okay. Maybe they're gone. Maybe they tried what they tried with Miranda and gave up."

Tarris ran his hands through his long blonde hair and fixed me with a stare from his luminous blue eyes. This close, I could see the grey circles under them from lack of sleep. "Do you really believe that?"

I hesitated, and that was enough for Tarris to pick up on. "Exactly. The longer we let them go without finding them, the longer they have to plot something awful."

"We're working on it," I sighed. "We can't find clues that aren't there. Be patient."

His fists bunched, and he stuck them angrily into the pockets of his coat. "I'm not going to let this go, Briar. These monsters radicalized my sister. They kidnapped Rick. He's still—" His voice caught.

Rick had been held in a cage for three days, taunted by cannibalistic mountain giants who'd planned to make him their dinner. For a Know-Naught, someone who was unaware of the magic underneath the world, it was a horrible introduction to the world of enchantments and monsters.

"How is Rick?" I said softly.

Tarris shook his head, his movements sharp and bitter. "He still gets nightmares. He'll wake up drenched in sweat, thinking he's back in that Grimmsdamn cage. He loves the Apple, and he's adjusting to it so well, but..."

Silence hung between us as a group of revelers bustled into the tavern behind us. "It's not even been six months," I said. "Rick's a strong kid."

"But he shouldn't have to be," Tarris said. "All of that only happened to him because he was with me."

"Cliché as it is, I have to say it, Tarris: none of that was your fault."

The smile he flashed me was tentative, and soon took on a slightly sinister edge. "I know, Bri. It was their fault. And I'm going to track them down and make sure they never hurt anyone again."

Before I could react to his sudden bout of vigilantism, Rick bounded over looking at his watch. "Sorry to interrupt, but we have to get going, babe."

It took him a second, but Tarris forced his face back into its usual cheerful elegance. "Sure thing. Just… think about what I said, Briar."

Rick's eyes narrowed with puzzlement, but he shot me his wide smile nonetheless. "Good to see you, Bri. We need to figure out a time all of us can do brunch at the Second Breakfast soon."

I squeezed his meaty shoulder before he and Tarris walked off. "Definitely. Enjoy the cabaret!"

Jacqui and Alice were already at the door to the Woodsman's Log. "Coming?" Alice chirped at me.

We made our way through the many nooks and corners of the tavern, dodging a gnome rugby team singing an incredibly vulgar drinking song and a slam poetry night that seemed to be catered to very mopey trolls. Trivia was held in a large stone annex on the backside of the building, on the other side of the outdoor patio. I think the annex used to be a church long ago; the wide, arched windows looked like they might have been stained glass once upon a time, before they'd been replaced after countless bar brawls. Now the interior was covered with concert posters, marker graffiti, and some strange, glowing runes that provided shifting amber lighting.

We approached a long, wooden table at the back that looked like it belonged in some ancient Viking drinking hall, already occupied by two men (boys? Boymen? Manboys? The mid-twenties are confusing). They were a study of contrasts, Antoine sitting rigidly straight in a tailored button-up shirt, Cade lounging in a pair of joggers and a hoodie.

To their credit, they'd reached some sort of détente in the six months since Antoine and I had begun working together. What started as some sort of macho pecking order catfight had petered out into a respectful-if-chilly distaste between the two of them, despite Alice's repeated suggestions that they "oil up and wrassle it out."

Antoine rose to his feet as we walked up, in some sort of polite gesture of etiquette that looked straight out of Downton Abbey. His smile was warm and genuine, and it lit up his chestnut eyes as I walked over to give him a *completely casual* side hug. Sure, the handsome knight and I had shared one spur-of-the-moment kiss after we'd saved the Apple from all-out chaos. But in the months since, we'd worked together on a variety of cases, with nothing more than a friendly embrace.

Speaking of which, I could feel Alice, Jacqui, and Cade stare as the hug went on just a breath too long. I extricated myself, one hand against the soft linen of his shirt. It was a light-brown gingham that probably set off his brown curls stunningly. If I were the kind of girl to notice those sorts of things.

"Nice pantsuit," Cade rumbled from behind me. "Did Sonic the Hedgehog put up a fight when you skinned him?"

I rolled my eyes, turned on him, and gave him a friendly slug on one of his meaty arms. As a Red Hood, patrolling the dangerous outskirts of the Afterwoods surrounding the Apple kept Cade in annoyingly good shape, and his tall frame made him the most intimidating guy in the room when he wanted to be. Usually he just wanted to crack jokes and eat nachos.

"Nice pajamas. Couldn't be bothered to put on real clothes?" I grumbled.

"They're called joggers and athleisure wear is really having a moment right now, you philistine," he grumbled in fake annoyance as we all settled down around the table.

Antoine gestured to a nearby server, who set down a tray full of flagons in front of us. After the thin, over-priced cocktails we'd had in the Otherworld, the frosty amber mead in front of me looked heavenly.

Somehow, I'd ended up between Antoine and Cade, so I had to constantly pivot my head back and forth as we chatted, getting all the casual small talk out of the way while we waited for trivia to start. Alice and Jacqui sat on the other side of the table acting like spectators at Wimbledon, watching as I talked Apple politics with Antoine and traded barbs with Cade.

Shit, were they actually right? Was I caught up in some teen drama bullshit?

Luckily, before I was able to come to any self-awareness, the rune light around us dimmed and a spotlight lit the ramshackle wooden stage on the other side of the room. Josefina Campbell, the Woodsman's Log's resident drag queen hostess, strutted onstage to the crowd's hoots and cheers. She was cosplaying as a sexy version of Donkeyskin, with patchwork fur just barely covering her. A stuffed animal donkey head dangled below her ample bosom and kept the costume from going full-on HBO.

"All right, dummies, quiet down," she said, her sharp eyes sparkling beneath the mock-scowl on her face. "It's trivia night, obviously, and you all are here to disappoint me yet again with the decline in public education standards. You know the drill, get your parchment out, no cheating, yada yada." She gave major side-eye to a table that was still murmuring as she pulled out a scroll of her own with a flourish.

"Time for Round One: Geography."

We all looked apprehensively around the table. Yes, we went to school in the Poisoned Apple, but we were still American; our knowledge of geography ended at the border to Jersey.

Josefina scanned the crowd with a superior smirk as she recited the first question. "Which famous Jazz Age hero led the first expedition through the Afterwoods to Drake Mountain? And, for a bonus point, how did the mountain get its name?"

Somehow, I'd been given the parchment and a pencil, which was laughable because my handwriting looks like a toddler attempting to write Nordic runes in a bouncy castle. It was always my least favorite job, having to make the executive decision of which of my friends was right and which were absolutely bullshitting.

"All right, well the second part is easy," Cade said from my right. "The cave at the base of the mountain has some sort of volcanic fissure that pushes out hot air, which the early explorers thought meant there was a drake nest inside the mountain."

"Really?" Alice said, cocking her head to the side. "I always assumed Drake was so rich he bought a mountain in the Apple with his Degrassi money."

"Cade's right, *mostly*," Antoine chimed in, a slight frost to his normally polite tone. "There are actually two caves at the base of the mountain," he said, as I hastily revised what I'd written down during Cade's monologue. "But as for the explorer… it was Sir Basil of Glaivesmill, wasn't it?"

Cade straightened up in his chair. "Actually, I know a lot of that area was charted by Lucian Lykos, the Red Hood ranger."

"Hmmm," Antoine said with a smile that had a few more teeth than his usual one. "Sir Basil was a Knight Explorer funded by the Crown—"

"Lykos had the advantage of his Red Hood training—"

"*Boys*," I chimed in, finally arriving at the answer. "Wasn't it Grav the Barbarian?"

Jacqui's eyes widened. "Oh yeah! Briar and I used to read a children's book series all about Grav and her adventures. *Grav and the Great Lich Caper, Grav versus the Sky Witch.*

"Yeah, the expedition to Drake Mountain was in *Grav and the Living Mountain.*"

To their credit, Cade and Antoine accepted our answer without argument, but still shot a few glares at each other while Josefina cleared her voice theatrically. "Our next category is Literature of the Italian Renaissance."

A collective groan issued from the crowd, but Josefina wasn't having it. "Quiet! Shut up, you ingrates. A certain fabulous diva got her degree in Classics and it might as well count for something. Now, who can complete this quote from Dante's Inferno: 'Do not be afraid; our fate cannot be taken from us; it is a…' what? What did Dante say Fate was?" She peered into the crowd expectantly as not a single person wrote anything down.

And it was in the confused hush that followed that all the screaming started.

Everyone in the room jolted. The yells were faint but seemed to be coming from all around us. All our eyes met, in that sort of horrible shared experience of something unexpected throwing the world out of kilter. The folks of the Poisoned Apple are generally pretty hard to rattle, but it wasn't every day the world turned into screams.

Finally, a girl with violent orange hair and pointed ears muttered, "Oh, for Freya's sake," and drew a wand. That one movement seemed to jolt everyone into action, and the twenty or so people in the room rushed outside. There were a few goblins smoking on the patio, but they were letting their pipes hang from their lips as they looked up at the sky in confusion.

It wasn't just one voice; it was dozens, at least. And it wasn't a unified, continuous drone; it was a mixture of short, sharp yelps over lower moaning sounds of pain. Each voice separate, distinct, and yet merging into a city-wide cacophony of rage and anguish.

And every voice was unmistakably feminine.

While the rest of us gaped, Alice had pulled her mirror out and began flicking the surface rapidly, summoning mirror messages and posts from all around the Apple. "Okay, it's being reported all over town… most reports coming from in and around Castle Fortnight." She paused for a second. "Okay, this is from one of my maid friends who's still in the castle, she says… it's coming from Princess Sumaya's room."

Jacqui's eyes narrowed in thought, as she ran through her nearly encyclopedic knowledge of Poisoned Apple Royalty. "Sumaya Olaad? It can't be. She's—"

"—asleep," Alice finished as she read the rest of the message. "She's screaming in her sleep. Sumaya has been under a sleeping curse for three years."

People in the crowd around us had taken out their mirrors as well and were sharing much of the same information.

"—has been asleep for two hundred years—"

"—Princess Morgana's eyelids are moving as if she's seeing something—"

"—like she's having a nightmare—"

I looked between Antoine and Cade, just like I'd been doing ten minutes ago when we'd first sat down. Between Antoine's connections with the knights of the realm, and Cade's position within the Red Hoods, they were both on call to deal with the strange and dangerous things that bubbled up in the Apple. They both looked back at me with steely determination.

At a certain point in life, you realize no one's galloping around the corner to save the day. That when things go to shit, someone needs to step up, and it might as well be you.

"All right," I said, resolve in my own voice. "I think it's time for me to go pick some flowers."

THE APPLE WAS TENSE as we made our way back to our part of town. Parents walked nervously, covering the ears of their children as the princesses continued to howl. The silvery wisps, who normally play a great game lighting the streetlamps across the city every evening, were flying tentatively from lamp to lamp, their glows dampened. A particularly enterprising ogre street hawker was already charging exorbitant prices for ear plugs he claimed were enchanted with the silence of freshly fallen snow. No matter what, there are always people ready to turn a crisis into a few bucks.

But even underneath the tumult, people were cautious, not panicked. Living in a world where anything can happen can be frightening, but in general, the Apple survives. At our hearts, we're New Yorkers with swords and magic wands. Whatever this new development was, we had dealt with worse, and between us all, we'd get through this, too.

At least that was what I kept telling myself.

Finally, we made it to the wide boulevard in Havmercy Park that led to our cottage. Maybe it was the impending crisis, but my shoulders always let out a little tension when I walk up the flagstones to our home. It's not pretty or fancy, just a jumbled plaster house with a thatched roof and more drafts than a hipster brewery. But in the three years we'd lived there, it had become my home, a place where my friends and I could talk and laugh and be happy.

Also, my bedroom has a bay window and there's no way I am going to find that anywhere else for the pittance we pay in rent.

We quickly set up our living room as a sort of situation room, just with more drying laundry and second-hand furniture.

Alice kicked her feet up on the cushy turquoise couch, sorting through mirror messages from the maids, footmen, and nannies she worked with at Castle Fortnight. Antoine and Jacqui paced around the living room, talking on their mirrors with their contacts among the Royalty. To keep track of everything, we'd gotten out our copy of the latest edition of the register of all the Royals in the Apple—it's thick and has the very pretentious title of *Noblesse*, but I'd used a Sharpie to rechristen it *Knobless*.

As the information came in, I made notes, compiling a list of which princesses were affected and any details about how the screaming had started. My head spun with all the names and titles, but I was mostly able to keep up. Cade busied himself in the kitchen, keeping a steady flow of tea, coffee, and flaky, delicious biscuits into our hands. Still, around ten I was flagging and pawned my notes off on Alice so I could get some air.

Opening the French doors out to our backyard, I stretched and luxuriated in the cool night air. My gardens were in their second bloom of the year, and the scent of roses welcomed me as I wandered the cracked stone paths to my favorite bench. Hundreds of roses on trees, bushes, and trellises surrounded me like old friends. At the far end of the yard, a dilapidated flagstone wall was all that separated us from the dark, deciduous mysteries of the Afterwoods.

It was lovely and relaxing as soon as I tuned out all the screaming.

The doors opened, and Cade came out with a pair of mismatched mugs. I smiled up at him as he handed over the one shaped like R2-D2. My favorite. "Chamomile?" I asked as the warm, delicate scent hit my nostrils.

Cade shrugged and blew on his own tea. "I know you can't handle any caffeine this late in the night."

I narrowed my eyes and smiled at him. "How do you know that?"

He treated me to one of his rare, wide smiles and ran his hand along the clipper-short blonde hair on the back of his neck. "Your room is above mine. I hear you pacing sometimes on the nights you have a late-night latte."

"You pay attention." The words escaped me, low and vulnerable, almost without a conscious thought. It had always been so easy, so *effortless* to talk to Cade, once upon a time. I sometimes forget how to communicate without disaffected snark.

"I've known you for… Perrault's panties, thirteen years? I've picked up a few things." He made eye contact, steady and sure, and my heart surged with forgotten emotion. Cade and I had once had… *something*. For a week at the end of high school, we had been together, before real life had intruded. And by real life, I mean me finding out I had used my burgeoning magic powers to bespell him to love me with a magic rose. Sometimes I think it was the best week of my life. Sometimes I forget how young I was then.

I took a steadying breath and played with one of the roses winding its way up the legs of the bench. That's one of the reasons we had all come back to the cottage, so I could stock up on roses for whatever was coming our way. I've got the power to put my emotions into roses and transfer those feelings to others. It's not supposed to happen; magic can do many things, but no spell is supposed to be able to change our hearts. That's why I'm a Free Spell: someone born with a weird and strange magic within them that defies even the fairy tale logic of magical law.

And the way I'd discovered my magic was in breaking Cade's heart. As soon as the spell had worn off, he'd known I'd… invaded him, somehow, without even knowing it. That his feelings for me had been mixed with my feelings for him, and he could never disentangle them. So we kept things light and casual and teased each other, and that had worked for the past five years.

So why did it feel like it wasn't working for us anymore?

I cleared my throat and tried to put us back on our normal terms, without even really knowing what that meant anymore. "Well, what do you think is going on here? With the screaming princesses, I mean," I quickly followed up.

"I don't know," he said, breaking eye contact and looking out at the trees of the Afterwoods. "All the princesses started screaming right around the same time, 6:13, in all different parts of the Apple. All of them were under some sort of sleeping curse—Jacqui confirmed that her princess friend who was merely taking a hungover nap was not affected. Most of them were in Castle Fortnight, but even those kept offsite were synced up. So it must be something affecting them from… outside?" He shook his head. "I fight monsters. This feels like something to let the wizards figure out."

"So just trust the authority figures to sort everything out for us? C'mon, when have I ever done that?"

I chuckled and jostled my shoulder into him playfully, in what I thought was an innocent bit of bro-ish tomfoolery. Instead, I just kind of… nestled into his firm shoulder and stuck there. The heat from his skin filtered through the light hoodie I was wearing, and suddenly the cool night felt unbearably hot. Cade's pale hazel eyes bore into mine, staring intensely at my sudden move.

They flicked down to my lips. I swallowed.

"Briar?" Antoine's soft voice carried across the garden from the open French doors. I jumped, like I'd been caught doing something wrong instead of just living my uncomfortable and confusing life. In the process, I spilled hot Chamomile all over my hand.

"Grimmsdammit, I—yeah, Antoine, what's up?" I grumbled. I'm pretty sure most romcom heroines don't swear like angry pirates when caught between their two hunks.

"I just got off an interesting call," he said. His voice was carefully neutral, and I thought maybe he couldn't see us huddled together in the dark garden. "I can tell you about it, if you want to come in. If you're… *done* out there." He turned and shut the door.

Something told me he could see us just fine.

"I, uh—we should go," I said, all but jumping off the bench as I tried to wipe my hands on my pajama pants.

"Yeah," Cade said, sounding a little… disappointed? Was I reading too much into it?

Son of a swan princess, this was all such a mess.

"Thanks for the tea, though," I said lamely as we walked in.

He turned before we got to the door and gave me a roguish smirk that almost made me trip. "Oh yeah? Did your hand like it?"

I snort-laughed and followed him inside.

Jacqui and Alice were seated at attention, so Cade and I settled ourselves on the threadbare stools near the kitchen and looked to Antoine. He looked practically unkempt, by his standards. Which meant he'd untucked his collared shirt from his chinos and undone a few buttons at the top. Was that a glimpse of auburn chest hair peeking out—

"Well," he started, cutting off my completely out-of-character mental ogling, "I just got off the mirror with the parents of one of the screaming princesses. They're concerned, and they want to hire us to figure out what's causing it." He gestured towards me, but somehow studiously avoided making eye contact.

Antoine had been the knight assigned to help me find Rick for Count Grimmour, and as much as I'd initially thought he was a stuck-up goody-two-shoes, that case was our origin story, and ever since we'd been teaming up to help people. Antoine was well-versed in Royal etiquette and knew a surprising amount of ways to kick out people's kneecaps, while I did the whole magic rose thing. Cade, Jacqui, and Alice lent a hand when they could, or when nothing good was playing on the mirror. It wasn't much, but we took cases for the people whom the Apple had turned its back on: tracking down Commoner children lost in the Afterwoods, helping little mom-and-pop shops stand up to organized crime in the shadier parts of town, and, on one incredibly delicious evening, battling the frosting ghosts which had infested Old Mother Marzipan's bakery in the Gingerbread Tenements.

I wanted us to have a cool, badass detective agency name like "Rose & Knight Investigations" but so far Antoine had shot down all of my ideas and forbidden me from wearing a trench coat. It's like he's deathly allergic to fun.

"I thought we didn't take jobs from Royals," I said.

"Who cares?" Alice countered. "We're investigating it anyways. We might as well take their money. Then we could buy more snacks."

There was a murmur of general agreement after the word *snacks*.

"Uh, it's not that," Antoine said. "It's who made the offer. Earl D'Lucien Ardor."

Jacqui's father.

All our eyes swiveled to Jacqui who stiffened. As far as a I knew, Jacqui hadn't been in touch with her family since their falling out two years previously. She took a ragged breath, confusion evident in her face.

"Oh, uh, okay. Why does my father give a shit about any of this?" she asked slowly.

Antoine sagged, clearly dreading what he had to say next. "It's… your sister, Jacqui. She's screaming."

Jacqui looked completely shocked. "Raye? But—Raye's asleep?"

"For about six months now." I knew Antoine well enough to know saying this was shredding him up inside, but he kept his voice steady, even. Trying to provide something solid for Jacqui to hold onto as her world spun out of control.

Alice recovered sooner than the rest of us from the bombshell, and scooched closer to Jacqui, immediately putting her arms around her. I moved just after, sitting clumsily by her side and putting a hand on her shoulder. It wasn't much, but it was all I could do.

"Raye," Jacqui said, talking more to herself than anyone else at this point. "How could they… they put her under a sleeping curse?"

"He—well, your father said it was her choice. She wanted it."

I bristled. There was a long and storied tradition in the Apple of princesses going into enchanted slumbers, in the hopes of meeting their prince and getting their happily ever after. As an added bonus, no one ages while under the effects of a sleeping curse. Royals sometimes brokered deals, matching their daughters up with princes who hadn't even been born yet. It didn't happen as often as it used to, but it was still one of those archaic, storybook practices that had just begun to be questioned.

Jacqui's face contorted in barely contained rage, but when she spoke, her voice had an icy, serial killer veneer. "And does my father know that you're connected to me?"

Antoine shook his head. "I don't think so. He didn't seem aware that I know you, or that Briar is my partner."

"Take the meeting," Jacqui said flatly.

"Jacqs," Alice started, "we don't have to—"

"Take it," Jacqui said, calmly disentangling herself from Alice and me and standing up. "Set it up, and I'm coming with you." She didn't wait for a response and walked out of the room.

We all just sat there for a moment, silent but for the constant drone of women's screams.

LATER THAT NIGHT, AFTER drawing my curtains, stuffing blankets into the crack underneath my door, putting in earplugs, and setting my mirror to play a white noise track called Alpine Snowdrift Serenity, I finally could almost forget about the shrieks outside. I'm a light sleeper on the best of nights, so this particular city-wide catastrophe was hitting me where it hurt.

All my noise-reduction efforts, however, did not drown out the scratch against the window just as I was starting to drift off.

I jumped up, grabbed the morning star from my dresser, and threw back my curtains.

"Jacqui," I squeaked out as blood pounded in my ears. "What are you doing, and—er, why are you a cat again?"

I opened a pane of my bay window to the sleek silver-and-white cat sitting on the sill, and she leapt casually through the window onto my bed. "You weren't answering when I pawed at the door."

"Sorry," I said, removing my ear plugs. "But again… why do you have paws?"

She shifted on the bed and looked away. "I didn't want to say anything. Bri, you've been so great getting my curse treated, and I'm almost completely cured, but there are still a few caveats they've been trying to work out."

My face grew hot. I didn't deserve her gratitude; Jacqui's ordeal had started when she'd eaten a cursed muffin basket sent to our house, addressed to Yours Truly and from whomever it was who was calling themselves the Arsenic Queens. So, when I'd gotten a boon from Count Grimmour, getting Jacqui treated by the wizards in the Curse Removal Department at the Academy of the Iron Wand was the least I could do.

"Caveats? So the curse isn't totally gone?" She shook her tiny, furry head. "Why?"

"The eggheads at the Academy aren't sure—the curse is different than anything the wizards have seen before."

Given that some of them were well into their third century of tenure, that wasn't a good sign.

"But Jacqs… why wouldn't you tell me?"

She turned and looked away from me. "Because… Briar, you did so much to get me treatment for my curse. I felt weird telling you there were a few strings attached."

"Then why now? Why are you a cat tonight?"

Even in her cat form, Jacqui never lost her Royal flair for the dramatic; she paused, sighed, and looked significantly out the window. "The moon," she said softly, as the full moon's light made her glossy coat sparkle.

"Oh. My. God. Jacqui, are you a—a *werecat*?" I covered my mouth with my hands and tried not to emit a delighted squeal.

"What? No, Briar. No! And I highly regret getting you addicted to *Teen Wolf*." She shook her head as I deflated. "My curse is mostly broken, but still active when I'm in the light of the full moon."

"Aww, are you sure? If you bit me, what would happen?"

She gave me a mock snarl. "Want to find out?"

We both chuckled and sat for a moment in the rich, comfortable silence only years of friendship can conjure. I could tell she didn't just come in here to talk about her curse.

"So that stuff about Raye…" I started, using the lower, serious voice I only bring out on special occasions. "Do you believe it? That she'd volunteer to go under a sleeping curse?"

Jacqui scoffed. "Not a chance. Raye was always so… vibrant. So alive. Why would she volunteer for that?"

"When's the last time you heard from her?"

"I got a card from her for my birthday, so… seven months? But that's not unusual. My parents do their best to keep her from having any contact with me. I have no idea who she bribed to bring me that birthday card. She's seventeen, Grimmsdammit."

I didn't know Raye that well, but I had clear memories of her as a young girl, dark-haired and bubbly. She seemed to thrive in the Royal spotlight that had made Jacqui bristle. Still, despite their differences, the sisters had always watched each other's backs. The hardest thing for Jacqui when she left Castle Fortnight to live with us Commoners was leaving Raye behind.

"Are you sure you want us to do this?" I asked. "Take a job from your father? I know how you feel about taking his money—"

Jacqui's eyes went steely in her feline face. "I've got to stand up to him. If he's done anything to Raye—" She shook her head. "Thanks for helping."

I shrugged. "We were already on the case. If we get to stick it to Daddy D'Lucien in the process, so much the better."

She butted her head against my arm, and I took a moment to scratch behind her ears. "Do you really think I'm in a love triangle?"

Jacqui gave a good-natured laugh, and her voice immediately softened. "Oh, one hundred percent. It is so obvious two out of three blind mice could see it."

I groaned and sank back onto my bed. "What am I gonna do, Jacqs?"

"Well, what do you want, Bri?"

"No idea. No clue. I mean, I could go for some pudding right now, but beyond that my feelings are a mystery."

"Okay, step one, figure that out. Then we go from there." She stretched and got up from where she was curled up on my bed. "Give yourself a deadline. Say you're going to figure out whether you want Cade, Antoine, or neither one of them by the time we finish our current crisis."

"So you're saying all I have to do is keep the princesses screaming forever and I'll never have to deal with this?"

Jacqui chuckled and jumped out to the window sill. "Get some sleep, Bri."

I closed the window, watching as the silver cat fur she'd left on my sheets transformed into Jacqui's long blonde hair as soon as it was out of the moonlight.

I ADJUSTED MY CLOAK'S hood to try to keep the early morning sun out of my eyes as Antoine and I waited in line to enter Castle Fortnight. The castle guard seemed to be showing extra scrutiny, probably to keep out the people looking to gawk at the screaming princesses. Or muffle their moaning with a pillow.

"Why are we doing this, again?" I said softly to Antoine. "I know a million ways to break into Castle Fortnight."

"For the third and probably nowhere near final time," Antoine said, his polite voice straining, "we're here on official business. We're allowed in."

"But this line is *so* long," I whined.

"Suck it up," he said with a wide grin. I lived for the times when I was able to needle him into being improper.

"We could still sneak off," I said, looking down at his shoes. "How are those slippers for shimmying up storm drains?"

"They're penny loafers, and we're almost at the front."

"Can I at least give them my fake identity, Lily d'Lis?"

"Is she any less annoying than you?"

"More so, I'm afraid."

Antoine rolled his eyes, and I shifted the heavy picnic basket in my arms as the guards called us forward.

One mostly painless interaction with medieval TSA later, we were walking along Chessboard Court, one of the major hubs of Castle Fortnight, named for the white and black cobblestones we walked along. Upscale food stands were set up all along the plaza, and I lingered wistfully near one whose chalkboard proclaimed, "I scream, you scream, literally everyone is screaming for Elsa's Handmade Ice Cream!" At least people were keeping their sense of humor about things.

We made our way up a wide, stone staircase leading to the part of the Castle known as the Aeries. A cluster of thin, pointy Gothic towers, the Aeries were joined by a knot of bridges, branching and connecting on different levels like a cat's cradle made from resplendent white stone. The bad news is many of the bridges are thin and precarious, but the good news is you can't fall far before hitting another level of stone beneath you. A giant, arching suspension bridge led us to the paired towers of the d'Lucien and Ardor families, Jacqui's childhood home. The two spires were separate at the bottom, and then about halfway up began to twist and spiral into each other; the architects had clearly changed their approach once the two houses had begun to intermarry.

A crisp and efficient concierge took us to a parlor near the top of the tower which sprawled out into an open balcony. Antoine thanked her heartily while I settled my picnic basket carefully on a settee, then rushed out to the balcony to take in the view.

Castle Fortnight is like if Helm's Deep had a baby with Times Square. It was less of a building and more of a miniature city all in itself. Every Duke, Sheik, Daimyo, and Grandee in the Apple had carved out some niche in the miles of battlements and balustrades that made up the Castle. Crude medieval fortress walls protected elegant wood pagodas and massive minarets. Sagging stone turrets leaned against flashy glass towers that looked like fairy-tale Apple Stores. Every time period, architectural style, and taste (or lack thereof) was represented. The level of wealth these towers signified was at once breathtaking and infuriating.

I looked out across the Aeries as the d'Lucien Ardors kept us waiting for twenty minutes in their spotless yet cold parlor. We were so high up, I could see the peak of Drake Mountain breaking the even horizon of the Afterwoods. Finally, the concierge (who seemed to have no problem just standing there silently like a Buckingham Palace guard) cleared her throat politely and announced, "The Right Honorable Earl Marchall D'Lucien Ardor and Lady Aurelle D'Lucien Ardor."

Jacqui's father marched through the door, the military medals on his puffed-up chest jangling with each rigid step. He was a barrel-chested man in his fifties, with a bit of elegant salt invading the borders of his pepper black hair. The maroon doublet and breeches he wore evoked the general's uniform I remember him prancing about in during my childhood. Even his sharp smile was a little aggressive, as if he were daring the world to disagree with his eagle-eyed evaluation of it.

A step behind, Aurelle swanned in, her arms drifting at her sides like independent entities. Her frilly blue ballgown was the exact same shade of periwinkle as her dewy eyes, which were expertly framed by the mass of curls arranged on her head like a blonde Mount Olympus. Sparkling silver jewelry punctuated her outfit, glimmering at her wrists, ears, and neck, to the point where she seemed to have a glimmering aura.

As soon as they entered, the room became a little brighter, the air became a little warmer, and a soft, pleasant birdsong seemed to drown out the screaming around us. I cringed, remembering what it was like to be in the presence of Jacqui's mother; Aurelle was one of a handful of Royals who still possessed Largesse, a form of magic that had mostly died out in recent generations. Reality gets a little pliant around Nobles blessed with Largesse—the sun shines on them like a personal spotlight, flowers blossom in all the colors of the rainbow, and birds have a weird tendency to do their chores.

Antoine bowed deeply, and I felt a curtsy overtake me as well. "Your Lordships," we murmured in perfect unison.

"Mister DuCarr, I thank you for accepting our invitation," Marchall said formally, all but ignoring me as he strode over to shake Antoine's hand.

"Oh," Aurelle said breathily, her eyes looking me over with the shrewdness that always took me by surprise, "but is that… little Briar Pryce?" She broke into a beaming smile. "Why, look at you all grown up! And a secretary to a knight! How lovely."

I bit back any response I had to being called Antoine's secretary and forced a smile. "It's nice to see you again, Lady d'Lucien Ardor."

"Oh, please, dear, call me Aurelle," she said with what seemed to be perfectly genuine warmth.

"Of course. Then, I'm sorry, Aurelle."

"Why, whatever for?" she said as I walked over to the settee and opened the top of the sturdy wicker picnic basket that I'd brought with me.

A furry grey streak leapt out of the basket, but it didn't stay in that form for long. Jacqui's transformation from cat to human wasn't squishy and biological; it was almost instant, a flash of silver light and the tangy smell of rusted silver, and suddenly a fully clothed human woman was sailing through the air. And as

Jacqui landed expertly on her wedge heels, her stylish navy duster billowing out behind her like a friggin' Valkyrie, I wondered, not for the first time, if she'd inherited a measure of her mother's talents.

The Earl and the Countess were stunned speechless. I took the moment to reach inside the picnic basket and dispel the enchanted moonstone (usually Alice's nightlight) which had kept Jacqui furry while we got into the castle. This exception to her curse was already proving to have advantages.

"Mother. Father," Jacqui said coolly. "I'm here to see Raye."

Shock, anger, and a bit of fear battled it out among Marchall's facial features. Aurelle seemed to recover more quickly. "Jacquinetta," she said casually, as if they'd run into each other at a dinner party, "what a surprise."

"Daughter," Marchall gritted out, "Why did—how are—were you just a cat?"

"Yes, Father," Jacqui said drolly. "I've been a cat on-and-off for a while now. Thanks for noticing."

"Your Lordships," Antoine intervened smoothly, "we wanted to bring Jacqui here to discuss taking your case. We all want what's best for Raye, and we think if we all work together, we can figure out what's happening to her and the other princesses."

"You—" Marchall turned on Antoine. "You smuggle my daughter into my demesne, which I have specifically forbidden her from returning to, and then expect us to continue our business together?" He shook his head, anger radiating out from him with almost as much palpable force as his wife's magic. "Tell me why I shouldn't call my guards and have you taken out in chains."

Marchall had oriented himself so he was only speaking to Antoine, but Jacqui neatly stepped into his line of sight, so he had no choice but to face her. "Because we're your best chance at helping your daughter. Your other daughter. The one you claim to care about."

Aurelle stepped towards her, eyes shining. "Jacqui, darling, we never said we didn't care about you—"

"You didn't need to say it. Marchall showed it quite well—" Jacqui said venomously.

"Young lady, I will not be spoken to like that—"

"*Everyone quiet*," I said, projecting my voice so I wasn't shouting, but filling the room with my voice. "The next person to start into family drama gets a rose to the face."

If my eloquence didn't win them over, my audacity seemed to stun them enough for the tension in the room to ebb a bit.

"Sorry, a rose?" Aurelle said tentatively.

"Briar's a Free Spell," Jacqui explained begrudgingly. "She can put magic into roses."

"One of the reasons we think we can help Raye," I said. "But we need your help. Your resources and connections will give us a reach we don't have on our own."

Marchall looked back and forth between us. When he spoke again, his voice was cracked and vulnerable. "You think you can help her?"

I nodded. "I think we're your best shot."

He met my eyes and gave a small, almost imperceptible nod. Then, with almost the same immediacy as Jacqui's transformation, the Earl put his haughty Royal façade back into place and looked at Antoine. "Why don't we go into my study and discuss details?"

Antoine looked to Jacqui, who rolled her eyes but gave a nod. Marchall led him through a door into the dimly lit room beyond. I bristled at the Royal's casual dismissal of his own daughter, but I knew Jacqui couldn't care less about getting a tour of her father's man cave.

"I want to see Raye," she said firmly as the door closed. Aurelle gave her a long look, and I couldn't tell what emotions were playing behind her wide, beautiful eyes.

"Come with me," she said, and walked out the way she'd come.

Jacqui looked over to me, her eyes a little desperate. I knew the strain standing up to her parents must have placed on her. In an instant I was at her side, hand around her waist. She reached up and gave my shoulder a quick squeeze as we followed her mother out to the spiral staircase in the center of the tower.

"It was a wonderful match," Aurelle said from a few steps above us. She daintily lifted her voluminous skirts to make her way up the stairs. "A nice young man from the Akitoye lineage. We were so happy."

Jacqui and I struggled to keep up, physically and intellectually. "Mom, what are you talking about?"

Aurelle turned to gracefully to give us an indulgent smile. "Raye's fiancé, of course. We arranged the match just a few months ago."

"A match? At her age?" Jacqui sputtered. "She's too young—and why did you have her put to sleep?"

Aurelle laughed, a tinny, musical sound that brought a hazy warmth to the stairwell. "I was seventeen when I met your father, dear. And Raye agreed to the sleep when she agreed to the match. Her husband-to-be is only eight. Give it ten years, and they'll be the most adorable couple."

My blood ran cold as we stopped on a landing with a set of wooden double doors. Even though I'd heard of Royals doing this—putting their daughters into the suspended animation of a sleeping spell to stop their aging while a prospective husband caught up—I'd never experienced it first hand, with living, breathing people I knew well. "Ten years?" I asked. "You're willing to miss ten years of your daughter's life so she can have some Royal power marriage?"

Without warning, Aurelle turned on me, her face wounded and furious. The light seemed to drain from the passageway as her words echoed through the air. "How dare you," she started. "I miss my daughter every day. But I'm her mother, and I supported *her* decision. It's what she wanted. Her prospects weren't great after the shame her sister brought on this family." She turned and walked through the doors.

I felt Jacqui tighten next to me as her mother's words landed. I wanted to say something, wanted to tell her it wasn't her fault—and then we heard shrieking from the other room.

It feels bad to say, but in the past fifteen hours, I thought I'd become desensitized to all the screams coming from the princesses. It was easy to think that when they were far, far away, and you could just think of it as noise, depersonalized and removed from its source. But standing in the next room and hearing another human wail like they were in pain activated every panicked, anxious reaction in my body. I felt Raye's screams deep in me, as if they were my own.

The three of us rushed into the next chamber, a rounded bedroom with the curtains drawn. Rich fabrics and tapestries hung around a giant four-poster bed that dominated the center of the room. Encircled by a gauzy shear canopy, Raye was completely still on the bed when we barged in, facing away from us. Her dark hair traced long, wavy paths along the bed beside her.

"Is she—" Jacqui started, and then her sister began to shriek, twisting in the bed like a wild animal. It was a deep, throaty scream, tearing through her vocal chords, seemingly equal parts pain and rage. I felt my eyes involuntarily begin to moisten, and a quick glance to the side showed tears making their way down Jacqui's face. After a few minutes, Raye started to quiet down, her slender limbs curling back underneath her head like she was just having a late-morning nap.

"This is how it's been," Aurelle said. "She's fine for long stretches, and then has these fits. I just—I hope she's not really in pain." Her voice was strained and quiet, but still managed to express almost as much anguish as Raye's screams had.

Jacqui sniffed and wiped a tear away from her eye angrily. Her whole body had softened, and instead of the fierce and rigid warrior princess she'd been downstairs, she looked like a worried older sister who had just seen her sister in pain. "We're going to fix this. We have to get Raye back." She reached out and put a hand tentatively on her mother's shoulder. Aurelle reached up and covered Jacqui's hand with hers, and for a second, they were just a mother and a daughter again.

"C'mon," Jacqui said. "Let's find Father and get a move on." She and her mother walked slowly out the door, with Aurelle giving Raye one final look of motherly concern before she left. I started to follow when Raye emitted a squeak, and something flashed in the corner of my vision. I bent down and pulled out one of the roses I'd slid into my boot for emergencies.

As Raye howled and thrashed in her bed, the rose in my hands glowed a sickly blood red color, its petals pulsing in perfect synchronization with the princess's shrieks.

ANTOINE AND I WALKED along the bank of the River Yester, just outside the walls of Castle Fortnight. Cooler heads had prevailed when we reunited with the menfolk downstairs, and the D'Lucien Ardors had agreed to give us their support. Jacqui had split off to go interview more of her Royal friends, to see if she could glean any sort of pattern about when and how the princesses of Castle Fortnight were affected.

Antoine and I walked along a mostly deserted tree-lined path, the canopy of leaves above us just starting to glow yellow in the midday September sun. The screams seemed to lull as we meandered, and my eyes drifted to the glistening water of the Yester. Just as my gaze settled on it, the surface broke and a pair of kelpie foals emerged from the river. I smiled as the jet-black horses ran along the top of the river, braying with delight as they chased each other haphazardly. The one in front shuddered briefly and became a little boy with a mane of shaggy black hair before scrambling up a tree. The other kelpie became a young girl, giggled, and climbed after him.

I hadn't told Antoine or Jacqui about what had happened with my rose—I knew I should have, but it was just so strange and personal that I needed a chance to come to terms with it myself. When I enchanted a rose, it changed color and sometimes even shape as it was filled with the emotion I imbued. But I'd never had something else affect the roses I carried. It was almost like I was an intermediary of some sort, unknowingly passing whatever magic was affecting the princesses on to the roses around me.

Which meant… was there some sort of connection between what was happening to them and my own power?

I cast that question aside as we approached the one place in the Apple that might have answers. The Academy of the Iron Wand sat on a hill at the edge of the city, its dreaming Gothic spires resplendent against the leafy background of the After-woods. Whereas Castle Fortnight had the feel of an extravagant fortress, the Academy's ornate stone buildings valued form over function. The Yester flowed through the center of the campus, a variety of arching bridges spanning the river as it babbled and wove down the hill separating the Academy from the rest of the Apple.

Normally the Academy is closed to the public, but Antoine and I flashed our brand-new Royal pennons from the D'Lucien Ardors. Small, enchanted triangles of fabric, the pennons gave us a lot of perks—access to the Royal's private Doors, expense accounts, and assistance from the knights and guards of Castle Fortnight. Plus, a 10% discount at Troll Foods.

As we passed through the looming wrought-iron gates, I noticed a palpable feeling of tension on campus. Wizards rushed across the quadrangles at decidedly un-wizard-like speeds, carrying stacks of books and armfuls of scrolls. I noticed one elderly wizard nearly fall off an arching stone bridge as she tripped on the hem of her sparkly robe. A muffled explosion came from a round tower nearby, followed by a string of decidedly unmagical exclamations.

"Should we assume from their current state of panic that the wizards also have no idea what's going on with the screaming princesses?" I asked Antoine as we wound our way through the flagstone paths of the Academy.

Antoine shrugged as we waited for two brown-robed wizards to levitate a series of crates along the path in front of us. "I imagine if they'd figured it all out, they'd have put a stop to it by now. But that doesn't mean they might not have useful clues."

We came to a wide Classical building with towering columns, a green slate roof, and an engraving over the door reading "Department of Magiphysics." Walking through the echoing hallways inside, the building felt much more deserted and sedate than the rest of campus. Antoine referred to a map and took us down a set of stairs to a door marked "Professor Tamsin Davies." After a few rounds of knocking, there was a series of thumps inside the office, and finally the door creaked open.

The woman on the other side peered at us through thick, cat-eye spectacles that magnified her kind eyes so they seemed to take up a third of her face. Her pleasant, freckle-splattered face registered confusion, and she reached up to scratch the astonishingly voluminous cloud of chestnut hair that circled her head. Instead of the traditional robes of a wizard, she wore a pair of jeans and a grey flannel shirt, although I noticed some golden runes stitched into the collar of her oversized green cardigan.

"Now, I am sorry to tell you that you two are most definitely in the wrong place," she said in a warm, musical Welsh accent.

"Professor Davies?" Antoine said, offering a hand. "I got your name from one of your old students, Ravenna Singh."

The woman gave a charming snort of a laugh and opened the door a bit wider. "Ravenna? My word, it's been a few years. How is she doing?"

"She's doing well," Antoine beamed, "and she speaks very highly of you, Professor Davies. May we come in?"

"Ah, sure. I've just put the kettle on," she said, turning away and letting us inside. "And please, call me Tamsin."

We introduced ourselves as we entered a charmingly cluttered basement room, somehow part office, part sitting room, and part laboratory all at once. Stacks of books lined the inset wooden shelving and spilled onto the thickly carpeted floor. The little light peeking in from the half windows near the ceiling was supplemented by a sparky yellow orb quietly bubbling like a lava lamp in the fireplace, emitting a delicate, heatless light. At the far end of the room, the worn carpets ended, and a ritual circle was drawn out on the floor in eerie, flickering blue runes.

After a few minutes, Tamsin emerged from a side room carrying a wooden tray with a mismatched tea service. She handed Antoine a tea cup that looked carved from some sort of eldritch crystal, while I got a chipped mug in the shape of Garfield's face. We settled in an overstuffed couch, and I noticed a rumpled blanket and a few pillows that suggested it was more often used as a bed. Tamsin took a sip of tea from her "Aberystwyth Is For Lovers" mug and perched on the one corner of her desk that wasn't covered in stacks of parchment.

"Now," she said abruptly, "as fond as I was of Ravenna, and as happy as I am to have guests, I'm still quite sure you've found your way to the wrong office. You have that hungry, naïve look of adventurers, and the biggest quest going at the moment is those wailin' rich girls. But for that, you'll want someone from the Curse Department, probably specializing in sleeping spells. I'd recommend Professor Maxwell—"

"Tamsin," Antoine started, "just so we are all on the same page, do you mind giving a brief summary of your specialty to Briar here?"

Tamsin stopped in her tracks and blinked. "Talk about my research? People are usually asking me to *stop* talking about my research."

I smiled. "Go for it. Just, er, slowly."

She nodded vigorously. "Well, all right then. So you know how the Poisoned Apple exists tied to the Otherworld, but slightly off?"

"Right, like any of the World Slips. They have tethers in the real world at specific locations. Mt. Olympus, Shangri-La, Atlantis…"

"Exactly," she said with excitement. "Now, there's plenty of research into how exactly our worlds intersect, how conditions in one world affect the other, what magic can travel through the Doors, et cetera. But my research is into alternative Slips—not the relatively stable, predictable worlds like the Apple, but temporary, possibly inaccessible worlds created by magic—um, sorry, why are you making that face?"

I realized my face was scrunched up with conversation. "My bad. This is the face I make when I encounter things that force me to completely rethink my worldview."

Antoine nodded. "That's what she looked like when someone tried to explain Bitcoin to her."

I turned on him. "We already have money! In the real world! Why do we need a whole new system of money for computers?!" I took a few deep, calming breaths. "All right, so in addition to living in a magical pocket dimension, there are *more* magical dimensions bubbling under the surface of this one?"

"Well, to put it simply, yes," Tamsin said, somewhat apologetically. "For instance, certain magical artifacts can trap people inside small, self-contained realms, or there are structures that can appear much larger on the inside than the outside—most of these are still pretty minor, and completely tethered to the world around them. You can think of them as just slight wrinkles in the fabric of the world, where more reality gathers that we're used to."

I nodded and tried to de-scrunch my face as much as I could. "Okay, so far, so good."

"Ravenna spoke very highly of your recent research," Antoine prompted. "The paper involving dreams."

"Well, my most recent publication was a theory that we all enter a massive, untethered World Slip when we dream," Tamsin continued. She beamed with amused self-deprecation. "It was *not* well received. The Grand Magister of the Department of Magiphysics called my theory 'piddly wink.'" She shrugged. "Academics can be wankers sometimes."

Things were starting to fall into place. I turned to Antoine. "And you think there's a connection between what's happening to the princesses and this… dream world?"

Tamsin jumped in before I'd even finished, shaking her head. "People under sleeping curses don't dream. It's a side effect of the curse."

"People in sleeping curses also don't scream and thrash around like they're having night terrors," Antoine countered. "That's why Ravenna thought of your research. She thought maybe whatever is affecting the princesses is getting to them—"

"—through the Dream Slip," Tamsin said. Her eyes were unfocused, her jaw was a little slack, and I could almost hear the neurons firing as her powerful mind exploded into action. "That would explain how something was affecting all of the princesses in the Apple at once. You said this was Ravenna's idea?"

Antoine smiled and nodded. "I'd forgotten how brilliant she was," Tamsin said, and she rushed over to a blackboard covered in runes and started scribbling.

I looked over at Antoine's warm smile as he watched Tamsin and found myself wondering who this Ravenna was. Antoine met a wide variety of people in his work as a knight, so of course I wouldn't know everyone he knew. I just didn't remember him mentioning her before. Or smiling like that before. It's funny, because he mentioned most of his friends. How come I hadn't heard of her? It's not weird. Just funny. Anyways.

I shook my head to clear it a bit. "So, what do we do? Go to the Dream Slip and figure out what is affecting the princesses from there? How soon can you whip us up a portal?"

Tamsin gave a warm, musical laugh. "Oh, no, my dear. See, my work so far has been completely theoretical. Over the next few years, I plan on doing extensive magical spectrum analyses to figure out the runic frequencies that might contain the Dream Slip. Then, possibly after a few decades, I might venture into sending small, inanimate objects into those etheric ranges—" Tamsin turned to take in Antoine's crestfallen face. "Oh. Right.

The princesses. I'm sorry, my friends, but there's just no rushing Academy magic."

She fell silent, and the three of us sat listening to the symphony of screams barely on the edge of our hearing. The Academy was far enough from the center of town that the sounds of terror were just a soft undercurrent, as if a guy in an apartment below us was watching *Saw* on loop.

I wasn't sure the Apple would last a week of this, never mind a decade.

Almost lost in the shrieking, I heard Tamsin mutter, "There has to be another—*Oh!*" Antoine and I jerked our heads to watch as she skittered over to her desk. "I swear it was in a folder—" I looked at Antoine, unsure if we were supposed to get involved in this conversation.

Just as I was feeling uncomfortable enough to stark speaking, Tamsin brayed, "Ah *ha*!" and withdrew a thin black folder from a pile of papers. On the front of the folder was the Academy of the Iron Wand's seal inside a pentagram. "Have you two ever heard of Free Spells?" the professor asked.

I grimaced. "I have." The last time I'd seen a folder like that, it had contained a detailed dossier on my own powers. The Academy keeps detailed files on anyone who might threaten their magical supremacy of the Apple.

"So I pulled this report a few weeks ago—it's not very thorough," Tamsin said as she flipped through it. "But the Academy has been able to verify a few reports of a Free Spell who is able to access people's dreams—his code name is The Oneirovore. Before all this princess stuff started happening, I had been meaning to follow up, maybe even try to track him down."

My ears perked up and I pushed myself up off the couch. "Tracking people down I can handle."

I SET MY MIRROR on my desk and rubbed my temples. It had been a few days of calling and visiting all the magical weirdos, ne'er-do-wells, and rebels I knew, but all I'd been getting were strange stories about the Oneirovore without any actual information. My buddy Silas, who splits his time between bartending and telling fortunes with a talking Tarot deck named Rider, claimed he'd been at a party where the Oneirovore had sent everyone on a kaleidoscopic vision quest into the collective unconscious. The Frazer Twins told me, in between shouting hexes at their downstairs neighbors, that the Oneirovore wasn't even human at all, but a spirit guide who had taken on physical form in order to bring about the End of Days. The Periwinkle Fairy said they'd hooked up once, but he says that about everyone.

I crossed off the last of the names on the list of sources I'd come up with and sighed, just as my mirror lit up with a call from Tarris. I tapped the cool glass surface as usual, but instead of Tarris's face appearing, the mirror glowed brightly and started to levitate out of my hands. I scrambled away and did a very awkward roll to take cover on the other side of my bed.

Overreaction? Maybe, but you can never be too careful with magic. One time an exploding magic mirror turned an entire building into frogs. Not just the people inside the building, *the entire building.*

The mirror spun a few times in mid-air, then settled face up on my desk. A fountain of sparks shot from the glass of the mirror, where a handful of them twirled and formed into Tarris's somewhat smug face. The twinkling lights made him look like a floating, fairy tale hologram.

"Grims*dammit*, Tarris. You nearly gave me a heart attack. What the elf is this?!"

The Prince was a notorious geek when it came to cutting edge magic, and his family's connections to the Academy of the Iron Wand gave him access to all the newest spells.

"They're calling it… SparkleCast," he said dramatically. When that revelation didn't have the desired effect, he sheepishly continued, "The wizards who developed it are much better at runes than they are at marketing."

"Well, at least do me a favor and say, 'Help me, Obi-Wan Kenobi, you're my only hope.'"

A cluster of sparkles rose out of the mirror, turned into a hand, and gave me the middle finger.

"What's up, Tar? Did you call just to terrify me with the inexorable advances of magic?"

"Nah, that was a side benefit," he deadpanned. "I hear you're getting wrapped up in this screaming princess business."

"Who told you? Alice?"

"Cade, actually. I ran into him at the gym, and you know how he likes to gossip when he lifts."

Something about that made me chuckle. Of course I knew that. My goofy friends were nothing if not consistent.

"But Briar," he said, and as his speech began to quicken, I was pretty sure I knew what was coming. "You have to be thinking what I'm thinking."

"That it's unfair that babies get to nap all the time when they don't even have jobs?"

"No—I mean, yes, I agree, but no. This has the Arsenic Queens written all over it!"

I stood up from where I was hunkered behind my bed and sat in my desk chair. "What makes you say that?"

Tarris started into a lecture that I swear he'd rehearsed before calling. "So when we last encountered them, the Queens were trying to take down the Multiarchy by sowing chaos and pitting Royals against each other. Their modus operandi was manipulating others using complex, non-Academy magic."

If Tarris saw my theatrical stage yawn, he gave no notice.

"The screaming princesses are already causing tensions to rise in the Apple, and by targeting the children of Royalty, the Queens are distracting their main targets so they can swoop in later and topple the Multiarchy. Whatever magic they used in the past is incomprehensible to wizards, which is why the Academy hasn't been able to figure out what is going on."

I involuntarily flashed back to my conversation with Jacqui a few nights before. *The curse is different than anything the wizards have seen before.*

"Bri, this could be our shot. If we can unravel this, if we could find out how they're doing this to the princesses, we could take down the Arsenic Queens."

"Tarris, I—" I sighed. The Prince made some good points. "I see what you mean, and it's possible your theory could be right."

The swirling sparks that made up Tarris's face seemed to glow brighter as he grinned. "Great. What can I do to help?"

"Get in touch with Jacqui—she's been liaising with the Royals, trying to get as much info as we can on how this thing started."

Tarris beamed and gave a salute. "I'm on it. Let me know if you find anything on your end."

"Will do. Later, Sparkles."

His mouth began to form an expletive as the spell ended and the winking lights fell harmlessly onto my desk, rolling across the surface and illuminating the junk mail I still needed to sort. I leaned back in my chair, balancing it on two legs while I thought. Could Tarris be right? Could whatever was happening to the princesses be some sort of evil plot to take down the Apple? I groaned. All I wanted was to make the screaming stop.

"Knock knock, hope you're not naked," Alice said as she blundered into the room. Boundaries aren't her strong suit.

I rolled my eyes and settled my chair back down on the floor. "Tell me you've got some good news."

Alice settled onto my bed and smoothed out her poodle skirt. "I've got news. Both of the good and bad variety."

"Let's start with the good."

"I talked to my buddy Diego who's a second footman to La Marquesa de Diamantes. He says he has it on pretty good authority that he knows where the Oneirovore will be tonight."

"Tonight? He has a time and a place? That's great." I paused. "What's the bad news?"

Alice grimaced, but I could tell she was secretly loving what she was about to say. "Don't worry. I've already got an outfit planned for you."

I STIFLED A YAWN as our uptown C Train rattled to a stop. Alice had been right about me not liking her news. I guess I'd been a chronic puppy kicker in a previous life because her source had tracked the Oneirovore down to a *club*.

The black dress she had loaned me was actually surprisingly comfortable. After a lot of whining on my part, I'd relented to letting her dress me up. I'd deny it under oath, but it was actually kind of fun to try on clothes and find a pair of chic boots in Jacqui's closet that could be rammed into an enemy's face.

Antoine always looked a little fancy, but he'd gone for a sleek, form-fitting purple shirt with a subtle floral design. In the scandal of the social season, he'd even left it untucked, letting the shirttails dangle over his grey slacks with wild abandon. It was almost like he was planning on having fun tonight.

I flipped through the dossier that Tamsin had loaned us. By Academy standards, it was pretty scant. "How come he gets such a cool code name? *The Oneirovore*. Latin for 'dream eater.' It's so badass."

"You were The Rose," Antoine said. "That's pretty cool, isn't it?"

I pouted. "Yeah, but they knew my real name. They barely know anything about this guy! He's practically a ghost."

"It seems like that's on purpose," Antoine said. "That's probably why he's not been spotted in the Apple in years."

Our crowded subway car finally released us. The platforms were crowded as usual, even on a weeknight at eleven. Apparently, this is the time when club people *start* their night. I do not approve.

For once, the frantic crowds and the diesel-soaked air of Manhattan felt more magical than the Apple, because at least here, the night wasn't polluted with the sound of screams.

Alice's info placed the Oneirovore at a grungy club in the Meatpacking District with the cringeworthy name WCKED. Very strictly, the magical Compact which binds all citizens of the Poisoned Apple forbids us from sharing the secret of its existence. But there are places like WCKED where the fey go to mix with non-magical Know-Naughts, and everyone seems to turn a blind eye. Probably because any raid of these clubs would probably reveal a dozen Royals slumming it with the oblivious residents of Manhattan.

WCKED was completely unmarked from the outside, and if it weren't for the large line queueing outside of the rundown warehouse, I'd think we were in the wrong place. The club-goers were a motley lot—some pierced goths who might have been goblins in human-looking fleshjackets, a few ethereally beautiful ravers, and a bachelorette party with adorable Minnesotan accents who were most likely in for a night of surprises.

Antoine made for the end of the line, but I jerked my head at him to follow me up front. "Briar," he said under his breath, "what are you doing?"

"I'm breaking the rules," I said with a smirk. He raised his thick, brown eyebrows, but I thought I detected the hint of a sparkle in the knight's eyes.

I slid a small white rose out of my purse and began to focus. I let my mind wander to the Aurora Borealis dancing in the northern sky, waterfalls that surge with thousands of gallons every second, and the way a bee can do a dance that tells his hive where to find honey. I remembered the awe I felt when my dad took me camping when I was six and I saw the night sky without the lights of the city to dull it, vast and dark and deep and dripping with stars. I let all that crackling wonder stretch and explore down my arm, through my fingertips, and into the rose. The white petals shuddered with the magic, and in an instant, they deepened to the dark indigo of a night sky, with tiny, sparkling constellations of stars across the petals.

The squat bouncer at the door barely looked up from his clipboard as I approached. "End of the line is that way, lady—" he started.

"Here," I said, offering him the rose. Probably expecting a bribe, he reached out before he'd even seen what was in my hand.

As soon as his fingers touched the rose's stem, his expression of hardened cynicism blew apart at the seams. His eyes widened, and the scowl that he wore as a uniform fell away. He looked Antoine and me up and down with a goofy grin on his face as he marveled at us, feeling all of the awe I'd just conjured into the rose.

I gave him a smile as I said, "Hi, we're really impressive, and we'd like to go into your club now." The bouncer nodded, seemingly too awestruck for speech, and undid the velvet rope blocking the doorway, much to the consternation of the rest of the people waiting in line.

Antoine was smiling as we went up the stairs carpeted in purple, but his tone held a scolding tone I was incredibly familiar with. "Are you sure you didn't overdo it?"

For once, I understood his concern. When we'd first met, I'd had a rude awakening that my power to give people emotions could sometimes last longer than I'd previously expected and could cause some unpleasant emotional side effects. "Not to worry," I explained. "I've been experimenting, and I've found those miniature rose varieties have a pretty short duration. He should be back to normal in five or ten minutes."

From outside, we suddenly heard the bouncer's excited shout. "Did you *see* them?! They were *amazing*!!!"

Antoine gave me a skeptical look.

"Okay, fifteen minutes tops. Maybe I got a little carried away."

We reached the tops of the stairs, and I could hear the heavy thump of electronic music coming from nearby. A few stragglers were loitering around a dimly lit lounge area, sipping drinks and wiping sweat from their faces. "What emotion did you use to get that reaction?" Antoine asked as we made our way towards the main entrance. "Celebrity crush?"

I almost tripped over my boots. His voice had lost its usual disapproving schoolmarm quality, and had a deeper, syrupy rumble that was almost—flirtatious?

I realized I hadn't said anything within a socially acceptable amount of time. All I had to do was respond with something, *anything*—"I was thinking of my dad," I blurted out. *Nope.* Something else. "He—when I was younger, he took me camping, and I was thinking of the first time I saw the stars outside the city, on a dark night in a forest clearing in the Adirondacks."

Now it was Antoine's turn to pause. He gave me a quizzical look, his lips curving into a smile. "What?" I asked him. "Did I already mess up the makeup Jacqui put on me?"

"No, not at all," he said, uncharacteristically tongue-tied. "It's just—even as well as I've gotten to know you, you still come up with ways to surprise me."

I felt heat come to my cheeks, and I silently rejoiced that my dark skin doesn't blush easily. Luckily, we were nearing the main entrance, and I soon found myself dealing with a whole new range of emotions.

Awe, first of all, although not the pure, childlike feeling of wondering at the natural world. WCKED's dance floor was a massive three-story space with scaffolding along the walls that gave the room an almost cathedral-like feel. Platforms stuck out at random intervals, where "costumed" dancers gyrated to the beat. A muscular dude with peacock wings jutting out from his bare torso twirled a level above an acrobatic woman made of an ice so clear that she refracted the laser lights shooting through her. The patrons on the main floor where an equally mixed lot— a coked-out hedge witch flailed in the middle of the floor, her arms leaving trails of runes in the air as she writhed, while a clutch of sirens in tight mini-dresses giggled and danced nearby, occasionally adding their floating, otherworldly voices to the thumping techno beats. A svelte young Indian man in mesh was vogueing so fast it looked awfully like he had half a dozen arms, and honestly, I wasn't sure if it was magic or incredible choreography.

The second and more prominent emotion was frustration, because it was *packed*, and no one seemed to be wearing a sparkling neon shirt with the phrase "I'm the Oneirovore" on it.

Were we just supposed to squeeze ourselves through the sweaty dance floor until we found a clue?

I turned to shout-complain at Antoine when a familiar voice came from the lounge behind us. "Well, hello there, beautiful. What a surprise."

Isaak Krakelev leaned on a table near the door, slowly swishing a tumbler of something purple and glowing. He wore a shredded black tank top that hung from his alabaster skin, and jeans with way too many buckles and straps. For once, his jet-black hair was a little disheveled, and a few strands hung down in front of his ice blue eyes.

Isaak had been a person of interest in my first case, the jealous ex-lover of Miranda Grimmour. In a fit of magical empathy, I'd accidentally absorbed his ever-present horndogginess and had almost gone home with him. Well, by "home" I mean the men's restroom. Regardless, he wasn't my favorite person.

Antoine stiffened next to me, but he remained still and looked to see how I would handle things. For my part, I groaned and rolled my eyes. "What are you doing here, Isaak?"

"Same reason as you, I imagine," he said, taking a sip of his purple drink. "*Indulging.*"

"Okay, cut the languid lothario shit. You're sweaty and alone at a rave; you're not exactly projecting an image of strength. We're here looking for someone called the Oneirovore. You know him?"

"I know a lot of people," Isaak drawled. "What's that information *worth* to you?"

All right, now he was pissing me off.

I grabbed another rose out of my purse and pointed it at his face. "How about you tell me, and I don't imbue you with the emotional equivalent of passing a kidney stone while being forced to watch a *Jerry Springer* marathon?"

Isaak's eyes widened, just a touch, but he remained draped on the table. "You wouldn't. The rumor going around the less savory parts of the Apple is that the Rose has lost her thorns. Doesn't play around with emotions the way she used to."

I met his eyes and stared into them. He was right, of course, but I wasn't going to let him know it. "Then maybe tonight is the night I do what you said. *Indulge myself.*"

There was a beat, and just as I started to worry he was liking the prolonged eye contact too much, he sniffed and turned away. "Fine. But you'll have to wait. He's just getting onstage."

I turned, and saw a man getting onstage behind the massive turntables festooned with lights. He was slim and tall, and his head was circled by swirling clouds, out of which a pair of eyes and a smile glowed. Above him, LCD screens blazed with a swirling design that read, "DJ DREEM EATR."

"He just… that's just his name? All we had to do was figure out the really bad spelling?" I turned and scowled at Isaak. "You continue to be completely useless. That didn't even count as a clue. We would've seen that if you hadn't bothered us."

Isaak shrugged. "Well then, go. Enjoy the music." I started to walk back towards the dance floor. "But remember, Briar, you owe me. And one day I'm going to collect."

I stiffened, about to retaliate, but he was right. In exchange for information that had stopped a civil war, I'd promised Isaak to deliver one rose on his behalf. No questions asked.

And only the very foolish break their promises in the Apple.

"So I guess the Oneirovore isn't as stealthy as we thought," Antoine said as we lingered on the edges of the dance floor. The music wasn't half bad—some soaring synth along with a heavily remixed version of the Eurythmics' *Sweet Dreams*. A little on the nose, but I found myself nodding along to the beat.

"I don't think he's worried about agents of the Academy of the Iron Wand tracking him down to this sweat fest." I looked over to see Antoine's ankle boots tapping in rhythm. Our eyes locked, and I felt something in my chest that's normally clenched tight begin to loosen.

"C'mon," I said. "We're not going to get to him in the middle of his set, so we might as well blend in." I gave him a smile, grabbed his hand, and took him deeper into the sea of dancing bodies.

I found us a pocket of space where we could dance comfortably without needing to actually touch each other. I was glad we had a little distance, partly because I wasn't sure where we were emotionally, but mostly because most of my dance moves involve a lot of frantic arm swinging.

The music smoothly transitioned to something more high energy, kinda cheesy but amazing to dance to. It felt good just to lose my body in the beat, and I incorporated enough head tossing that I didn't have to look awkwardly at Antoine. Dance like your maybe-crush isn't watching, as they say.

I was able to sneak in a look at Antoine between shimmies, and I almost fell. He looked… *cool*. At some point he'd rolled up his shirtsleeves, leaving the veins in his well-muscled forearms out for the world to see. Antoine's dancing wasn't flashy or showy; he just sort of rode the beat, looking suave and completely at ease. A shift of his shoulder there, a twist of his hips there—*damn*.

He saw me staring and gave me an irritatingly cocky smile as he grooved.

I shook my head yet couldn't help but smile back. "All right, knight boy, where did you learn to dance like that?" I said as I danced a little closer. So I could hear him. Obviously.

"Paris," he said. I raised my eyebrows at him. "I lived there for a summer, learning their fighting styles with a street gang, *Les Courgettes en Colère*."

"I don't speak French, but they sound pretty tough."

"They were. But also incredible dancers. We'd go to this one discothèque in Montmarte…" he trailed off with a fond, nostalgic grin.

I looked at him, trying and failing to picture him rolling up to a French club with a posse of rhythmic hoodlums. I vaguely remembered him mentioning his time in Paris before, but realized I couldn't fit it into a timeline of his life. For someone with whom I had spent hundreds of hours, shared countless meals, and fought alongside with blades bared, I was still learning who he was. While Cade seemed to know every nook and cranny of my past and present, Antoine seemed to be a mysterious labyrinth that was unfolding into the future.

And the sexy enigma was dancing closer and closer to me.

It was imperceptible, at first. One movement would bring him closer, dangerously, flirting with the boundaries of my personal space and filling the air with an electric charge. But then the music would seemingly bring him back to where he was, and I would think that I'd imagined it, out of paranoia or wishful thinking or both. Then a few beats later, an arm, a leg, his hips, would suddenly start to fly into the danger zone, only to pull back a few seconds later.

So I started to move towards him. Suddenly, Antoine wasn't retreating. He was only advancing, until we were so close, I could feel the heat coming off of his skin. There was only a thin layer of air separating us, although it was like a magnet was pulling us closer. I looked up, and his carefree attitude was gone. His eyes burned with intensity, and a slight smile on his lips dared me to move even closer, reach out and—

"Briar," he said, a little throatily.

"Yeah?"

"They're switching DJs."

Grimmsdammit.

I whirled around, just as a tall girl with braids was taking over the turn tables. DJ DREEM EATR was casually heading down the stairs offstage, heading for a door in the back corner of the room.

"Let's go," I said, starting to wind my way through the crowd. Antoine and I are about the same height, but I'm way less polite, so I bulldozed my way through the dancefloor with ease as he followed.

This was a rave, not a Justin Bieber concert, so there wasn't any security or barrier between the dance floor and the dingy hallway that seemed to serve as the backstage area. We turned the corner just as the Oneirovore reached up into the swirling crowd surrounding his head. He did *something*, and suddenly the cloud dissipated, and he was just a lanky guy a few years older than me, wearing a hoodie and some torn jeans. His curly dark hair could probably use a trim, and his brown skin didn't do much to hide the dark circles under his eyes. He opened a nearby cooler and took out a lethal-looking energy drink.

Antoine and I traded a look. I'm pretty sure neither of us had any clue how to approach him now that we'd actually tracked him down. I gave a slight hand wave that I hoped indicated that Antoine should try his particular brand of charm and diplomacy before I was my usual unfiltered self.

"Hey, nice set out there, man," Antoine said, somehow sounding convincingly like a raver bro when I know for a fact he can list fifteen varietals of Darjeeling.

The Oneirovore turned and gave an easy smile. I noticed he had striking hazel eyes that were so bright they were almost amber, and his grin had something comforting and vaguely familiar about it. "Thanks, dude."

He gave us a quick look up-and-down and seemed to figure out we were from the Apple. It's usually not too difficult to tell a fey from a Know-Naught; we fey have slight differences in mannerisms, literally otherworldly qualities that make us stand out. It's not the same for everyone; for some, it's a stilted, almost medieval style of speech. Others have a bouncing gait that's more used to cobblestones than concrete. Whatever it is, you can tell we aren't from the world of time sheets and 401(k)s.

"Hey, listen, I heard you might be able to help us," Antoine said. "We heard you might have certain abilities that—"

As soon Antoine said the word "abilities," the Oneirovore freaked. His eyes widened with panic, and before I could react, he'd thrown the can full of sickly-sweet energy drink at my face and bolted for a nearby stairwell.

"Oberon's balls!" I sputtered in shock, wiping the green liquid out of my eyes in time to see Antoine dart after our target. I skidded in the puddle of energy drink but found my footing as I followed them.

The stairwell we'd chased him into was lit only by the light coming from the exterior doors, and all three of us slowed down as we stumbled down two flights of stairs. The Oneirovore slammed through a door that seemed to be from a completely different building than the one we'd left—I didn't think it was magical, just weird architecture. New York is full of weird, winding basement spaces, from abandoned subway stations to old bootleggers' hideaways. The Poisoned Apple is just one of many secrets scattered throughout the five boroughs.

Antoine made a series of hand motions that either meant *I'm going to circle around and cut him off* or *I like it when people use a circular motion while tickling me*. Either way, he ducked down a side hallway, leaving me to follow the Oneirovore through the door.

I ran into a defunct industrial kitchen, barely visible in the dull red light of an exit sign behind me. I palmed a rose and threw a little of the stunned shock I'd felt when I'd been doused in energy drink into the blossom, giving it a sickly green glow.

In the light, I could see another door across the long, narrow room. There was no way the Oneirovore could've reached it in the few seconds of lead time he'd had, so where was—

A frying pan flew towards my face from the darkness, and I glimpsed movement from the far corner of the room as I ducked, the pan handle clanging painfully off my shoulder. I swore and flicked the rose in my hand forward, flinging the petals like glowing, magical darts. They swarmed like acid green fireflies towards the Oneirovore, but at the last second, he grabbed a tray off a nearby countertop and used it as a shield, deflecting the petals harmlessly into an industrial sink. I responded by shouting some words that referenced the male anatomy in impolite ways.

He made it out of the kitchen, far enough ahead that the door had closed completely by the time I got there. I slammed my already bruised shoulder into it, wincing as I came through into another stairwell, this one straight down to a heavy wooden door. As I watched, the Oneirovore placed his hand on it and chanted a few phrases that sounded Russian, making a series of runes glow purple along the doorframe. Something told me that if he got through that door, we wouldn't be finding him again anytime soon. I only had a few seconds.

With a slightly unintimidating shriek of "Maaaaaarrry Poppppinnns!!!" I leapt onto the bannister butt-first and threw myself down the stairs. The wood was bumpy and nearly threw me off, but a childhood of shenanigans served me well, and I was able to keep my momentum going until I reached the Oneirovore. At the last second, probably shaken by my battle cry, he began to turn, but I barreled into him, taking him down onto the floor with my full weight on his back.

He gave a few half-hearted attempts to break free, but he was a pretty slender guy, and I had all the leverage in the situation. Finally, he sighed and tried to shrug as best he could.

"Fine, you got me. What the hell do you want?"

"First off," I said, still panting a bit from the exertion, "I want to say that spin move you did with the tray in the kitchen was really cool. Major props."

He gave that crooked smile again. "Thanks. What was that spell, anyways? Some sort of magic flower power?"

I snorted. "I'm not a hippie, I'm a Free Spell."

At my words, I felt some of the tension leak out of him, and I decided to give him a display of trust. I got off him and offered my hand, pulling the lanky guy up to his feet.

"You're another Free Spell? You're not from the Academy?"

"Nope," I said. "Just another magic freak who could use your help."

At that moment, the door above us clanged open, and Antoine burst in. He took in the scene. "Oh. Is everything all right? The hallway I took to cut him off was a dead end."

I looked at the Oneirovore's gleaming eyes and found myself, almost without reason, trusting him. "Yeah, I think we're all right."

WE GRABBED A TABLE upstairs in the lounge area to talk. The Oneirovore's real name was Linden, and he became even friendlier when Antoine bought him a LaCroix.

"So you haven't heard anything about what's been happening in the Apple?" I said, sipping on a beer.

Linden spread his hands wide. "I haven't been back in the Apple in months. I mix with some fey here when I have a gig, but in general I've tried to leave that place behind." I could smell the sharp scent of anger on the edge of his words, but there was also the deep, loamy smell of past hurt underneath.

Oh, right. I can smell emotions. It's one of my Free Spell things. Let's move on.

"Why?" I said. "Was the Academy closing in on you?"

"Those nerds?" Linden snorted. "Nah, they were sniffing around but I got the sense they just wanted to know more about me. But let's just say I don't fit into the perfect happy little dreamworld of the Apple."

I nodded. Sometimes, seeing the cookie-cutter princesses of the Apple in their ballgowns, walking through the spotless halls of Castle Fortnight, I felt the same way. I knew how it felt to be different, the hurt that comes from not fitting in. It's a spindle that keeps on pricking.

I mean, as hurt as I was, I would never become a DJ, but still. I knew how hard breaking from the mold of the Apple could be.

Antoine filled Linden in on the events of the last few days, from the princesses' first screams to our meeting with Professor Tamsin. When he'd finished, Linden sipped his LaCroix stoically while we waited for him to respond.

"And in summary, I'm basically your only lead to help save your best friend's sister?" he said finally.

"Well, and the rest of the princesses under sleeping curses. But yeah. We don't really have much to go on other than your… whatever you do."

Linden gave a short, somewhat bitter chuckle. "Listen, I want to help, but my…," he lowered his voice as a group of ba-dass raver chicks walked by, "*powers*, or whatever, aren't under my control. They just *happen*. It's not a gift, it's my own freakin' curse."

I didn't need to sniff his emotions to tell he was being genuine. I'd said the same words at various points in my life.

"I get it, Linden," I said. "I really do. I still screw up with my powers, sometimes. There's no guidebook for us to follow, no step-by-step recipe to let us know how we're 'supposed' to do this. That's the price we pay for being able to do something no one else can do."

"But what if I make it worse?" he said quietly.

Antoine and I looked at each other and shrugged. "The Apple is pretty screwed up right now," I said, "The princesses seem to be in horrible, unending agony, and everyone who has to listen isn't much better off. But the silver lining is, I'm not sure you can make it much worse."

Linden screwed up his bright eyes in a fake scowl. "Is this supposed to be a pep talk?"

I gave a big yawn. "Shut up, it's late."

"It's barely midnight."

"I stand by my original statement," I said, standing. "Now are you coming back to the Apple or not? We can meet up with Tamsin in the morning."

"I, er…" Linden looked at his can of LaCroix like it was going to give him all the answers. I've known oracles who use tea leaves, coffee stains, or pigeon shit to tell the future, but never overpriced sugar water.

He met my eyes steadily. "I'll give it a try."

My mouth broke into a wide grin, and after a moment his face mirrored mine. "That's all we can ask."

"But umm… I need a place to crash."

AN HOUR LATER, LINDEN was curled up downstairs on my couch in a pair of Cade's old Witchdale High Athletics sweatpants and a concert t-shirt for Britney Scythes, the Apple's most violent Britney Spears tribute act. I had barely been able to keep my eyes open all the way home, but once I got into bed, it felt like my mind couldn't stop racing. I tossed and turned for a while, but the muffled drone of screams echoing through the Apple kept worming its way into my ears.

Finally, I dragged myself out of bed. If I was going to be stuck awake, I might as well be stuffing my face with cookie dough. Eyes barely open, I stumbled down the stairs into the living room, where I noticed a flickering light still glowing.

Linden was sitting on the sill of one of the windows wearing a flowing blue bathrobe that looked incredibly comfortable. His dark hair reflected the orange tones of a roaring fire in the fireplace, which had definitely not been lit when I'd tucked him in earlier. The sound of princesses screaming mixed with a roaring wind outside from a storm that must've picked up since we'd gotten home.

"Nice robe," I said by way of greeting. Linden looked up at me quizzically, and I noticed the tired circles under his eyes were gone. In fact, his face looked fuller, healthier, even happier.

"Don't mind me, I'm just going for a midnight snack," I said as he continued to stare. "You want anything?"

Finally, he got up out of the window in a whirl of—was his robe satin? It was much nicer than any other clothing in the house, and it made me wonder where he'd been hiding it.

"Briar?" he stammered. "Is that—really you?"

I paused. "Uh… yes? Why wouldn't it be?"

"How are you here?"

Something… off about the whole scene started to gnaw at me, and I chuckled a little nervously. "Are you okay, Linden? Did you snort some pixie dust at the club?"

Before he could respond, a flash of lightning lit the house in stark relief, and I jumped. *Someone was standing just inside the front window*. My heart started hammering into my throat, and a horrible voice in my head started questioning if I was somehow stuck in a horror movie—and if so, was I the Final Girl or the comic relief who dies early?

I took a shaky step forward towards the figure, and suddenly recognition blossomed. "Alice? What the hell are you doing?" She was stock still, staring out the window with a blank expression.

She didn't respond. By this point Linden had walked over and was peering at me, somewhat rudely.

"What's going on?" I said, an edge of panic in my voice. "Is she sleepwalking?"

"It's really you," Linden mumbled, almost to himself. Then he seemed to snap out of it. "Briar, you're in a dream."

I started to respond, paused, took a breath, freaked out a bit, and finally felt my heart start to pound again. "What?"

"This has never happened before," he continued. "I always just… show up in dreams. By myself."

"So like, our minds traveled into Alice's mind?"

Linden shrugged. "I don't know about you, but I'm really here. Physically. Usually I can exert a little influence over the dream, but mostly I'm just an audience member." As if to demonstrate, he gestured with his hand and a can of LaCroix suddenly appeared. He cracked it and took a sip.

Another flash illuminated the house, and I walked to Alice's side. Her eyes were unfocused, and her mouth was a little open, watching out the window with dread. "Alice?"

"Dreamers are usually a bit… out of it," Linden warned.

I started to answer him, until I caught sight of what Alice was looking at outside.

The shrieking outside was not just the sounds of princesses, but a vast, swirling tornado, ripping its way through the Apple. As I watched, a row of cottages was thrown violently into the sky, wood and straw ripped apart like a child's toy. Next, the storm bore down on Castle Fortnight, the intensity of the wind and screams growing as stone towers fell into each other, the loose stone debris picked up into the whirlwind.

My mouth went dry, and I stepped back from the window.

"Pretty messed up, huh?" Linden said nonchalantly.

"Is this… this isn't real, right?" I said. All of my senses, all of my emotions were screaming that the world around me was ending.

"Nope. We're fine. Unless your friend has any divinatory powers?"

I shook my head. "Besides a freaky ability to predict who is going to win *The Bachelor*, she's just as clueless as the rest of us."

"Then, yeah. Dreams can be horrible. Or amazing. Mostly they're just weird. You have to just sorta sit back and—"

His words were interrupted by a sharp rap on the door, three precise knocks with an epilogue of ominous foreboding. Linden and I just stared at each other. Despite his laid-back words, I could tell he was also a little spooked.

"Should we get that?" I asked. I wasn't familiar with dream protocol.

I was saved from indecision when Alice walked slowly past us, moving like she was being driven by an unseen force, her limbs limp like a marionette's. She stood before the door, and it opened of its own accord with a horrible languidness.

A man and a woman stood outside, clad in matching black business attire and ominous scowls. I've never met them, but somehow, I knew they were Alice's parents from her descriptions of them: her father, looming and disapproving, his surgeon's hands clutched severely in front of him, and her mother, her eyes sharp and disapproving, taking in all the details of the scene in front of her like she was constantly prosecuting a case.

"Daughter," Alice's father said coolly. "It's time to come home."

Alice's eyes fluttered, and a spark of awareness lit in them. "What? I am home."

"Don't be ridiculous," her mother said harshly. "Your home is with us. In Fargo."

Still in a stupor, Alice shook her head sluggishly. "No. No, I'm not going back there. I live here now. I love it. I love the Poisoned Apple."

Her parents turned to each other and shared a look. "Darling," her father said, "we've been over this."

Then they both pivoted their heads, nearly robotically, and trained their cold eyes on Alice. When they spoke, it was in a monotone, terrifying unison.

"There is no Poisoned Apple."

As they said the words, the roof of my house tore off with a deafening roar, and the winds of the tornado rushed all around us, tearing the living room to shreds. Everything began to swirl around me, the rug ripping out from under my feet and causing me to stumble. Plates shattered in the kitchen, thrown like clay pigeons into the wall, while a horrendous groan preceded the floorboards starting to splinter and rise. Finally, the force of the gale grew too strong, and my feet began to scrabble for purchase on the floor as I was drawn up and up and—

"It's not real," Linden said. In the midst of the chaos, he stood completely still, his robe unruffled. "It seems like you're in a tornado, that it's going to pull you apart—*but it's not real.*"

My fear-struck brain took a moment to process his words, but slowly, the truth began to sink in. I took a gulp of air, and after a shaky exhale, my feet found solid ground again. With a slow, strange detachment, I looked around as my living room was turned to debris, shards of our broken magic mirror adding a sparkle to the horror.

"It's not real," Alice echoed from behind us. As I turned to her, the entire scene shifted, and instead of the rubble of our cottage, we were in a stark, white room. The padded walls were covered in twisted, scratched-out words, designs, drawings. I saw the words *curse*, *witch*, *princess*, a rudimentary drawing of Castle Fortnight, and a trio of stick figures that bore a heart-wrenching resemblance to Alice, Jacqui, and me.

Alice was curled up in the corner, except it wasn't the rebellious, fashionable, badass of a girl I knew. She looked younger, thinner, and haunted. Instead of her iconic, choppy style, her hair was a long, drooping mess that covered her face and laid listlessly on her hospital gown.

"It's not real," she said one last time, before the entire scene in front of me disappeared into darkness.

"HELL YEAH, MOTHERGOOSER," I swore triumphantly under my breath as I flipped a pancake perfectly on the first try. It was just past sunrise, and I'd destroyed the kitchen almost as much as the dream cyclone had while making Alice's favorite chocolate-chip Nutella pancakes. I hadn't slept much after being jolted out of the Dream Slip and back into my bed, and rather than mull over the Big Questions I had about how that had all happened, I decided to make breakfast. I even gave Linden a twenty and told him to go get some fancy coffee from our favorite neighborhood café, Pour Over the Rainbow.

As luck would have it, Alice came downstairs just as I'd finished the first batch of pancakes. As an honest-to-goodness morning person, she practically bounded down the steps in a

She-Ra nightshirt and fluffy skull slippers. She stopped in mock horror when she saw me awake and cooking.

"First the princesses screaming, and now people are getting possessed?" she said, plopping down on one of the stools along our breakfast bar.

I stuck my tongue out at her as I handed her a plate stacked with pancakes. She eyed them warily. "What are these for? Did someone die?"

"Can't I do something nice for my best friend without you assuming there was a death?"

"Not before ten A.M. you can't."

I laughed despite myself. "Okay, you're right. They're sort of apology pancakes."

Alice had already started pouring maple syrup and whipped cream on them. "Whatever it is, I forgive you."

"Thanks—uh, do you remember any dreams from last night?"

She shook her head as she stuffed half a pancake in her mouth with a guttural moan of delight.

"Well, this is going to sound bonkers, but you know the guy who slept on our couch last night? He and I went in your dreams."

Alice looked thoughtful for a moment but kept stuffing her face with pancakes. "Oh," she said between mouthfuls.

"I guess that just happens to him, and for some reason I got pulled along for the ride. It must be a Free Spell thing. But still, even if I didn't mean to, it felt like an invasion of privacy. So please accept these apology pancakes." I dumped two more on her plate and bowed my head.

Alice gulped and took a swig of the milk I'd gotten her. "Bri, don't worry about it. No harm, no foul."

"But what I saw seemed really... personal. It was kind of messed up, to be honest."

"Well, yeah. It's a dream. A weird fragment of my subconscious filtered through whatever physiological state I was in after eating that bunyip burrito before bed."

Even for Alice, this seemed like she was handling this way too nonchalantly. "But there was a tornado, and the Apple got destroyed, and then you were in a *mental institution*." I gestured dramatically with my spatula.

"Oh, that one?" Alice shrugged. "Yeah, I used to have that all the time when I first moved here." She looked at me critically. "Are you okay? I'm sorry—I remember that one being sort of headtrippy. Do you want to talk about it?"

"I—are *you* apologizing to *me* for having a disturbing dream that I crashed with unknown magics?"

"I mean, don't expect any pancakes," she said with a wry grin.

I turned off the stove and sat down next to her with my own (slightly less towering) plate of pancakes. "So, do you actually think that? Are you worried the Apple is all some sort of hallucination that you're having in a padded cell in North Dakota?"

"Briar," Alice said, her voice getting firm and serious, "*of course not*. Not really. Sure, one time when Jacqui and I did pixie dust I thought we were all figments of my imagination, but I also spent an hour convinced I should write a screenplay for a dark, gritty reboot of the Kool-Aid Man."

"I would still watch that," I said under my breath.

"I know you would," Alice said warmly. "But really, Bri, I'm fine. I have my issues with my overbearing parents, sure, but the one thing I'm grateful to them for is making me go to therapy when I was in high school. Weirdly, they thought it would fix me and make me commit to going to Loyola for pre-law, but talking through some of my shit was actually what inspired me to move to New York. And then discover the Apple."

I gave her a smirk. "Would you say you… *fell down the rabbit hole?*"

She groaned and hit me with an oven mitt.

I grinned. Alice didn't talk about her life before the Apple very often, except in passing references and snide comments. "Well, I'm glad you did all of that. Otherwise I wouldn't have met you. And gotten that somewhat terrifying view into your subconscious."

Alice brightened and gave me her full smile, which could light up a stadium. "Same. Besides, if my worst fear is that I'm living a life so awesome and magical that it seems unreal, I must be doing something right, huh?"

At that moment, the front door opened, and Linden came in with a cardboard carrier full of coffee. Outside of the Dream Slip, he was back in sweatpants and looked a little tired. The smell of caffeine and Nutella finally brought Cade and Jacqui out of hibernation, and pretty soon we were all camped out, eating pancakes in our PJs and talking shit. Linden seemed to fit right in, and I was delighted to discover he had a sarcastic pottymouth almost as biting as mine. It was nice to have a little normalcy before a long day of epic questing. In the middle of Jacqui's story about a dinner party her parents threw where she'd swapped out the Dom Pérignon for shrinking syrup, there were three perfectly timed raps on the front door.

As soon as I saw Antoine's expression as he stood on our front step, however, I knew the fun was over. "Have you looked on your mirror?" he said grimly.

I groaned. "No. C'mon, we already have one Apple-wide crisis. How can it get worse?"

By way of answering, he walked past me and pressed a few runes on our giant, golden framed magic mirror. The surface rippled for a few moments before resolving into a distinguished

Royal speaking to a crowd in one of Castle Fortnight's large plazas.

"Who's that?" I asked apprehensively.

"Baron Landgreaves," Antoine said angrily. "Some third-rate minor Noble trying to make a name for himself."

The Baron was handsome, in a silver fox sort of way. He was standing in one of the many courtyards in Castle Fortnight, dressed conservatively in a severe grey doublet and a black cape. His wide-jawed face was perfectly arranged into an expression of disapproval and sympathy.

"—and my fellow citizens of the Apple, this cannot continue. Our daughters are literally screaming out in pain and confusion. They need us to protect them." He paused as the onlookers cheered. "They need us to get this city in order. To return to the stories that form the bedrock on which our world is built. For too long, we have sacrificed our cherished traditions and deeply rooted identities in the name of ill-conceived progress. We must again take up the mantle of noble heroes, of staunch protectors, and save these damsels in distress."

Another roar of agreement from the crowd.

"That's why I've called on the Multiarchy to authorize a special task force of our greatest heroes to take on this quest. This group, the White Knights, will root out whoever is harming the princesses of the Apple, defeat them, and bring back the happily ever afters that we all deserve. Thank you!" The Baron ended his speech with a strong, confident smile, sweeping his arms dramatically towards the gathered crowd. The footage cut back to the usual pair of animated statues who read the local news.

A knot formed in my stomach as I exchanged glances with my friends. Taken individually, the Baron's words were mostly innocuous platitudes. Who doesn't want to help the princesses? It was easy to get swept up in the force of his strong, macho act.

But the instant I started really considering his words, his glowing praise of tradition and identity, it all started to take on a sinister stench.

And the pieces of troll dung in the audience were eating it up.

"One of my guard friends tipped me off this morning," Antoine said, breaking the nauseous silence. "She said these White Knights the Baron is calling together are being given absurd amounts of funding and free reign to do whatever they deem necessary to complete their quest."

"It's a power grab," Jacqui said quietly. "He's using the situation with the princesses to consolidate military power, start investigating anyone he thinks isn't in line with the 'traditions' of the Apple—"

"Let's not get too far ahead of ourselves," Cade cautioned. "Maybe he truly wants to help—"

I shook my head. "I really, *really* don't like this, but it's not our problem, yet. The best thing we can do is figure out whatever is going on before the lunkheads the Baron is recruiting have the chance to cause any real harm."

Looking around, I wasn't sure I had done a great job convincing my friends. Jacqui, in particular, had crossed her arms and was giving me a look that said this wasn't the last I'd hear about this.

"C'mon," I said to Linden and Antoine, "we've got to get to Castle Fortnight. Tamsin wants a chance to examine the Oneirovore and Jacqui's sister."

Linden blanched and rolled his eyes. "Yippy. Just let me change into something more appropriate for being experimented on."

THE D'LUCIEN ARDORS HAD loaned us a parlor near Raye's room, and Tamsin had wasted no time setting up a makeshift lab—currently, she had Linden in a protective pentagram and kept throwing purple powder at him, then looking through a crystal at his aura and making copious notes. I don't know if it was good thaumaturgy, but it was definitely fun to watch.

Seemingly satisfied after the thirteenth repetition of all this, Tamsin closed her notebook and looked up, almost as if she were noticing Antoine and me for the first time. "Now, Briar, you said you followed the Oneirovore—"

"You can just call me Linden—"

"—you followed Linden *into* the Dream Slip? In an astral form or were you there corporeally?"

"Honestly I'm not sure. I remember falling asleep first, but I don't know if I took my body along for the ride into Alice's dream. Did I look very solid to you?"

Linden shrugged as a I looked at him. "I didn't notice you floating through any walls or anything, but also there was a tornado so it's possible I missed something."

Tamsin began pacing and speaking under her breath. "It's possible if their auric frequencies resonated, the Oneirovore's talent pulled in another nearby Free Spell in its wake—"

Jacqui entered the room, looking worried. "Raye seems to have quieted down. If we want to have Linden try to make contact with her in the Dream Slip, now might be our best chance."

Everyone in the room turned to look at Linden. His hazel eyes widened, then set into a determined gaze as we all made our way into the hallway. Walking beside him, I could see his hands clenched, and I smelled the sweaty undercurrent of apprehension billowing off of him.

"You okay?" I said softly, dropping back behind Jacqui, Antoine, and Tamsin.

Linden swallowed, the scent of his nerves filling the hallway. "I dunno. My power isn't something I'm used to turning on and off like a spigot. It's more of a horrifying side effect I try to avoid."

"Linden," I said, trying to keep my own nerves out of my voice, "I get it. I spent a long time running from my power. Or using it in a way that made me feel gross. But they're a part of us, good or bad. And once we accept that, then we can try to use them to help people."

Linden shook his head and refused to make eye contact.

"Hey," I repeated, grabbing his wrist. "You can do this. That girl in there needs you. So go let your freak flag fly." He gave me a strange look and a bit of a snort-laugh, but I could smell a puff of relief at my words.

Raye's bedroom was much the same as the last time we'd seen it, mostly empty and shrouded in darkness. We formed a semi-circle around the foot of the canopied bed. Raye was quiet, but even in her slumber, her face was twisted in an expression of fear.

Jacqui stared at her sister. Most people wouldn't even notice the tremor in her chin as she held back tears, but I'd seen that face grow up and knew it better than my own.

"All right," she said, turning towards Linden and walking towards him. "How does this work?"

"I, uh," Linden swallowed. "I'm not exactly sure."

"Sorry, what?" Jacqui said, her anxiety flipping into anger. "You aren't sure? You're just going to go fiddle around in my sister's head?"

"Jacqui," I said, smoothly interspersing myself between them, "we just need to give Linden some space to work."

"But—" she started, but I raised my eyebrows and guided her back to the other side of the room without much resistance.

"And Linden," I said, putting my hands on his shoulders and guiding him towards the gauzy, wavy canopy that surrounded Raye's bed, "just relax. Take all the time that you need, and I'll be right by your side."

"Briar?" he said, not looking at me, but instead staring into the diaphanous fabric in front of him.

"What is it, buddy?"

"Did you mean that literally?"

I turned to see what had caught his eye, and I saw that the two of us were no longer in Raye's bedroom in the d'Lucien Ardor Tower. We were in an old pine forest, the knotted branches covered in miles of the same looping, semi-translucent material from Raye's canopy. A thick white mist covered the forest floor, at times seeming to merge with the draping curtains draping across the landscape.

"No, I did not," I muttered. My voice felt weirdly muffled, and I realized there weren't any other sounds in the forest: no wind in the trees, no birdsong in the branches, nothing. Even the mist on the ground seemed to hang and float, stagnant, without movement.

"Well," I said, pushing down the slight unease building in my stomach, "good job. You made it into Raye's dream. And brought me along for the ride."

Linden looked distant, slowly moving his eyes around the dreamscape. "This feels... off."

"What do you mean?"

"I've been in a lot of dreams. A lot of nightmares too. There aren't many hard rules, but every one of them has always been in motion. I've never seen a dream so static."

"Is that a bad thing?" I said. "Maybe this dream is actually going to be restful."

As if on cue, the pine-needle-covered ground below us began to tremble, a throbbing pulse that began to quicken its pace from a dull heartbeat to a frantic spasm. I grabbed Linden's arm to steady myself, and somehow between the two of us we were able to stay on our feet. I looked around, panicked, but where do you run when the whole world is shaking apart?

"Briar?" a small, hoarse voice whispered, cutting through the chaos. Ten feet away, clad in a gauzy white shift, Raye stood with her arm against the trunk of a tree.

"Raye!" My legs started moving almost of their own accord, pumping against the shuddering earth. The mist had begun to swirl and boil around me, but I kept moving through the nightmare, sure that if I could just reach Raye, if I could just get to her—

The ground erupted in front of me, and I scraped my palm against a tree's bark to slow myself down before I skidded into whatever was emerging. A twisting arm of thick roots writhed out of the ground, shaking dirt loose as it flailed. Its long, curving thorns made it look like someone had squeezed an echidna through a toothpaste tube. Raye was just on the other side of the vine, a look of terror in her pale blue eyes as they stared at me. In my periphery, I could now see a dozen other princesses in the woods, all beset by their own monstrous plant snakes.

I tensed, watching the root's movements as it swayed, trying to time it so I could get to Raye. In a deeply distant part of my mind, I was aware of the sludgy, regurgitative sounds of earth cascading as a dozen more thorny vines launched themselves from beneath us, closing the three of us in on all sides. Linden slid to a stop next to me, panting. "Briar, we gotta go. We need to get out of here—"

But before he could finish, I'd thrown myself across the wall of thorns rising from the earth. The majority of my mass made it, but my left shoulder screamed with pain as a thorn stuck into it, spinning me with my own momentum and flinging me to the ground.

Raye closed the few steps to me as I straightened, and my arms opened, as if I could protect her from the hellscape of thorns around us. She reached out her hand, and I grabbed it in both of mine. It was delicate, soft, but very warm and alive.

"Briar, what's—" she started, before a vine looped itself around her chest.

"*No!*" I screamed as the vine began to jerk her away from me. I gripped her arm with all my strength, my boot heels digging uselessly into the dirt underneath me. Despite my entire weight, I could feel the vine pulling Raye away from me.

Our eyes met, then, in that brief moment of equilibrium while I was able to keep her hand in mine. I could see the whites of her eyes completely around her iris, tinged with pink and the sheen of tears. They were the eyes of someone who thought she was going to die.

"Raye," I said, the words tumbling out with whatever air was left in my lungs. "Hold on. We're coming for you. You're not alone in here. Jacqui and I are going to—"

With a mighty tug, the vine ripped Raye out of my grasp, up into the treeline where she was blocked from view by the violently waving curtains hanging in the trees. She screamed, and I saw a web of thorns coming towards my face before something hit me from behind and the world went black.

I WOKE UP ON the floor of Raye's bedroom, tangled with Linden from where he'd slide tackled me, with enough force to knock us both out of the Dream Slip. Raye's screams continued on this side of reality, and as I staggered to my feet, I saw her thrashing on the bed. Knowing what I knew, I could almost see the vines still curling around her.

"Rumpelstiltskin's red rear," Jacqui swore. "What just happened?"

I shook my head and offered a hand to Linden as he groaned and got up. "We were in the Dream Slip. It got messy."

"I was right," Tamsin said hollowly. "All my theories, about the Dream Slip, the connections between dreamers…" She trailed off, but a slightly giddy smile lit her face.

"Briar, are you okay?" Antoine said, looking at my shoulder with panic. There, stuck into my shoulder, was one of the thorns from the vines in Raye's dream.

"What the f—OW!" I said as Tamsin stepped forward and yanked the thorn from my skin. I immediately clamped my hand over the wound. It felt mostly superficial, but still stung like a witch.

"This came from the Dream Slip?" Tamsin said, eyeing the thorn hungrily and turning it over in her hands. "I've got to run some tests." She scurried out of the room, and Raye began screeching, so the rest of us followed Tamsin into the hallway.

"What did you do to my daughter?" an icy voice said from behind us. I turned to see Aurelle standing with one of her handmaidens, a scroll clutched in her hand. Jacqui's mother was wearing enough silk to make a kimono for a giant, dozens of flowing layers of sparkling indigo and violet that made her look like a glitter-soaked bouquet of carnations.

I felt heat rise to my face, but as much as I tried to speak up to defend our actions, I found myself unable to speak. In fact, I was finding it almost hard to breathe. *It's her Largesse*, I realized. The sheer force of her magical Royal presence was keeping us all tongue-tied like naughty schoolchildren.

Jacqui seemed to have built up some resistance to it over the years, because with gritted teeth she was able to force out, "We're working on it, Mother. Briar and Linden were able to make contact with Raye."

All of a sudden, the feeling of a hand at my throat was gone, and I took in a shuttering breath. Aurelle was back to the dainty image of Nobility, as if she hadn't just been magically choking us.

"You spoke to my darling Raye? Is she okay?" she said, her wide eyes turning to me.

"I—we only spoke briefly," I said, trying to hedge my bets. I didn't want to alarm her. "Raye is hanging in there. She's being very brave."

Aurelle's eyes moistened with tears, even as her mouth set itself with determination. "Good. That's my girl," she said softly, surprising me with the force behind the words. Then, in an instant, she flounced back into Disney mode. "I have other matters to attend to, but please update me with any developments." She turned in a wide circle, her dress twirling out with enough sparkle to make my eyes burn.

Once we were safely ensconced in Tamsin's makeshift lab, I briefly described the dream as Antoine put a poultice on my shoulder and bandaged it up.

"So these vines burrowed through the ground and started attacking princesses?" Jacqui said. She'd been pacing and re-pacing an infinity sign into the plush Persian rugs of her family's parlor.

"Yeah, it got a little *Tremors*," I said. "They just burst up all through the forest."

"What I don't get is," Linden said, sipping a wine cooler he'd bullied a servant into bringing, "whose dream were we in? I thought it was Raye's, but then there were other princesses in there too."

"Was it some sort of—" I started.

"—collective unconscious?" Antoine said, finishing my sentence.

"I was going to say Vulcan mind meld."

"Then who was dreaming up those scary plant worms?" Linden said.

"No one is," Tamsin piped up. She had been examining the thorn she'd pulled from my shoulder for the last ten minutes through a series of lenses, orbs, and what looked to me like cast-iron opera glasses. "This thorn didn't come from the Dream Slip."

"What do you mean?" I asked, struggling to keep up with her.

Tamsin looked up from the thorn, blinking, and seemed to remember the rest of us in the room. She gave a smile, and with a flick of her wrist, she sent the thorn floating to the middle of the room. "The thorn isn't made of dreamstuff. It's from the real world, and it seems to be made of runes." She spoke something quiet and guttural, and the thorn began to glow with golden light, forming into streams of swirling runes. After a moment, the light exploded out, and a huge, three-dimensional image of the thorn filled the parlor, searing in the afternoon sun. The glimmering points of energy that made up the picture floated serenely, passing through the chandelier in the middle of the room.

"How much do you all know about basic thaumaturgical theory?" Tamsin asked. My look of abject terror was echoed in the faces of Jacqui, Linden, and Antoine. Tamsin chuckled. "Okay. To vastly oversimplify the first decade of training you'd receive at the Academy of the Iron Wand, magic is a language. Wizards work spells by forming runes into basic, primitive sentences. Each rune is like a phoneme in linguistics—more or less meaningless on its own, but they can be linked together to form words. And eventually, with enough runes, you can start linking those words together to form basic sentences."

Jacqui nodded. "That sounds sort of like what they told me in the Curse Removal Department. They said my curse was like a contract with reality, and they were trying to find the loopholes and expand them out until the whole thing was null and void."

"Sounds like a complicated curse," Tamsin said. "To expand the metaphor, even the most powerful wizards alive have only mastered enough runes to form spells equal to the complexity of a paragraph or two. And it takes them years."

I caught Linden's gaze, and I didn't need my magic nose to guess he was thinking about the same thing. "What about Free Spells? How do they use magic?"

Tamsin adjusted her glasses. "Naturally, there are a lot of ways to use magic, just like there are a lot of ways to use language. Witches and shamans use it almost more like poetry—they're still making sense, but there are fewer rules, and its more about emotion and intention than syntax and grammar. And Free Spells haven't been studied as much, but from what I understand, your magic manifests… more like scatting."

"I'm sorry," I said, "did you just say my magic is the linguistic equivalent of animal poop?"

"No! Scat like vocal jazz improvisation. Scooby-doo-wop-dee-wop, and such," she finished weakly, wagging a finger in time to her half-hearted singing. "You're using the same sounds and phonemes a wizard would, but twisting them to your own purposes, until you're able to do something very few people can do."

"Cool," I shrugged. "We're the Ella Fitzgeralds of magic. I'll take it. So what does all this have to do with these thorns?"

Tamsin walked to where the thorn was floating, gazing up with reverence at the galaxy of golden motes swirling around the room. "Each one of these sparks represents a spell more complex than anything I've seen in forty years at the Academy. If most wizards cast spells in sentences, this thorn contains the magical equivalent of James Joyce's *Ulysses*."

There was a moment of silence.

"It's a really long, complex, and confusing novel."

We all nodded as if we got the reference.

"Whoever or… *whatever* made this spell, they use magic at a level completely unheard of in the history of the Apple. But it is clear that these thorns were sent by someone. The princesses aren't screaming by accident."

I looked to Antoine, who usually keeps his cool, even in situations where everything around us is topsy-turvy. His mouth was agape, and I could see the whites around his brown eyes as he stared up at the golden lights weaving their way around the room.

I caught a whiff of panic starting to fill the room (*she who smelt it, dealt it*, a voice from inside me said wisely), so I took a deep breath and tried to steady myself. "Okay. Wherever these things come from, however they were able to get to the princesses within the Dream Slip, they were created for a purpose, right? Which means we can approach this the way we would any other case. Just because they have alien magic of godlike proportions, we can still figure out a motive, determine a list of suspects, and track down the perp."

"And then what?" Linden said.

"To be determined!" I nearly shouted.

"Wait," Antoine said, speaking up for the first time since Tamsin's lecture. "If this thorn, and whatever spell is affecting the princesses, is made of magic, aren't we forgetting another option? What about Prick?"

"Woah, rude, my name is Linden—"

"No," I cut Linden off, as I rummaged in my messenger bag, "he means this." I drew out a thick, silver dagger with the design of vines inlaid on the hilt. Even in the sunlight, a subtle glow traced the outline of the thorn-shaped blade. "This is

Prick." I held it up so Tamsin and Linden could see. "It's forged dwarf iron capable of disenchanting most magic."

Tamsin peered closer. "Grimmsdamn. Where did you find something like that?"

"Graduation present from my dad," I said warmly. Good ol' Pops. Somehow in all his years working as a gardener at Castle Fortnight, he'd saved up enough to buy me a hefty magical artifact.

"Briar," Jacqui said, "you know I love you, but you're not putting that dagger anywhere near my sister. Not until we know what it's going to do to her."

"Well, what if we test it first? How about we see if it's able to dispel the thorn?" Antoine suggested.

"What? Are you joking? This thorn passed into our world from the Dream Slip," Tamsin said, her voice thick with tension. "It could advance my research decades—hell, it could revolutionize modern spellcraft! If we could reverse engineer—"

"If Prick can destroy this spell, it will end everything. The princesses—*my sister* will be free from whatever torment they're in," Jacqui said.

"But if you just give me time, the things I could *learn*—"

"No. My sister is in pain *now*." Jacqui wasn't angry, but I'd never heard her so firm in her life. "You've got to decide, Tamsin. Are you here to expand your research, or are you here to help the princesses?"

There was a pregnant pause, but it delivered early. "You're right," Tamsin said, shaking her head. "I'm sorry. Of course you're right. Let's give it a try." She flicked her hand and the thorn floated over to me.

I grabbed it out of the air and held Prick with my other hand. "Well, here goes nothing. Or, I guess, here goes the fate of the Apple. Either way."

I swung Prick in a straight arc to take off the tip of the thorn. Prick's powers only require the smallest cut, but I wasn't taking any chances, and the blade sliced through the air with more force than was strictly necessary. As soon as its edge touched the green surface, a silvery tingle shot through my arm, and Prick bounced off the thorn and out of my hand. There was a deep, ringing gong-noise, vaguely reminiscent of one of those bowls they use at yoga classes (or at least at the few Alice had dragged me to).

Jacqui's shoulders sagged, and I could tell she was secretly hoping this would be the end of it. "Nothing's ever frickin' easy in this town."

"Yeah," I said, stopping to pick up my dagger. "Easy doesn't make for good stories."

Tamsin had the empathy not to look too pleased that her experimental material wasn't damaged by my attack, but she picked up her opera glasses and peered across the room. "Huh," she muttered.

"Did you get something from that?" I asked.

"That ringing noise," she said. "It almost sounded like…" She adjusted the lenses and got closer. "It can be caused by two equivalent etheric valences comingling…"

"And in layperson, that means…?"

Tamsin put the opera glasses back in her cardigan pocket. "The two spells interacting probably have the same source."

"Wait," I said, still trying to decode what she was saying, "You're saying my dagger and whatever is hurting the princesses could've been made by the same person?"

"I can't determine that precisely, but it's very likely. And, not to be condescending," she said, "but even without my extensive knowledge of the arcane, both the spells in the Dream Slip and your dagger have a strong theme of thorns."

Damn. She had a point.

"There's something else," I said reluctantly. "When we were in Raye's room the first time, something happened with my powers. I couldn't tell exactly what, but it seemed like the spell that was affecting her was going through me and into a rose."

"What?" Jacqui said, whirling to face me. "Why didn't you say something before?"

"I dunno—I thought maybe it was a coincidence that my powers freaked out while I was near Raye, or that my own emotions were going haywire after seeing her… like that."

Navy snipers have less intense stares than Jacqui when she's riled, but after a moment she nodded begrudgingly. "Okay, I guess. But what does that mean? There's a connection between this thorn, your powers, and your high school graduation gift?"

Tamsin nodded, a slight frown on her lips. "I am in the habit of regarding any coincidence as a connection we do not yet understand. And that makes sense that only someone with such advanced magics could create your dagger—where did your father get such a rare and powerful artifact?"

"I don't know," I said. "It was a gift, so it seemed rude to ask. But my dad was a gardener at Castle Fortnight before he retired; there's no way he could've afforded something like this on Looking Glass Lane."

Antoine shook his head. "You can't find forged dwarf iron at Macey's."

"Alight, well then it looks like I'm going to go visit my dad in Witchdale and ask him some questions," I said, grabbing my messenger bag and throwing it on my shoulder.

"I'll come with you, Briar," Antoine said, a bit quickly.

Jacqui looked between Antoine and me and I could detect the ghost of a smile on her lips. "I'm going back to the house to check in with Alice," Jacqui said.

"Linden," Tamsin started, "would you mind coming back to the Academy with me? I have a few spells I'd like to try. You're going to have to be asleep for them, though."

Linden spared a glance at me, and I nodded. "Sure," he said. "I never turn down a free nap."

I hitched up my messenger bag, pleased as my friends all split up—it felt good to at least be doing something. Mysteries always felt a little overwhelming at the start, a big tangle of questions and connections that didn't make any sense. It was only as you started pulling at the threads that the true shape of the thing came to light. And it felt good that this was one mystery I wasn't exploring on my own.

Maybe I was right. Maybe we would be able to solve this like any other case.

My mood soured as we walked down the tower stairways, their stone walls echoing with the sound of Raye's screams.

WITCHDALE IS ONE OF the closest things the Apple has to the 'burbs. The fences are white-picket, the cobblestones are well-maintained, and the will-o-wisps never forget to light the regularly placed street lamps. Sure, it's a little boring compared to the chaos of the Apple proper, but it was a gorgeous place to grow up.

Antoine and I walked around a leaf-shaded curve in the road. Around us, the older residents of Witchdale trimmed their hedges, puttered in their yards, or sipped apple lemonade on the porches dotting the neighborhood.

"Ah, property ownership," I muttered as a pair of witches on brooms cackled overhead. "Modern society's least believable fairy tale."

Antoine chuckled. "Are you sure you're okay being around this much vegetation? Especially right after those vines attacked you in Raye's dream." I could tell from the timbre of his voice he was genuinely concerned.

I squinted at him. "I'm fine—why do you ask?"

"You've had some bad experiences with plant life in the past." When my face was still scrunched in confusion, he elaborated. "Remember our first case? You almost got killed by a Blighted Oak in the Afterwoods?"

"Oh right! I thought you were talking about when I saw the revival of *Little Shop of Horrors* on Broadway." He chuckled, but I failed to repress a genuine shudder. "That puppet was *terrifying*."

Antoine smiled but gave me one of his patented Serious Looks. "Just take care of yourself. All of this jumping from dream to dream sounds disorienting."

For once, I bit back a witty retort and thought on his words. He was right—beyond what was happening to the Apple, this case was becoming stranger than what I was used to. And maybe connected to my own magic? My own father? I swallowed, not able to speak for a moment. "Thanks," I squeaked out.

"I'm here if you want to talk," Antoine said quietly, his voice warm. I had no doubt he would be there for me, whatever I needed. But the prospect of opening up to him like that scared me more deeply than any murderous greenery.

I nodded my thanks at him, still not trusting my voice, and he took that as a sign he should move on to lighter topics. "When was the last time you visited your dad?"

"A few weeks ago, actually. Witchdale is kind of a pain to get to from Havmercy, but we did a brunch for his birthday."

Antoine quirked an eyebrow. "Are you two close?"

"Of course. He's the best. My dad was a single dude in his thirties when I was left randomly on his doorstep, and he raised me with no complaints."

"And did you cook this birthday brunch for him?" His tone sounded dubious.

"Hey! I can cook when the circumstances require. I just rarely do because I'm lazy." I realized that sounded like a much stronger counter-argument in my head.

"You'll have to prove that to me sometime," Antoine said, a glint in his eyes. I immediately avoided eye contact and looked at a nearby yard.

"Oh, Balrog butts," I swore. "Look at that."

I pointed to a red sign on a front lawn with bold white lettering. It read WHITE KNIGHTS WELCOME HERE.

Antoine went still beside me. "They already have merchandise?" I sputtered.

"Something tells me they've been waiting for this for a long time," Antoine said. "They were just preparing for a crisis to come along and give them the opportunity."

I shook my head. "You sound like you're about to make a helm out of tinfoil."

"It's only a conspiracy theory until it's proven," Antoine said wryly.

I stormed off down the road and we came to my dad's cottage, a small, white-washed colonial that he kept spotless. Rain or shine, my father spent every day of his retirement in his gardens, and it showed. Dense ferns spilled over the flagstone paths, and ivy traced a maze of trellises and gates. It turned what was a fairly modest little house into a gorgeous oasis.

True to form, my dad was out in the front yard in his overalls, hard at work with a trowel. He was never a large man, but as he aged into his fifties, he'd kept a wiry strength even as I grew half a foot taller than him.

"You need help, old man?" I said good-naturedly as I let myself in the front gate.

"Sure," my dad said, getting to his feet with a surprised chuckle and big grin. "Do you know anyone who knows a perennial from a hole in her head?"

I chuckled and gave him a big hug. "Good to see you, Pop. This is my friend, Antoine."

"Nice to meet you, Mr. Pryce."

"Call me Hank." He gave Antoine a handshake and a clap on the shoulder. "Great to meetcha."

"Dad, we have a few questions—"

"Honey, it's a beautiful day. My amazing daughter is visiting. First things first, we're having tea." I started to protest, but no matter how old I get, my dad can still give me a look that clamps my mouth shut. "Antoine, have a seat at that table over there, and we'll bring some out."

My dad ushered me into his small, cozy kitchen and we began working in tandem to brew a pot of tea, as we'd done countless times throughout the years. Whatever feelings Antoine had dredged up softened as I went through the familiar ritual. It felt good to be back in this kitchen, to know exactly where my dad had kept his mugs since I was a child. Even the tile floors were familiar as I shuffled across them, chipped but meticulously scrubbed, until finally I perched on the stone counter as we waited for the kettle to boil.

"Antoine seems nice," Dad said in his softest, non-confrontational yet infuriating tone.

"He is," I said. "He's a great *friend*."

He made a *hmm* noise while he pulled out some spoons.

"C'mon, Pop. Out with it. You're obviously fishing."

"It's just nice for you to bring a boy back home," he said. "Or anyone, of course."

"He's my partner, Dad. My *business* partner."

Dad opened up a jar of loose-leaf tea and gave it a good sniff, rolling a few leaves in between his fingers before giving a satisfied nod. "And how does the handsome knight feel about that? He seems very smitten with you."

"Really? You picked that up in the thirty seconds you've known him?"

He gave me a grin as the kettle began to rattle and whistle. "What can I say, I'm that good."

I groaned. "Why is everyone so obsessed with me dating someone?"

"I'm your father and, whether you're dating someone or not, I want you to be happy. Despite your best efforts at being miserable."

I poured the kettle into the pot. "I do not try to be miserable."

"Really? You don't find it easier to stay cynical and sarcastic than make new choices that might be scary?" He looked at me with raised eyebrows and kind eyes.

"I don't—I'm not—" I sputtered. "I fight monsters and use public transit. I'm fine with scary."

He shrugged and smiled. "Fighting a basilisk is one kind of scary. Putting yourself out there to possibly get rejected is another." I started to speak but his calm voice cut through mine. "So is letting go of a high school crush."

Steam rose from our teapot as I sagged onto the counter and crossed my arms. Pops knew me better than anyone, and clearly, he'd thought of these particularly insightful truth bombs in advance and prepared an arsenal. "I never really talked to you about Cade," I managed.

"You didn't have to. I saw enough to figure out what was going on. And I knew you'd get through it. Heartache is tough, but eventually we move on."

Again, my voice seemed to vanish as my thoughts swirled. "I'm not even sure what or who I want. What if I'm not ready?"

"You won't be."

I made a face. "Thank you for the support."

"Life's always happening, my darling. Doesn't matter if we're ready or not. Sometimes you have to take the plunge and figure out how to fly on the way down."

I paused. No matter how self-absorbed I was as a teen, I'd quickly learned the value of listening to what my dad said. Even when I did the complete opposite of his advice. "And what if it blows up in my face again, and I just get the emotional stuffing kicked out of me?"

"It might. The only way to avoid that is to stay safe, wrap yourself in bitterness, and never try."

The truth of what he was saying landed heavily in my stomach. I had been deflecting, avoiding whatever it was that was happening with Cade and Antoine. It was so much easier to make a joke of it and pretend it was something Jacqui and Alice were inventing.

A small rose in a vase on the windowsill started to flicker, its petals flitting from white to an anxiety-producing orange, the changes in color matching the pace of my racing heart as my magic spilled out of me, uncontrolled.

My dad's eyes flicked to the rose, and then to my face, holding my gaze with a steady compassion. "Breathe, honey. It's okay."

The sound of his voice reached straight to my lungs, bypassing my thought-logged brain. I took a large, if unsteady, breath in, and the colors on the rose started to calm down. The floor under my feet stopped spinning as I continued to breathe, deep into my stomach.

"Feel better?" my dad said quietly.

I nodded. "I'm still losing control sometimes."

"And you're also getting better at dealing with it. I've never seen you get back to normal that quickly." He grinned and tossed me a scone. "I'm proud of you, hun."

I took another breath and gave him a shaky smile. "Thanks. It hasn't been easy. I'm not exactly working with an instruction manual."

"None of us are. But if you can figure out the mysterious, impossible power inside you, I think you'll be able to figure out your boy problems."

I chuckled despite myself. My father was right. If I wanted things to change, I'd need to start doing things differently. But that would have to wait until after I'd saved the Apple. *Again.*

He removed the strainer and placed it delicately in the sink. "Tea's ready."

I sniffed and wiped the tears someone must've put in my eyes. "Any more emotional gut punches you want to land before we head back out?"

Dad wiped his hands on his overalls and wrapped me in a warm embrace. "You're incredibly strong, but growing up is difficult. Just don't be too hard on yourself, okay?"

I let out a tense breath. "Thanks, Dad. Really."

He made for the door, leaving me to carry the tea tray. "Anytime, sweetheart."

We set up our impromptu tea party on a cute metal café table Dad kept in his backyard, under a wisteria tree heavy with blooms. My dad was annoyingly kind and interested in Antoine, but eventually I was able to move us away from small talk and describe what we'd discovered so far about the princesses.

"So we came here," I said, warming my hands on my mug, "to ask you where you got Prick, and who might have made it."

"I'm sorry, I don't know who made it," my dad said. "I just got a delivery one day to the cottage."

I sagged. Of course there'd be more to the story. "Anonymously?"

"There was just a note that said 'For Briar' and explained the enchantment. It was right before your graduation, so I assumed that was when I was supposed to give it to you."

I took a calming sip of tea. "So you just gave your daughter a powerful magical item of dubious origin? No questions asked?"

My dad looked me steadily in the eye. "I trusted you. And I had a wizard friend check it out and make sure it was curse-free. You had just found out about your powers, so this seemed like a good thing to have as you were learning to use them. I figured you couldn't do too much damage if you also had a way to remove spells from people."

"Dad, why did you never tell me any of this?"

He shifted uncomfortably. "Bri, I dunno. You were going through a lot, with your powers, with…" A quick glance towards Antoine let me know he wanted to talk about Cade, but he stopped himself. "You were still so young. And I didn't know much, so it seemed cruel to give you more questions you couldn't answer."

I slumped back in my chair. "Crap. So maybe the same person who sent Prick to me five years ago is the one messing with the princesses now."

"Could be," Antoine said.

"Sorry I couldn't be more help, kiddo."

I reached across the table and put my hand on his. "You were plenty of help, Dad. Thank you. But we should probably go check in with Jacqui and Alice and see if they've been able to dredge up any leads."

"Thank you for the tea, Hank," Antoine said warmly as he stood. I gave my dad one last hug as we said our goodbyes.

"Everything okay?" Antoine said as we walked out of the yard.

"Sure," I semi-lied. "Why do you ask?"

"When you and your dad were in the kitchen, every rose in the garden went haywire for a few minutes."

So much for handling my powers.

"We… had a chat" I said.

Antoine nodded. For a part-time knight-detective, he was good at not prying. "As long as you're okay. Family can be a lot sometimes."

I sighed. "I'm mostly okay. I love my dad, but man, does he know how to get under my skin. For good or bad."

"Sure. Our family knows how to push our buttons because they made our buttons."

"That's very wise for a meathead knight."

Antoine waggled his eyebrows. "I heard it on a podcast, I think."

"Briar!" My dad's voice rang out from behind us. He came running up. "I found it."

"Found what?" I asked as he drew something from his overall pocket.

"The note. That came with Prick."

Somehow, as he handed the parchment over, I knew what I'd find. It was the same parchment, the same acid green ink, as the note that had come with the cursed muffin basket that had turned Jacqui into a cat. The same handwriting as the kidnappers who had stolen Rick from the mortal world.

The mark of the Arsenic Queens.

Grimmsdammit, Tarris was going to be so smug when I told him.

WE CAME HOME TO my house to find Jacqui, Alice, Tarris, and Rick hard at work in the living room. The floor was covered in poster boards and writing utensils. My friends all laid out on the floor drawing and writing while our mirror played old seventies folk-protest songs.

"Baron Landgreaves made an announcement," Jacqui explained over the sounds of Joni Mitchell. "They're having a kickoff rally in Liars' Square to announce the White Knights' plan to help the princesses."

I looked around at the posters they were making with slogans like NO ONE'S DAMSEL and FANTASY, NOT FASCISM. "And I assume you guys are going to be there as well?"

"You're damn right," Alice said with a wicked smile. "There have been mirror posts all day from people who are showing up to tell those assholes what they think of them and their regressive plan for the Apple."

I nodded, a warm pride for my friends filling my chest. "I'm in. Someone hand me a marker."

As I drew a picture of a princess raising a clenched fist, I told everyone about our trip to Witchdale. As soon as I mentioned the possible connection between the spell affecting the princesses and the Arsenic Queens, Tarris threw down his paintbrush and jumped to his feet.

"Yesssss, I told you!" Tarris shouted as he sprang up onto my couch in glee. "I knew it! I was totally right. Take that, nerds!"

Rick looked partway amused, partway embarrassed. "You'll have to excuse him. He gets excited."

"It's all connected!" Tarris said, bouncing slightly on the cushions. "I bet the Arsenic Queens are working with Baron Landgreaves—hell, maybe he *is* the person behind all the crap they've done!"

"I'm not sure a sexist authoritarian would call himself a queen—" I started.

Tarris waved his hands as if he were flinging my comment to the side. "Whatever. Maybe he's trying to throw us off the scent."

I was skeptical. It felt too easy, too pat for someone who had thrown the Apple into crisis to then immediately set himself up as the savior. From what I knew of the Arsenic Queens, they acted through agents and cat's paws, never stepping out of the shadows. If anything, maybe this Baron was just another one of their unwitting dupes, like Miranda Grimmour.

"For now, it doesn't matter," Jacqui said. "We can't let Landgreaves or the bootlickers who look up to him spread their bullshit unchecked. We're showing up to that rally."

LIARS' SQUARE WAS NORMALLY one of my favorite parts of the Apple, a haven for street peddlers, buskers, and other misfits who'd gotten kicked out of the pristine walls of Castle Fortnight. But today the gaudy stalls of enchanted tchotchkes and souvenir armor had been cleared, and a large stage had been erected in the far corner. Billowing red tapestries hung on either side, with stylized white logos of a knight's helm.

Again, I was impressed with the branding going into this misogynist nightmare.

There were a few hundred people milling about the plaza—it was hard to judge, but it seemed like about two-thirds of them were here for the protest. Royal Guards had set up a blockade to separate the White Knight supporters from the picketers. It seemed like people were being peaceful for now, but I was wary. Underneath the glare of the hot sun, I could catch the sharp, metallic smell of tension.

Crowds always put me a little on edge, which I know is a funny thing to hear from someone who grew up in a city. It's one thing weaving through a packed subway platform—it's something else when a large group of people is all standing in one place, especially in an emotionally fraught display. There's something about the way that my ability picks up a crowd's emotion that is disturbing—it's like everyone's feelings are amplified, and the normal boundaries between one person and another are loosened. One time at a Yankees game, I smelled how an umpire's call had whipped the crowd into a frenzy, the rage spreading from one fan to the next like embers across dry leaves. The scent of righteous anger became dizzying, and all over whether one guy had caught the ball before another had touched his foot to a rubber mat.

The stakes were higher here.

Ever the social butterfly, Alice met up with a few of her maid friends and led us over to a group of protesters gathered in the shade of an oak tree growing to the side of the pentagonal plaza (obviously, a place called Liars' Square isn't going to have four sides). The demonstrators were a motley group—more women than men, more young folk than old, but other than that, it was all types. A kind-eyed old man in a knitted pink hat was blowing bubbles out of his corn-cob pipe next to a pair of leather-clad dryads with more metal piercings between them than most Slipknot concerts. My eyes filled with tears of pride when I saw a resolute group of young goblin girls in school uniforms march by, their glossed lips set with determination.

Trumpets sounded a fanfare from the stage, and, as one being, the entire crowd turned to face the stage. Baron Landgreaves stepped up the stairs at the back of the stage, waving to the crowd with a big smile on his face. He'd ditched the more formal outfit from his mirror message in favor of a collared shirt with the sleeves rolled up—the kind of look Know-Naught politicians employ to appear like the kind of person you can have a beer with. Or at least what their publicists, stylists, and focus groups think gives that impression.

The Baron stepped up to a podium, also adorned with the sigil of the White Knights, and held his hands up for the crowd to quiet down. He'd been met with a mixture of cheers and jeers, but from his smug grin, it seemed like he'd only heard the former.

"Good afternoon, my fellow citizens!" he said, his voice booming from the amplification charms in his podium. "Thank you so much for coming out today. I am honored you all are participating in this historic mission, at a time when the Apple needs us the most."

The crowd of anti-Knights booed, and surprisingly Landgreaves acknowledged us. "I know not all of you agree with what we're trying to do for the Apple. There's been a lot of misinformation spread about our noble quest. But I'm here to engage with you, to show you how we're going to help. I just hope you'll listen and we can have a respectful debate."

Alice scoffed from beside me. "If it's a debate, how come he's the only one at the podium?"

"Without further ado," the Baron said, cutting off the disgruntled murmuring around us, "I'd like to introduce you to a very special girl." He gestured, and a pair of knights wheeled in a gurney, on top of which rested a sleeping princess with thick, gorgeous black hair. "This is Princess Ayesha, of the Sultanate of Scheherazade. Ayesha has been sleeping peacefully for over three decades, watched over by her family until her groom-to-be is born. She—"

Without warning, Ayesha shot up in bed, her face contorted by the scream ripping through her throat. The knights grabbed her shoulders as she thrashed, eventually easing her back down onto the mattress as she flailed. The Baron looked on, shaking his head with downcast eyes.

Like the smell of sewage rising from the storm drains after a heavy rain, fear began to ooze from the crowd, supporters and demonstrators alike. It was one thing to hear the princesses scream from the tower tops far away; it was very different to see it in person. Hell, I'd seen Raye's behavior up close and personal, and it was still hard to see Ayesha thrash in complete terror. After a few moments, she settled down, returning to a fitful, murmuring sleep.

"Ladies and gentlemen of the Apple, this is what is happening to the young, innocent princesses of Castle Fortnight. Something is torturing them, causing their blissful sleep to be turned into a nightmare. I'm sorry to show you such a shocking display, but I think it's important you know what we're up against."

There was murmuring in the crowd, and even the most adamant of the protestors seemed to at least be considering his words.

"I'm going to be honest with you—we don't know what is causing this. We don't know what could be affecting all of the princesses, all at once. But we're committed to figuring it out, to saving our princesses. And we need your help."

As much as he made me bristle, the Baron was a spellbinding speaker. The entire crowd, supporters and demonstrators, was hanging on his every word. It was the force with which he spoke—the absolute *certainty* that he projected into his speech. Eradicating all nuance, eroding all detail, and brushing away any chance of disagreement. Whether he truly believed in what he was saying, in his heart of hearts, I couldn't say. But to the people of the Apple, he presented himself as an infallible man with a plan.

"We can't do this alone," the Baron continued. "The quest ahead of us is going to require all of us working together. Coming together to protect the Apple in its time of need. It may require sacrifices of us all. Of our time, our effort, of our usual way of doing things. The White Knights are going to stop at nothing to save the princesses, but we need your support. We—"

Ayesha's scream pierced through the air, and everyone in the crowd jumped with surprise. But there was something different about her—no longer was she crying out in pain. She was yelling in rage.

The two knights came from where they were standing at the back of the stage, but before they could reach her, Ayesha leapt out of the gurney, landing unsteadily on her feet. She moved in fits and jerks with her eyes closed, like someone had shot a sleepwalker full of cocaine. Somehow, she still could sense the world around her, as she cocked her head at the approaching knights and bared her teeth. In a flash, she shoved the gurney with both arms, and it slammed into the leftmost knight with unnatural force. He crumpled onto it as the other knight advanced on Ayesha, his hand going for his sword.

"Sir Terrence—" the Baron shouted, having put the podium between himself and the action. But before he could continue, Ayesha took two faltering, uneven steps and jammed her palm into the center of the other knight's chest; the burly man jerked backwards like he was in a bad wire-fu movie, sailing through the air and smashing into the wings of the stage ten feet in the air.

"Joseph Campbell's junk," I swore. Ayesha had turned and was doing an uneven zombie walk towards the Baron. And given the way she'd Supergirled those two knights, I couldn't imagine this was going to end well.

On one hand, seeing that asshole get torn apart by a slender princess would've felt great. But if the Apple was already in a frenzy, seeing the White Knights' charismatic leader martyred in front of them wouldn't end well for the princesses.

I was going to have to save his ass, knowing full well I was probably going to kick it later.

There were probably about forty people between me and the stage, and even if I could get there, the Royal Guards' barricade was in my way. So I clambered up on the lowest limb of the tree beside us, looking over the heads of the dumbstruck crowd. I had about ten seconds before Ayesha got her super-strong hands around Landgreaves's neck.

I dug deep, thinking how much I needed to protect the Baron, to prevent any more violence from pushing the Apple further down the road to chaos. He was my number-one priority at the moment—everything else could wait until after I'd averted catastrophe. I opened my palm, and a small rose I'd tucked into my sleeve leapt into my outstretched hand. The petals immediately turned the bright, urgent orange of a traffic cone, a vibrant copy of the rose I'd accidentally created in my father's kitchen. I took a deep breath, brought the bloom to my lips, and blew.

The petals flew off the stem in a rush, flying like darts towards the stage. In a second, they struck the knight who'd been hit by the gurney, and he jerked with sudden energy. Somehow, I could feel the bruising in his abdomen where he'd been hit, could sense the cloudiness of his head from where he'd smacked it.

Get up, I thought, trying to force him to move through his mental fog. *Get on your feet.*

The knight staggered up, clawing at the gurney to give himself enough leverage to life his armored body. He swayed but was able to get his feet underneath himself.

Now go.

The knight took a few uneven steps forward, breaking into a slow run. As he did, Ayesha threw the podium aside, heaving the heavy wood away from her like it was made of foam. Now there was nothing between her and the Baron.

GO! I screamed in my head, and it was like an invisible wind pushed the knight along. He slammed into the Baron at a full gallop, and the older man was taken down with a satisfying thunk onto the surface of the stage. Seconds later, the princess lurched forward in an animalistic pounce, her hands splintering the wood where the Baron had been just a few moments before. The Baron and the knight scrambled towards the back of the stage as a lone wizard in a White Knight robe ran up the stairs. Ayesha turned to face them, another shout of incandescent rage spewing from her lips. But the wizard shouted something back, ancient words I couldn't follow. As he did, glowing purple chains sprang into existence, wrapping around Ayesha's petite frame. She was able to grab the first chain and snap it between her hands, but soon more bindings followed, and she couldn't keep up. Soon, like a five-foot-two King Kong, she was wrapped in chains no matter how much she struggled, and she collapsed, shrieking, to the ground.

"Briar," Antoine said from below me, "we need to go." The crowd began to disperse, panic making people pushy and agitated. Antoine, Jacqui, Alice, Tarris, Rick and I were able to stick together among the rush out of the plaza, following the general pandemonium out onto the streets of the Apple.

We stepped off of the street into a little playground alongside Lovers' Lane. Where a playground in Manhattan would have a plastic castle or pirate ship, this park had a little miniature version of the Chrysler building for kids to pretend to be bankers or insurance salesmen or whatever. The grass is always greener.

"Is everyone okay?" Antoine asked. We all nodded, but it was clear the scene had rattled us. A few of the other protestors still filing out of Liars' Square were crying or holding each other; I saw a burly orc comfort his even burlier friend who looked like he'd gotten trampled in the mad dash to exit the square.

"Briar," Jacqui said, still slightly out of breath, "what in the name of Tom Bombadil's taint did you just do?"

"I'm—I'm not sure. I was trying to stop that princess from turning Baron Landreaves into a puddle of SpaghettiO's in front of the entire Apple."

"Why?" Tarris's voice cut through the air like a vorpal sword. I turned to look at him, and I'd never seen an expression of such intense hatred on his face. "Why would you save that monster?"

I took an involuntary step back from the prince. "You think I should've let him die? Tarris, c'mon. That's not who we are."

"Maybe it should be," he muttered. Everyone in our little makeshift circle looked at him. "Maybe that bastard should pay the price for what he's doing to the Apple. For everything the Arsenic Queens have done."

"Tarris?" Rick said, his voice gentle. "Babe, that's—"

"I'm going back to Castle Fortnight," Tarris said. "Let me know when you guys are done playing heroic quest and ready to fight back."

He whirled on his feet and stormed off, the chic cape he was wearing providing a dramatic flourish. Rick looked after him, then turned to me. "I'm sorry," he said, putting his hand lightly on my arm. "He's—he's just upset. I'm going to go try to calm him down. I'll be in touch." Rick followed quickly after his boyfriend.

"But Briar," Antoine said, "what did you do? That didn't look like your normal emotion magic. It seemed like you were… *puppeteering* that knight."

I shook my head. "I don't know. I was just trying to make him feel protective of the Baron." The memory of the knight's bruised torso made me wince. "But when the rose hit, I felt somehow connected to him—like my magic was a two-way street between us."

"Is that normal?" Alice asked.

"Nope. Not even normal for me."

"Free Spell weirdness aside," Jacqui said, "Tarris had a point. The White Knights are looking more and more suspicious every moment. Why are you protecting them?"

"I loathe that slimeball," I said. "But if the Baron is responsible, why did he almost let himself be pummeled by a princess?"

"Maybe they weren't expecting them to go all *Walking Dead*," Jacqui mused. "Or gain super strength."

"You guys," Alice said, her voice getting serious, "do you think that is going to start happening to all of the princesses? That they'll go from having nightmares to sleep walking? And sleep smashing?"

Everyone paused for a moment to consider it. "Maybe," I said lamely.

"That's why I agree with Tarris!" Jacqui insisted. "We need to go after the White Knights. Hard and fast. Take them out and figure out a way to stop what they're doing to the princesses."

"Believe me, I want to stop this," I said. "But if we jump to the conclusion that they're responsible for everything without evidence, we might be letting the real Arsenic Queens get away."

"Then let's get evidence," Antoine said. "I did some digging and got a hold of some of the Baron's financial records. From there I was able to get the address of his Manhattan penthouse. If we can get hard evidence, maybe we can either nail him or exonerate him."

I thought for a moment. "I have an idea. But let's swing by the Academy. I'll explain on the way."

THE SUN WAS SETTING over the Hudson as we walked the bougie streets of the Upper East Side. Linden had somehow found the time to change into a striped tank top under a crumpled lavender suit, and he was watching the assorted trophy spouses and dog walkers around us like they were aliens.

"I dunno, Bri. I feel like living in this neighborhood by itself is enough evidence to prove the Baron is unspeakably evil." He peered over his oversized round sunglasses as a couple bickered over which Instagram filter made their Pekingese look slimmer.

It had taken a lot of convincing to get Antoine to agree to my plan, especially considering that I'd insisted he stay behind. But if the Apple was about to devolve into a pit of punching princesses, we needed to throw a few hail Morrigans.

"And you're sure you don't have anything a little more… inconspicuous to wear?" I said, eyeing his plaid socks and Converse.

"As someone who has routinely bluffed his way into parties he can't afford," Linden said, "The worst thing you can do is appear like you don't want anyone to notice you."

Per usual, I'd raided Jacqui's closet for something expensive to wear. Unlike the Crayola blue pantsuit, the blouse and skirt combo she'd suggested was understated and elegant. I'd been able to find a pair of tomboyish Oxfords in Alice's room that even gave me enough traction for breaking and entering.

We walked up to the address Antoine had given us, a sleek glass skyscraper with a terraced top, like some sort of futuristic ziggurat. Barely anyone passed through the large glass automatic doors, and a pair of immaculately suited doormen surveyed everyone who passed.

"How come no one is coming in and out?" Linden said as we lingered, trying to pretend we were deep in discussion and not casing the joint.

"Probably there aren't many people actually living there," I muttered. "Buildings like that are usually a lot of second homes, pied-à-terres, and investment properties."

"So wait, rich people pay millions of dollars for these places and then don't even live there?"

"There are about six vacant homes for every homeless person in U.S.," I said, remembering one of Jacqui's more recent rants. "It's really messed up. But let's hope the Baron's place is one of the vacant one as the moment."

Linden raised his eyebrows and moved to walk by my side. "Just walk confidently, don't make eye contact, and don't break stride," I muttered.

"Please," Linden said. "I got into the VIP section in Coachella no problem. I only got kicked out for stealing Solange's LaCroix."

I shot him a sideways glance, the corners of my lips tugging upwards against my will. "What?" he said. "You didn't think this was baby's first B&E, did you?"

The glass doors slid open before us without a sound, and luckily the doormen were just as silent. But I had no doubt they were sizing us up, ready to pounce if we caused the slightest problem.

The lobby was designed in the sort of empty, minimalist style that actually takes a lot of money to pull off. A royal purple carpet led from the front doors to the elevator, and two giant, abstract glass chandeliers twinkled in the dusky sunlight coming in through the floor-to-ceiling windows. A marble desk ran the entire length of the room, behind which sat a very severe-looking attendant. She struck me as somewhere between a mean librarian stereotype and the evil henchwoman of a Bond villain.

I was pretty sure if I undid her tight bun, she'd unravel like Weezer's sweater.

She was much more interested in us than the doormen had been, and my gut kicked as we kept walking. The attendant did her best to initiate eye contact, but I'm a New Yorker, Grimmsdammit, and I have seen people defecate three feet away from me on the subway without going so far as to acknowledge them. I let my gaze slide off her and towards the elevator.

"Miss?" she said, lightly enough that I could believably pretend not to hear it. "Excuse me, *ma'am*?"

That got my attention.

I whirled around, and grabbed the small tea rose I'd been wearing on my lapel. I cast my mind back to when I was younger, the time when Jacqui had tricked me into thinking that the Tooth Fairy wasn't real. She was just being a bratty six-year-old, but I fell for it, hook, line and sinker. I've done a lot of growing up since then, and I don't believe as easily, but I remembered how that felt. Accepting what people told me without question. Thinking the world was just and good. The feeling of being gullible.

I felt a bittersweet twinge as that buried emotion of naiveté fluttered down into the rose, turning it the speckled blue of a robin's egg.

"Here, this would look great in your hair," I said as we approached the desk. The concierge raised her hand in semi-disgust, as if she were about to knock the rose out of my hand. But as soon as her fingers grazed the leaves, her eyes widened behind her thick-framed glasses.

"Oh my," she said, her voice shedding the reptilian hardness that most high-profile customer service workers adopt. "How lovely." A soft smile lit her face becomingly as she put it behind her ear. For once, I wasn't lying. It did look great.

Her adorable expression almost made me forgive her for calling me "ma'am." *Almost.*

"We're here to prepare Mr. Landgreaves's suite for his arrival," I said. "You should have received a call about it."

Her brow furrowed lightly for a moment, but then smoothed. "Hmm, yes. I'm sure I must have. And do you have your new keycards? We updated the system last month."

"We requested a new one, if that's all right," I said. She immediately nodded, the magic making her swallow whatever I said.

"Let me get a new one for you," she said, turning to a flatscreen monitor in front of her. "If you'll just wait a moment, miss."

Finally.

After a few minutes of rapid typing, the attendant gave us the keycard and a warm smile as we walked to the elevator. I had to waive the keycard just to make the elevator's keypad work, and felt a slimy sort of satisfaction hitting the button marked *Penthouse.*

"So why don't you do that rose stuff more often?" Linden asked as the elevator zoomed upwards. "That was so cool!"

I shifted uncomfortably. "I used to. It used to be my job—enchanting people for the Royals. But I found out it was doing a little more to people than I originally thought."

"What do you mean?"

"I can't completely control it. Giving that concierge gullibility so she wouldn't question our story is one thing, but what if it doesn't wear off? What if she gets a drink after work and some pickup artist takes advantage of her?" I shook my head. "Now I try to only do it when it's necessary." I thought of the other night when I'd enchanted the bouncer at WCKED and felt a stirring of shame. It was a hard habit to break.

"I get it," Linden said, his voice getting uncharacteristically quiet. "I used to think going into people's dreams was all fun and games. But then I saw some things—" His voice caught, and he stopped talking for a moment. "I get it."

"#FreeSpellProblems, right?" I said, trying to lighten the mood as the elevator came to a stop. "Get ready."

As I expected from seeing lots of rich people's apartments on *Law & Order*, the elevator opened directly into the Baron's penthouse. A grand foyer of grey marble opened in front of us, with stairs leading between two columns to the rest of the apartment. I put my finger to my lips, and the two of us stepped out of the elevator.

All the lights I could see were off, and we paused to listen for a moment but only heard vast, expensive silence. I shrugged, and we continued up the stairs. If anyone was lurking in the dark, I had more roses in my pockets.

We walked up into a gaping, open-plan living room, with a view of the skyline along two sides. The furniture looked like it cost the equivalent of the GDP of a small country, done in a severe black leather that came across as aggressive and masculine. "Someone's been reading too much *Fifty Shades*," Linden murmured.

"Ew," I said. "Please don't make me picture the Baron reading erotica."

The living space was fairly bare, like a hotel that no one really lived in. Same with the Baron's bedroom, which was decorated with dark red silk and a lot of mirrors, which made me think maybe Linden's estimation of Landgreaves's décor inspiration wasn't far off.

Finally, we found his study, a wood-paneled room with a mahogany desk that looked like it weighed as much as a truck. Here, the Baron was a little messier, and papers spread out over the blotter on the center of the desk.

"Bingo," I said, immediately regretting that I didn't have a cooler quip. "Let's start going through all this."

"Man, is detective work always this much reading and bookkeeping?" Linden complained as he started rifling through a file cabinet.

"Sadly, yes. With occasional interruptions of mortal danger."

"Fun," he deadpanned.

"It's a living," I said, scanning over what looked to be lease agreements. "Not all of us can make money wearing a silly helmet and clicking play on a laptop."

He stuck his tongue out at me. "DJing is just one of my many hustles. And I'm not making Diplo money yet. It's not easy out here in the real world."

I looked across the desk at him. "Why did you leave the Apple? It ain't perfect, but the rent has got to be cheaper than Manhattan."

Linden shrugged his bony shoulders and looked away. For once, I could see him struggling to form a response. His face softened, and he lost some of the armor of snark I'd grown to associate with him.

"I didn't fit in," he said simply. "I tried for a long time to make it work, to follow the fairy tale, but it became too much. I knew I'd never be happy while I was still living with their expectations wrapped around me."

I weighed his words and nodded. "I get that. It's not easy, with the Old Stories always breathing down your neck. Sometimes it's hard to feel like you are allowed to write your own. Was it being a Free Spell?"

He shook his head. "Not really. I mean, that didn't help, but... I don't know. The Apple is all about princes marrying princesses and living happily ever after. And I don't want that."

I nodded at him, giving him space.

"I don't think I want that with a princess. Or a prince. Or anyone. And I was sick of feeling like that was some sort of crime."

The scent of his genuine emotion was like freshly cut grass, and I put the papers I'd been reading down and went over to pull him into a hug.

"Linden, that's absolutely fine. If the Apple feels like a place where you can't be yourself, where you feel like anything less than awesome, then screw them."

After a moment, he squeezed my shoulder and pulled back. His eyes were a little wet, but he was smiling. "Thanks, Bri."

"And whatever you want romantically, just remember your happily ever after isn't going to be alone. You've got friends. I am way too stubborn not to stick around."

He nodded and wiped his eyes. "All right, can we find something incriminating so we can take this asshole down?"

We spent a few hours combing the office but found nothing besides a few redacted memos that might've implicated him in some light insider trading (I took some mirror pictures just in case). I was putting the last set of files back where we'd found them when we heard the elevator doors open.

My heart immediately started pounding, but I took a deep breath and turned off the light in the office and silently closed the door.

This was all part of the plan.

I grabbed another rose from the breast pocket of my blazer and focused. I remembered a house from our neighborhood in Witchdale that was down at the end of a forgotten cul-de-sac. It was a crumbling, ramshackle cottage surrounded by overgrown weeds that I knew drove my father wild. Random junk was scattered all around the house, broken furniture from a variety of time periods, dozens of shattered wind chimes, and mason jars full of strange samples, suspended in muddy brown liquid.

And everywhere, bones. Most small enough to be from animals, but some we couldn't be too sure about. The neighborhood kids called the woman who lived there the Bone Witch, and while many had claimed to see her, there were never any confirmed sightings. We just knew she rearranged the strange objects around her house sometimes, maybe in the dead of night.

Nobody liked to go by that house. There was always a sense of unease, of being watched. Something was off, and people didn't want the wrongness that permeated that place to stick to them. That uneasy dread flowed through my fingertips, and the rose tuned the same mottled yellow color as the Bone Witch's rotting wooden walls.

Keeping my focus, I plucked the petals from the stem and sprinkled them across the door jam. They shimmered slightly in the dark room, making Linden's face glow in the mustard light.

Lights went on in the rest of the apartment, and I could hear the Baron's resonant voice as he hung up a call. Not long after he entered, his footsteps echoed through the hallway and approached the door.

My breath caught, and Linden and I looked at each other in panic. All we could hear were his strident footsteps, getting closer and closer to us. I closed my eyes and focused on the petals at my feet, willing them to work.

The steps came right outside the door and stopped. Everything froze for a second, and I was sure the Baron would be able to hear my heartbeat thumping even on the other side of the door. We were trapped, and if the Baron found us, there was no place to run. Linden and I locked eyes, mirror images of each other's fear.

Then, after what felt like forever, the Baron walked away.

I slumped, relieved that the ward had worked. I had only figured out how to do them a few months before, and, like eve-

rything else having to do with my power, I still didn't completely understand it. But I knew if I supercharged a rose and left it
simmering, I could make a barrier that sent out waves of an
emotion if anyone approached. As an added bonus, the effect
was fairly short-lived, wearing off soon after a person left the
ward's presence. Which meant no guilt about disrupting some
dummy's emotional equilibrium!

Linden gave me an impressed thumbs up, and for once I
was glad I could still use my power in a way that didn't make
me feel like I needed to shower.

For the next forty-five minutes or so, we heard the Baron
puttering around in his bedroom next door, listening to some
cringe-worthy '80s love ballads. Finally, the Bryan Adams quieted down and the lights clicked off, leaving the penthouse
silent. I gave it a few minutes, then risked a whisper.

"You ready?"

Linden shrugged. "I've never tried to enter a neofascist's
dreamscape in an attempt to interrogate him."

"Me neither. But there's a first time for—"

That's when the study around us disappeared.

I COULD TELL I was in a dream, this time. I was almost used
to the weird, wispy nature of the subconscious scene around me,
a little hazy and insubstantial like it had been made from frosting by a supernaturally talented reality show baker.

We were on the Highline, right near Chelsea Market, on a
beautiful summer's day. Just as it would be in real life, the elevated park was jammed with tourists enjoying the weather.
Children ran along the tree-lined path between the buildings,
and tourists from all over the world snapped pictures and point-

ed out landmarks rising up around us as we walked suspended in the cityscape. But the proportions were all a little off, the angles of the skyscrapers not quite perpendicular. We weren't walking through the Manhattan I knew; we were walking through the Baron's idea of what the city *felt* like.

"Hmmm," Linden said from next to me. "This is a lot less unpleasant than I'd thought." He was still wearing his light purple suit, and with a sweeping, dramatic gesture he summoned a LaCroix for himself from the dreamstuff around us.

"If we keep doing this, you're going to have to teach me how you do that," I mused, looking around at the crowd. I didn't see the Baron anywhere.

"What fun is that?" he smiled. He created a ballcap that said "I'M WITH STUPID" and plopped it on my head. "Now you've got to keep me around."

I pouted at his shitty taste in hats, but before I could respond, a scream shattered the carefree atmosphere around us. A classically beautiful blonde stood by the railing of the Highline, looking out at the Hudson and gripping the railing for support. Her white dress billowed around her like '50s pin-up calendar, and I felt a little sick.

"They're coming!" she shrieked, before literally swooning into the muscular arms of the man next to her.

Out in the middle of the river, not far from the Statue of Liberty, the water was bubbling, disturbed by something underneath. From our vantage point, we could see a dark patch in the water grow larger as whatever was underneath got closer to the surface. A mass of dark, tangled strands broke through the river, water pouring off of what eventually became a forehead.

Godzilla-like, a female form rose from the Hudson, towering over the buildings of Manhattan. The water rocked and roiled as her limbs unfurled, splashing aside the Staten Island Ferry like it was a bathtub toy.

I recognized Princess Ayesha from the Baron's ill-fated demonstration at the rally, but the dream version of her looked wilder and more monstrous, with yellow eyes looking hungrily at the city. She threw her head back and gave an echoing roar.

Around her, more giant princesses started to push through the surface of the water.

Ayesha's battle cry broke the people around me out of their horrified reverie. Everyone started screaming and running for the stairs down to the main level, pushing and shoving in their panic as the princesses began to descend on the island.

Linden looked at me, dumbstruck, and I grabbed his hand. "C'mon," I shouted over the chaos, "we need to find the Baron."

"What the hell is all this?"

"If I had to bet, a very overblown metaphor for male fragility by way of a B-movie. But they can't hurt us, right? It's not one of those 'if you die in a dream, you die in real life' things?"

Linden shook his head. "I don't think so. But given everything weird that's been going on in the Dream Slip, I'd rather not find out. Dream deaths still hurt like a Mother Hubbard."

I gave him a nod, and we started running towards the nearest stairs down to 10th Ave. As we were maybe fifteen feet away, a giant glass slipper stepped between the high-rises and slammed down on the Highline, cracking the concrete like it was made of popsicle sticks. Linden was able to pull me back in time, and together we skidded, barely halting our momentum before we slid off the edge.

Without pausing, we turned, running towards the next stairwell a few blocks uptown. Sirens were screeching across the entire city, the noise so much it made my head pound. Another princess to our side was being dive-bombed by a police chopper; she roared like King Kong as she tried to knock it out of the air. The sweet summer dream of a few moments ago had turned into a carnivalesque nightmare.

"Where do you think the Baron is?" Linden yelled, clearly getting out of breath.

"He thinks he's a hero," I said, darting around a slow-moving family (even in an absurd dream disaster, *tourists are so slow*). "So my guess is he'll be waiting around in the wings for things to get really bad, then step in to save the day."

We made it to the stairs, which were jammed with people trying to get down off the Highline, now visibly shuddering after being damaged. The smell of smoke was heavy in the air as the princesses continued their attack and the city crumbled. Finally, we made it down the stairs and out of the press of bodies. 10th Ave was a wasteland, dotted with cars flipped by the princesses and piles of rubble from the crumbling buildings.

"Briar," Linden called out from behind me as he caught up, "this is looking pretty bad. If your theory is right, shouldn't the Baron have already—"

Before he could finish, another stunningly gorgeous woman gasped dramatically. I swear she was a carbon copy of the woman on the bridge, just with red hair this time. "Look! Up in the sky! It's the White Knights!" she cheered before fainting.

Gandalf's giblets, this dream was getting old.

Per the sexist plot device's instructions, I looked to the sky, where a giant red robot was descending through the clouds. It looked like a mechanized version of a medieval knight, with the familiar helm logos of the White Knights. In its right gauntlet, it had a sword that looked like it had mated violently with a chainsaw, producing a glowing red monstrosity with a serrated edge.

"Fear not, citizens!" the Baron's voice boomed out from the robot, loud enough to echo around the entire island of Manhattan. "We're here to protect you."

The force with which my eyes rolled probably also echoed around the city. "Great, he's gone full *Power Rangers*. How are we supposed to interrogate him now?"

Linden squinted up at the sky. "I could probably teleport us up there."

"What the elf, Linden? You could teleport in dreams this whole time? Then why have we been fleeing in terror?"

"I need a place to teleport us *to*. The princesses were smashing everything around us."

"Still, my feet hurt and I hold you responsible."

Linden stuck his tongue out at me. "Do you want to get up there or not?"

"Lead the way, Nightcrawler."

He wrapped his arm in mine and closed his eyes. For a moment, nothing happened, and then the dream world shifted around us, and we were in a medieval version of the bridge of the Starship Enterprise. Wizards sat at long desks, manipulating glowing red runes in front of them. A few rugged-looking knight-types steered the robot, looking through an opening at the front of the room that showed the city as we zoomed between buildings. We must've landed in the helm.

At the center of the room, in some weird cross between a captain's seat and a throne, the Baron barked orders at his men (because of course all the attendants around us were men). His lackeys looked upon him with such fawning admiration that it made me sick to my stomach. We were definitely in his fantasy.

In perfect dream logic, nobody paid us much attention as we approached Landgreaves. Before we were in earshot, Linden leaned over to whisper in my ear. "Remember, dreamers don't like being shaken out of their delusions. It's best if you try to talk to him as if this were all real."

I groaned. "Can't I just kick his ass?"

"If we want him to let slip something useful, we need to play by the rules of his game."

My eyes narrowed, but to Linden's credit he looked sorry for having to suggest it. "Fine. But can you conjure me up a pen and notepad? I'm going to need some props."

Linden plucked the ballcap from my head, crushed it between his fingers like potter's clay, and reformed it into a bright blue notepad. He rolled another bit of dreamstuff between his fingers to make an elegant quill like you'd get in a nice stationery shop on Looking Glass Lane. Disguise in place, I approached the Baron.

"Baron Landreaves?" I said, trying to keep my intense hatred for him out of my voice.

"On the bridge of my ship, you'll address me as Captain," he said, not taking his eyes off of the scene outside the robot.

I gripped the quill very tightly, but, somehow, I was able to squeak my voice out through the rage aneurysm building in my left temple. "*Captain* Landgreaves, I'm from the Havmercy Herald. We're working on a piece about your heroic efforts to combat the princesses."

My play to his ego was well-received, because immediately he turned in his chair to face me with his beaming politician's smile. "Are you now? About time our movement is recognized by the mainstream media."

"Obviously you've responded so quickly to the threat—can you tell our readers how long you've been preparing for this battle?"

"This battle specifically?" he asked. "How could we? This threat came out of nowhere. But we've been preparing for something, and now we can finally put all our plans into motion."

"What plans are these, exactly?"

The Baron gave what I'm sure he thought was a charming chuckle and tapped the side of his nose. "All in good time, my dear. Suffice to say, this sort of danger has been brewing for a while. There's only so far you can push society before the natural order has to reassert itself. The Apple has become a place I barely recognize. After that incident earlier this year—that Grimmour girl, taking up arms against the Multiarchy?"

He shook his head, which gave me time to recover from this revelation. Miranda's father had put some serious effort into covering up her failed insurrection, so I was stunned this clown had heard about it.

"When I was young, the princesses of the Apple were respectable. They had class—they were truly regal, you understand? They understood that true Royalty doesn't have anything to prove. They were content with their place in society. Now, look at these monsters." He gestured to the princesses flying by outside the robot. "They never wanted equality. They have always wanted to tear down everything the Poisoned Apple stood for. But they've played right into our hands."

I looked at Linden, who, bless him, looked about as ready to kick the Baron's shiny white teeth in as I was. I shook my head subtly. As much as it was killing me, he needed his teeth where they were to continue talking.

"They thought they'd beaten us," the Baron continued. "They thought they'd built a new world where heroes like us were obsolete. But this is exactly the chance we've been waiting for. We're going to get things back to the way they were. And the secret," his voice got quieter, more conspiratorial, and he beckoned me so close I could feel his stale, cigar-tinged breath as he whispered, "is in their blood."

I shuddered just as a siren blared from across the bridge. "Incoming!" a dream-extra yelled, just as the floor jolted violently. "One's got us by the leg."

Everything inside the robot was descending into chaos, and Linden grabbed my shoulder. "We need to get out of here!"

"One more thing," I said, stepping towards the Baron's chair.

I'm not a violent person, by nature. People annoy the hell out of me sometimes, but my dad always taught me living well is the best revenge. But I can throw a punch when I need to, and there are a few very select situations where I find it necessary.

His jaw gave a satisfying crack as I hit it, and the pain that shot through my wrist was totally worth it.

The Baron looked at me, a mixture of rage and fear in his eyes. I gave him a small wave as Linden grabbed my hand. "I'm going to see you when you wake up, asshole, and that's when your real nightmare is going to start."

There was another moment of the world lurching around me, and suddenly Linden and I were on a skyscraper rooftop, watching the city explode into a Michael Bay wet dream. Before us, the mecha-knight was straining to fly away from a princess with her hand grasping its ankle. With ferocious strength, the giant woman jerked the robot down, using her other hand to grab the knight's sword hand before he could slash her. A loud whirring noise burst from the shoulder joint as the princess ripped the arm from its socket, tossing it and the sword into Washington Square Park like discarded laundry. Then she squared up with knight, twisted her body, and raised a fist to smash in its head.

As the giant princess turned, her hair flipped over her face, and I saw it for the first time.

Princess Jacquinetta D'Lucien Ardor slammed her subway-car-sized fist into the helm of the White Knights' robot, and all around us the dreamworld went dark.

LINDEN AND I STUMBLED through the space between worlds and back into the Baron's study. I collided with one of his side tables, sending an expensive yet tacky lamp to the ground. In the room next to us, I heard the Baron wake with a start, and his feet hit the ground as he scrambled out of his bed. Linden and I nearly fell over each other as we booked it out of the office and into the hallway. Luckily, we weren't far from the elevator, and I still had the key card. If we could get in—

"Stop right there." The Baron's voice was ice hard, no trace of the slimy charm he'd had during our dream interview. The sound of gun cocking a bullet into its chamber punctuated his command.

Guns don't work in the Poisoned Apple. Whatever alternative laws of physics our World Slip runs on, gunpowder doesn't translate. The dwarves have been able to rig some fairly unstable rune-powered muskets, but you've got about equal odds of hitting your target or liquefying your trigger finger.

So I'm not used to having a finely tuned death machine available at the local Walmart. Or pointed at my back.

"Raise your hands. Turn around."

Linden and I followed his orders. The Baron was barefoot in his pajama pants, his expensively cross-trained torso bare. A sleek chrome pistol was trained at us, and the Baron's eyes bored into us as he stepped past the door to his study.

"Who the hell are you? And how—how did you get in my head?" he growled. At least he seemed as shaken as we were from our trip through his kaiju nightmare.

I stared at the gun, panic welling up inside of me, looking for a place to release. We weren't in the Apple, where elves enchant armor with reinforced moonlight and the right riddle can stop a crossbow bolt; no fairy tale was going to stop that bullet from leaving the chamber.

The baron's feet brushed one of the rose petals I'd used to set up my ward earlier, and somehow, I could sense an escape hatch opening in my mind. The feeling of being totally helpless, of knowing that a slight pressure from a man's finger could send lead into my heart, that I could be annihilated without a thought, surged through me, and I willed it into the petals across the room. Instantly, their glow shifted from yellow to orange and started to stir.

"Start talking," the Baron said.

"Or what?" I said, the words bursting forth from me as the petals started to gather into a small whirlwind. "You're gonna shoot us in your own penthouse? Even you're not rich enough to get away with that."

"Want to bet?" he snarled, flicking the safety off.

I did.

At my mental command, the petals flew upwards in a whirl, swirling and fluttering like a swarm of angry wasps. They went straight for his eyes, dive bombing him in desperate attacks. With each swipe, I could feel the hopelessness and fear I'd spelled them with ooze into the Baron; he yelled and brought up his arms to defend himself, but the petals were all around him.

"Briar, c'mon!" Linden said, tugging at my arm.

I drew another rose. If the Baron wanted to change the world back to the "good old days," then maybe he'd appreciate it if I gave him an emotional hard reset. The light pink blossom in my hand drained of color, turning to the cracked ivory of a blank parchment. I knew that if I just gave it to him, I could rewrite him. Start fresh and maybe make a worthwhile human being.

"*Briar*," Linden said, shaking my arm so the rose fell out of my fingers. As soon as it broke its connection with me, the petals turned back to their normal color, and my mind cleared a bit.

I was still going to stop whatever regressive shit the Baron was doing, but I wasn't going to do something I wouldn't be able to take back.

Without another word, I left the Baron cowering in his penthouse, under attack from my swarm of rose petals. In a blind rage, I grabbed the fancy leather attaché case the Baron had left on a bench by the entryway.

The lobby attendant barely looked up from her desk as we rushed out of the elevator. Maybe having two disheveled "assistants" leaving the penthouse at midnight wasn't uncommon in this building. We caught a mostly empty crosstown bus through Central Park to get to the Belvedere Door.

"So do you want to… uh, talk about any of that?" Linden said lamely as we settled into some crusty felt seats in the back.

"About which part? The fact that the Baron is concocting some evil plan with princess blood, or that my best friend was a monster lurking in his subconscious?"

"I was gonna ask about you going all Dark Phoenix with your magic roses, but whatever you feel like." He paused expectantly. "Or we don't have to."

I let out a breath I hadn't realized I had been holding for the past twenty minutes. "Oh yeah. That. It's happened before, during our boss fight with Miranda on top of Grimmour Tower. I just get so… *angry*, and it's like the magic inside of me gets uncorked." The memory of that day, of the rose petals swirling around me as we fought high above Castle Fortnight, made my eyes water. "It scares me."

"Have you ever done anything with it?" Linden asked quietly, no hint of judgement in his tone.

I shook my head. "I've never given into it, at least not yet, but I feel like… it's always there. Just on the other side of my magic, waiting for me. It gives me the feeling that I could go beyond just changing people's temporary feelings. That if I wanted to, I could go further—I could totally dismantle a person's self and rebuild them."

"But you haven't, right? So the next time it rears its ugly head, you'll say no."

I turned to face him on the hard plastic of the bus seat. "How do I know that? Honestly, the only reason I haven't done something horrible is because of other people. On Grimmour Tower, Antoine stopped me from using my magic on Miranda. And if you hadn't grabbed me back there in the Baron's apartment…"

"Briar, take it from someone whose life has been a series of disturbing deep dives into the human subconscious: we are all capable of some really messed up shit, deep down. When the lights are off and our minds are free to imagine anything they want, we can all become monsters. But just because we have those terrible impulses doesn't mean we give into them. In the light of day, with good people watching our back, we say no. And that's way more important than what we might feel like when we're in the dark."

I looked away as what he was saying hit home. "This is us."

"You're right, this is who we are. Slightly broken people trying our best to make things better—"

"No, I mean this is our stop." I pointed out the window to the bus shelter we were slowly approaching.

"Oh. Right. That too," Linden said sheepishly as we left the bus.

Central Park technically wasn't closed yet, but the dark had cleared out all the joggers and tourists. It also made the fey inhabitants of Manhattan bolder, and as we walked the paths to Belvedere Castle, we passed a gang of spriggans standing in a circle, laughing and passing around a joint. Further down, a cute surfer-dude selkie was holding hands with a burly guy as they snuck off to the Ramble.

Belvedere Castle glowed with a sepia light, rising out of the trees in front of us like a fanciful Thomas Kinkade. A teenage couple stood at the edge of the landing, looking out at the lake and giggling as they handed a 40 back and forth between them. Judging from the points of their ears, they were residents of the Apple out for a little rebellious fun in the Other World. I smiled as I remembered those nights with Jacqui and Cade—getting a bottle of cheap wine and sneaking into Manhattan to drink and chat and laugh.

We made our way to the main tower, to the door that would open for anyone with magic in them, no matter the time of day. Many considered the Belvedere Door to be the main entrance to the Apple, and it had always been one of my favorites. Walking the fanciful stone tunnels that led from Here to There always felt like a bit of a treat; there were other Passageways that were more dramatic, more convenient, or more efficient, but none of them gave you that *Through the Looking Glass* feeling like Belvedere.

At the bottom of the tower's stairs, a door invisible to the mundane eye welcomed us into the Apple's embrace. "So what's the plan, boss?" Linden said as we passed through its rune-etched arch.

"Honestly, it's getting late. I don't think we're going to get much more done tonight—let's head back to the house and try to get some actual sleep."

The ancient brickwork around us became more and more decrepit, letting in the cool air and the lush smells of the After-woods the farther we walked. Soon, the walls around us were nothing more than ruins, suggesting the activities of humans long ago as we fully entered the forest.

""Evenin' Miss Briar," a voice came from the side of a broken stone archway in front of us. Horace, my favorite Doorman, was on duty, and seemed to be having his afternoon tea at midnight. He sipped politely from a chipped mug that looked like it might have been from the Regency era. "And hello to you too,

Mister Linden. It's been a while." His wrinkled face split into a wide smile.

"Heya, Horace," I smiled. I hadn't seen the eccentric older man in a while, and I'd always found his friendly, slightly gossipy interest in the people who came through this Door charming. "Isn't it a little late for tea?"

"I haven't been sleeping well, on account of the world descending into a hell orchestra of shrieks," he said casually, adjusting the sleeves of his green velvet suitcoat. "Scone?" He offered us a plate, and I eagerly thanked him and grabbed a slice. It was already made up with clotted cream and a thick rowan-berry jelly.

"I hear you and that Knight of yours are working on fixing things," Horace continued. I wasn't surprised—the man's ability to hear and remember rumors was so scary, I often wondered if he wasn't some sort of ancient, incredibly nosy forest god.

"We're trying," I sighed. "You hear anything that might help?"

"I've heard a lot of things. I heard the Alchemist's Guild poisoned the princesses to make them scream so they could sell more sleeping potions. Other people think it's a cadre of wealthy Royal property developers trying to drive down housing prices in the neighborhoods surrounding Castle Fortnight. One fella came through here saying that the princesses are screaming because the Poisoned Apple is not following the sacred commandments of the great and terrible R'hathpunzel, She Whose Hair Shall Ensnare The World."

"Oh man, that cult sounds awesome," Linden said, also snacking on a scone.

"I wish I knew if any of it was true," Horace said, looking down at his feet. For once the dapper old gentleman looked truly tired. "It's just so hard to focus on anything when the whole world is screaming."

"That's why I stay off Twitter," I said sympathetically, putting my hand on his shoulder while licking clotted cream off of the other. "Take care, Horace."

"Give 'em hell, Miss Briar."

I smiled and took a scone for the road. "Don't worry. I fully intend to."

LINDEN MUST HAVE USED up his dream magic for the evening by the time we got back to our house, so I was able to get my first night of uninterrupted sleep in days. By the time I woke up, the house was quiet, so I meandered down into the kitchen, where Cade was just finishing his morning protein potion.

"Where is everybody?" I yawned, adjusting the front of the old EntStock t-shirt I'd slept in.

"Linden is still asleep, so for once you're not the last one up," Cade replied with a grin.

"Hey, we had a bit of a busy night last night. I think dream jumping and getting a gun waved at us earned us a rest?"

"A gun?" Cade said, standing up from the stool he'd been sitting on.

"It's fine," I said, waving my hands. "I'll tell you all about it—where are Jacqui and Alice?"

"They went to the Second Breakfast to meet up with Tarris. I waited behind to drag you along when you woke up."

The Second Breakfast was our favorite neighborhood brunch spot, so there would be no dragging necessary. "You could've just gone with them and left a note to meet you there."

Cade turned away to wash out his potion bottle, and I swear the morning sunlight revealed a slight blush on his cheeks. "I don't mind. I'm ready whenever you are."

I spread my arms in mock offense and blew a tangled strand of dark hair out of my face. "What, you don't think I'm ready for brunch like this?"

Wiping his hands on a kitchen towel, Cade turned back to me and gave me a wide smile. "If anyone could pull off torn pajama pants at the Second Breakfast, it's you."

I felt my face get hot, and if my skin were as light as Cade's, I'm sure he would've seen me blush. Instead, I forced a chuckle and ran upstairs to get dressed.

A few minutes later, we stepped out into the lazy sunshine of the Havmercy morning. It had been over a week of hearing the princesses scream nonstop, but in a weird way, the people of the Poisoned Apple were adjusting to the new normal. We passed a group of pixies doing yoga in the park, their ears covered with giant headphones to block the noise. Cade held me back briefly to stop me from getting hit by a pair of little boys in crowns as they raced down the cobblestones, weaving between the people walking through our sleepy neighborhood.

"I heard you went back to Witchdale to see your dad," Cade said as we walked along the edge of a farmer's market in Pig King Plaza. "How's Hank doing?"

My hands clutched with emotion as I thought back to my conversation with my dad, especially the part that had centered around Cade. "He's good. The usual. So kind and also so able to get under my skin."

"That's family," Cade said with a smile. "I always liked your dad."

"He always liked you," I said, catching his eye. "I think you were the closest thing he had to a son."

"He always came to my jousting matches. Even when you weren't there."

I rolled my eyes. "Wow, five years later and you're still bringing that up. I went to most of them!"

"I know," he said warmly. "I would always scan the stands to see you before a big joust."

My voice caught in my throat, and I walked in silence for a moment. "Did you think we'd end up like this? Back in high school, I mean."

"End up like what?" he asked.

I thought for a second about what I actually did mean. Friends? Roommates? …something more? But I chickened out and made the safer choice. "Solving mysteries, saving the Apple, attempting heroics. You know." I waved my hand generally to encompass the entire range of our shenanigans.

Cade chuckled. "I thought I was going to be a Royal champion jouster, before my shoulder injury. But yeah, I always figured you were destined for something amazing and ridiculous. Even before we knew you were a Free Spell."

I snorted. "Amazing and ridiculous, huh? Sounds like something they'll put on my tombstone."

Cade slowed as we turned the corner onto Rampart Drive, just a few blocks from the Second Breakfast. Maybe, like me, he wanted to linger a bit, enjoy being alone together for just a moment longer before the rest of our chaotic lives caught up with us.

His voice got low and serious, and he turned to face me. "I had a lot of thoughts about what would happen after high school. With us."

My heart began to pound, and the panicky, amazing feelings I'd felt around Cade as a sixteen-year-old girl started to swirl around my head. I fiddled with the hem of my paisley shirtdress and cleared my throat.

"I'm sorry," Cade said quickly, before I could respond. "I shouldn't say stuff like that. Briar, you're my friend and I don't want to make you uncomfortable and—shit, I'm sorry." He was blushing in earnest, and suddenly his six-foot-four frame crumpled in shame, like a puppy hit on the nose with a rolled-up parchment.

"No!" I said, putting my hands out in front of me. "No, Cade, *I'm* sorry. I just freeze up whenever we talk about us. It's a lot. With our history." The words spilled out of my mouth, and I almost felt a ringing in my ears as panic set in.

"I know, it's a crappy thing for me to bring up. You're moving on, and I hope you know how much I want you to be happy—"

"Moving on? What do you mean?" I tried to catch my breath and plant my feet. It would be really embarrassing if had to steady myself on Cade's arm. His very thick, muscular arm.

Cade looked away, and I could smell a pungent waft of jealousy, shame, and resignation. "You know, Antoine," he mumbled so I could barely hear.

"I—Antoine and I aren't together," I stammered out.

Cade's clear eyes peered back at me cautiously, seeming to alternate between a piercing green and a yellowish brown in the variegated sunlight of the Commontown streets. "But there's something there, isn't it? With you guys working together so much…"

My stomach did a kickflip Tony Hawk would be proud of. A large part of me wanted to lie, to say whatever I could to make Cade feel better and to avoid more awkwardness. And honestly, if I hadn't just had a surprise therapy session with Hank Pryce so recently, I might've just said what he wanted to hear. But I was a big girl, and I had to be upfront with one of the people I was closest to in the world.

"There might be something there," I said quietly. "You're right. But Cade—I don't know. I still think about you, about us—it's just a lot. I know I really did a number on your head in high school when I gave you that rose—"

"You didn't mean to," he said quickly. There was a hint of hope in his eyes as he leapt to my defense. Cade never let anyone speak ill of me, even when I was the one being critical of myself. "I know that, and I've forgiven you—"

"Right, but still. Our history is a Gordian knot of high school fantasies and awkward guilt, and it's a lot to untangle. I think when things just settle down…" I trailed off. I had no idea what I thought might happen when my life stopped being a cosmic game of Whack-A-Mole.

Cade straightened his spine, looking at me with a look that I hadn't seen from him in a long time. Supportive, accepting, and above all, kind. For all his snark and his skill with an axe, Cade was one of the kindest people I know. Somewhere deep down, I knew however things worked out, I'd still have him on my side.

"I get it, Bri. We're kind of in the middle of an existential crisis. But on the other hand, I feel like I'm old enough now to know that life never really settles down. Never really stops. Especially for people who live the kind of lives we do. And I don't think either of us are becoming accountants and moving to the suburbs anytime soon."

I snort-giggled despite myself, picturing Cade trading in his axe for a briefcase and a Roth IRA.

"But the thing is Bri, we can't keep running away from this. For me, for you—we can't delay things forever because it's not the perfect time. We fight despots and slay monsters. I think we can handle a conversation about how we feel about each other. What we want."

I was suddenly very conscious of where we were, standing on a street corner in our neighborhood in the sun, with the bustling residents of the Apple rushing by us as if nothing was happening. A trio of witches flew through the azure sky above us, their good-natured gossip high above the bustle on the streets below. Life kept surging around us, and Cade was right. It was always going to be a jumble of magic and curses, Royals and monsters, joy and chaos.

I took a deep breath. Somehow just saying all of this, putting it out there instead of keeping it locked up tight in my head, made me feel a hundred pounds lighter. I felt like I could float up and join those witches in the clouds.

But first I had a city to save.

"You're so Grimmsdamn right. What do you say, after this princess thing is over, we get a bottle of wine, sneak into Central Park like we used to, and we don't come back to the Apple until we've figured things out?"

Cade's crooked smile could've matched the lights of Manhattan, and he nodded. "That sounds amazing and terrifying."

I felt my own face light up in return. "Then we're on the same page."

He opened his arms wide and before I knew it, I was pressed up against him, my head finding the familiar cradle of his shoulder. I squeezed, knowing that Cade was one of the few people I never had to worry about holding too tight.

It did feel good to be on the same page as him. But part of me still wondered if that page was the start of a new story, or the end of a chapter.

THE SECOND BREAKFAST WAS a big, airy building with lots of windows and an assortment of comfy, second-hand furniture that made you feel like you were having a cozy morning meal with friends who were much, much better cooks than you. So far it had remained successful enough to stay in business but not popular enough to get infested by Brooklyn hipsters.

Flora, the owner and head cook, jumped off of a stool near the entrance as we came in and wiped the flour off her hands. "Cade! Briar! You made it. All your friends are in the back." Her rosy cheeks matched the red scarf tying back her long auburn hair, and she looked every inch the welcoming landlady of a country inn. Even if she was almost three feet shorter than me.

I leaned down to give the Little Person a big hug. Flora's cousin Scuff worked with Cade in the Red Hoods as a medic, and his legitimate medicines had saved my ass more than once. His less legitimate concoctions had also given us some pretty legendary house parties, so I always had a soft spot in my heart for the McCorryn clan.

"Shall I whip up the usual for you two?" she chirped, giving us a warm smile.

"Yes, please! Thanks, Flora. I hope everyone isn't giving you too much trouble."

She cackled. "I'm just glad someone is giving those White Knights some trouble. I booked out the whole back room for you guys, as long as you need."

"Thank you so much," Cade said, beaming. I knew his regular order here involved a quantity of breakfast meats that would make Gaston go vegan. "Have you had any more problem with those giant rats in the basement?"

A few months back, Cade and I had helped her clear her cellar of an infestation of giant, squeaking rats. It was a little bit like a bad video game tutorial, but she'd repaid us in many, many drinks.

"Not a squeak," Flora said. "All thanks to my noble heroes."

"Hey, that's what neighbors do, Flora," I said. "After all you've done for us—you're the best."

She squeezed my arm. I wasn't lying—Flora really was the best. She'd done more for the neighborhood of Havmercy than a dozen Royals, giving jobs to locals in need and slipping baked goods to anyone going hungry.

Cade nodded. "Thanks so much for letting us take over your back room."

"Any time, darling," she beamed, bustling away towards the kitchen, hopefully to make my favorite Nutella-banana crepes. "Whatever you guys need, let me know. An army runs on its stomach, after all."

I understood what she meant by army when I made it to the backroom. The long wooden dining table in the center looked like a mix between a military control room and the Mad Hatter's tea party. Mugs, mimosas, and marmalade were scattered amongst a giant map of the Apple, scattered with notes and pins. A half-eaten cheesecake stood in for the White Tower, the Royals' high-security answer to Guantanamo Bay, while someone had used the crusts from a half-dozen pieces of avocado toast to fill in the border of the Afterwoods. Parchment after parchment was filled with Alice's loopy handwriting, listing her contacts spread throughout the city, somewhere between a medieval rolodex and the beginnings of a massive community network.

Jacqui, Antoine, Alice, and Tarris stood around the table deep in discussion, but stopped when I entered. Jacqui, Antoine, and Alice gave me warm hugs, but the Grimmour prince still seemed irritated with me judging from his blasé wave. Flora arrived not long after I entered with my crepes and a steaming pot of English Breakfast tea with milk and honey, just the way I liked it. I had to be restrained from proposing marriage to her right then and there.

Through mouthfuls of gooey hazelnut goodness, I described the events of the previous evening to them, only leaving out the detail about Jacqui's presence in the Baron's dreamscape. They were rapt; one of the advantages to my life being a swirling fountain of pandemonium is I get some great stories out of it.

When I finished, they almost immediately launched into an argument over what it all meant.

"Of course he would deny responsibility for starting all of this," Tarris growled. "He's a master manipulator—"

"Why would he lie in a dream?" Antoine said, absentmindedly shuffling through pages of parchment.

"Briar said it seemed like they were just taking advantage of the opportunity," Cade said. "I trust her instincts."

Tarris glowered as Jacqui drained her third espresso. "I'm going to get a refill," she said, getting up from the bench where she'd been perched.

"I'll give you a hand," I said quickly, following her out of the backroom as the others continued to argue. We wove through the bustling brunch-goers, making our way to the long oak bar that lined the back of the restaurant.

"You still had half a pot of tea," Jacqui said astutely. "So what did you want to talk about away from the boys?" She turned to me as she plopped onto a stool. "Is it about Antoine? Or Cade? Or *Linden*? He's cute in a kinda skinny, raver sort of way—"

"No, not any of that," I said, waving my hand. "Although I'll fill you in on the emotional dressing down my dad gave me later. This is about you." She quirked an eyebrow. "And the Baron."

Jacqui's blue eyes, bright with the promise of incoming gossip, lost their shine as she angled her face away from me under the pretext of flagging down a waiter. "What do you mean?"

I waited for her to put in her order for more espresso and a croissant before continuing. "I saw you in his dream. You were the final monster that attacked his robot just before he woke up." I paused. "It was actually really badass. You were taller than the Empire State building."

She sighed. "It's not—it's not a big deal. If it were at all relevant to our investigation, I would've said something."

"Jacqs," I said, grabbing her hand, "I'm not asking as a detective. I'm asking as your friend. How do you know him?"

"He had dealings with my family." I noticed the bright red blush of shame coming to her cheeks, and I stayed quiet until she continued. "My father was in business with him, and, when I was about fourteen or so, they tried to create an alliance between our families. The Baron took an interest in me."

My gut roiled at her words, but I just nodded and gave her hand a warm squeeze.

"He decided I had potential to help continue the Landsgreaves line and wanted me to marry into his family. In a generation."

"You mean—?"

"He wanted me to take a sleeping curse, so the son he'd just had could take me as his wife. I'd go to sleep for fourteen years and wake up when we were the same age."

I shuddered. "Jacqui, I'm so sorry."

She shook her head, dismissing my concern for her like she didn't deserve it. "Don't be. I ate it all up. The promise of an advantageous match to an influential prince… I was so steeped in my parents' Royal bullshit that I barely even hesitated before agreeing."

I tried to hide my surprise at this, lest my shock came across as judgment. "You were fourteen. Giving that choice to a *child* that age is monstrous. And I'm sure your parents were pressuring you—"

"But I wanted it, Bri. I was willing to very literally put my future on hold to try to get what I thought would be my happily ever after. How can I pretend like I'm fighting the Baron's misogynist shit when I was so willing to buy into it the second I got the offer?"

"Woah there, cowgirl," I said as a waiter arrived with her croissant and espresso. "You can't blame yourself for believing in the stories you were told your whole life."

"I should've questioned them. I should've told the Baron to shove his offer up his professionally landscaped ass."

I snorted at the imagery. "When we're young, we just listen to the stories we're told. But we're adults now. Kind of. So that means we get to tell our own stories."

Jacqui nodded, hiding the tenderness I saw in her eyes with a sip of espresso. "Yeah," she squeaked out. "Yeah, you're right." We both looked around at the happy breakfasters around us, talking and laughing over the distant sound of screams. Just a few weekends ago, we were them, giggling and gossiping over a table full of syrup and carbs. Now it felt like the world was ending.

I sighed. "So what happened with the Baron? Why aren't you in the big sleep?"

Jacqui looked sheepish. "When I said yes, they took me to meet my husband-to-be in his nursery. And I asked if he was going to get any less wrinkly by the time I had to marry him, and the Baron got very upset."

I laughed. "Now, that sounds like the Jacqui I know."

"Not long after, my family's business dealings with the Baron went sour, and so the curse was called off. My parents blamed it all on my display of 'cheek' and never really forgave me for it. So in a way, all of that led to me leaving Castle Fortnight and our weird, brilliant lives in Commontown. So, cheers, I guess," she said, raising up her little espresso cup.

"All's well that ends well. And I guess making fun of Landgreaves's son was enough to make you a symbol in the Baron's head of dangerous, outspoken women. So that's pretty awesome."

My best friend smiled as she hopped off her stool and started back to our war room. "You're right. Now let's see if we can figure out a way to make the Baron's nightmares come true."

THE CAMPUS OF THE Academy of the Iron Wand had a significant White Knight presence as Antoine and I made our way to the Department of Magiphysics to meet Tamsin and Linden. Our planning at the Second Breakfast had hit a standstill, so getting Tamsin's mirror message was a welcome respite from our increasingly outlandish speculation about the Baron's evil plans. I shuddered involuntarily as we walked past another passel of White Knights standing on one of the quads, testing out some sort of enchanted crossbows. I watched a Knight fire a bolt into a target, only to have a swarm of iron chains erupt out and wrap the target like a mechanical octopus. The meaty warrior gave his friend a high five and whooped like a Grimmsdamn frat boy.

These were the guys people were trusting to solve the princess crisis?

Tamsin was excited to see us when we entered her basement office, fluttering around and throwing books and various pieces of lab equipment off of her couch so we'd have a place to sit. "Your friend Alice has been giving me reports about more princesses behaving oddly." She launched into her lecture without much chit chat. "Not many, but a few have started attacking people like the one did in Liars' Square. Only a handful so far, but it's got me thinking."

"Can you speed this up?" Linden called from the other room. Tamsin had ushered him into the kitchen area before she'd opened the door for us.

"Explaining the nuances of transdimensional magic takes time, dearie," Tamsin called back kindly. "Now, from the princesses' new behavior, it's safe to say the nature of the curse affecting them is changing, and what's more, it's changing at a nonstandard rate."

She looked expectantly at Antoine and me, somehow thinking this was going to make sense to us. When it didn't, she frowned and continued. "Meaning, of course, that the new effects are spreading through the Dream Slip from a point of origin."

A couple neurons in my brain weakly fired in the face of Tamsin's brilliance. "Wait, so you think you could track the disturbances in the Dream Slip to whatever is causing the princesses' curse?"

"No," Tamsin said smugly, "*I* can't do that. But I was able to create something that will allow someone else to."

She paused for a moment. Nothing happened.

"Linden, my darling, that was your cue," she sighed.

"Oh, right," Linden mumbled as he came out into the main room of Tamsin's lab. He was wearing what looked like the lampshade collars you give to dogs post-surgery, only this one was covered with intricate swirls of runes and sigils. From the back, a wire projected out over his face, dangling a clear, pointy crystal in front of him like he was an angler fish.

I couldn't help it. I burst out laughing.

"Oh, ha ha," Linden deadpanned. "I'm so sorry my outfit, which is going to *save the Apple*, amuses you."

"You look like a community theatre production of A Midsummer Night's Dream costume-designed by a neural network."

"Hey, I didn't design it—" Linden started.

"You look like the most pathetic member of the PAW Patrol," I gasped out between wheezes.

"Briar, come now—" Tamsin started.

"Are you done?" Linden scowled.

"I could probably come up with a few more, but I'd have to keep looking at you."

He rolled his eyes but couldn't hide his smirk.

"What does it do?" Antoine said. His voice sounded professional, but his eyes sparkled with mirth—he'd never admit to enjoying my antics.

"The crystal acts as a focus to heighten Linden's awareness of the Dream Slip," Tamsin explained. "It should allow him to home in on the disturbances in our world and figure out where they are coming from."

"That's amazing," Antoine said. "How did you figure out how to detect the disturbances?"

"She had help," a clear voice from the other room said, nearly making my heart stop. A gorgeous, lithe young woman a few years older than me stepped into view. Her long, dark hair flowed almost seamlessly into the fur collar of a mid-length black dress that looked like it belonged in a trendy Elvira reboot. She had caramel skin and a pointed, vulpine face that peered at us with amused dark eyes.

"Ravenna," Antoine said, straightening in his seat and getting up. "You always were fond of dramatic entrances."

"Some things never change, eh?" she said, drawing him into a deep hug. "How have you been, Boy Scout?"

I got up from the couch and made sure to ignore whatever twisty feelings I got in my gut as I watched them hug. After what I thought was an inordinately long time, they separated, and Ravenna turned to me. "And you must be Briar! I've heard so much about you. And heard how much you like the collar I helped design."

I stammered, which just made the young woman give me a wicked grin. "Honestly, I probably could've made it more subtle, but who doesn't love some rhinestone runes?"

Linden glowered at Ravenna and Tamsin. "I can't believe you left me alone with these two."

"How have you been, Rav?" Antoine said. I tried to remember the last time I'd heard him use a nickname for anyone and failed.

"Just got in from Tír na nÓg a few weeks ago! The druids there are doing some really exciting stuff with blending arcane runes and shamanic incantations," she gushed.

"Ravenna's brilliance was never going to reach its full potential being confined at the Academy," Tamsin said, beaming at her former pupil.

"Well, I was happy to get your call," Ravenna smiled. "Not every day I get to help save the Apple by designing accessories."

"Does your latest fashion statement also work?" Antoine said, a hint of teasing mischief in his voice.

Linden nodded and took a breath. He closed his eyes and concentrated until the crystal hanging over his head began to glow red. His eyes still closed, he turned in a small circle; when he faced the back corner of the room, the crystal's light turned an emerald green.

"That's where the disturbance in the Dream Slip is coming from," Tamsin said, her voice quiet and serious. "If you follow the crystal's glow, you'll find whoever or whatever is causing this."

The rush of hope I felt was quickly dampened as I saw the color drain from Antoine's face. "That way?" he said. "Are you sure?"

Tamsin nodded grimly as I racked my brain trying to figure out what direction Linden was facing—what we all would soon be facing. Tamsin said it just as my mind reached the horrifying conclusion.

"The Afterwoods. Whatever is affecting the princesses is coming from beyond the edges of the Apple. I can't tell how far, but I know it's out there."

The Afterwoods. Where the darkest creatures from every fairy story lurk, growing twisted in the wild magic that seeps through each tree root. A place where Things That Go Bump lie in wait for a child to lose their way and stray from the path. A place that makes the Black Forest described in so many Grimm tales look like Prospect Park.

We were going to need lots of trail mix.

WE WENT BACK TO my house to meet up with the others, who'd left the Second Breakfast because, as Jacqui put it, "if I had another frittata, I'd start screaming louder than any of the princesses." Tamsin had stayed behind at the University to work on her runes, so my ragtag team consisted of Antoine, Cade, Alice, Jacqui, Tarris, Linden, and Ravenna, whom Antoine had invited along. We'd made two French presses of coffee and sat scattered amongst the mismatched furniture of my living room. It was like the Fellowship meeting at the Council of Elrond, except with more thrift-store furniture and Doritos.

It didn't take long until Antoine and Cade disagreed on the strategy of our fool's errand. "If I put out the call through official Red Hood channels, we could get a full battalion of rangers to escort us through the woods. That might be our only chance—" Cade repeated for the third time.

Antoine shook his head. "It's too risky. We don't know who in the Hoods could be sympathetic to the White Knights. And our best chance is to travel light with a small group to avoid alerting all of the creatures of the Afterwoods to our presence."

Cade started to growl a response but stopped himself and took a short breath. His hands clenched as he turned to me. "Briar, what do you think?" His eyes held mine, and I couldn't help but think back to our conversation that morning, the promise of what might be waiting for us at the end of this journey.

I shook my head to clear it. As someone who had lived through three Spiderman movie franchises, I had learned one thing: heroics first, romance second.

"Antoine is right," I said. I looked downward as I said it but was slow enough that I still saw Cade's face fall. "You know I value what the Red Hoods do for the Apple, but it just takes one authoritarian meathead to leak things to the White Knights for things to go pear-shaped. I don't want the Baron deploying his forces to the Afterwoods and mucking up our chance to help the princesses."

Cade radiated anger, but gave a sharp nod as what I was saying sank in. I tried to shoot him a sympathetic look, but he turned away, so I focused on Antoine. "Who would you put in this small group?" I asked.

"Cade knows the Afterwoods the best. I can back him up in a fight," Antoine said diplomatically. "We need Linden to track the disturbance, and Ravenna to keep his collar in working order. And you," he said, giving me a warm glance that made the tips of my ears go hot, "are our Free Spell wildcard."

I've been called worse.

Jacqui stood up from her weathered green armchair. "I'm coming. I need to help, to do *something*. My sister—"

"—needs you here," Antoine finished firmly. "We're fighting on multiple fronts. It's just as important that you, Alice, and Tarris keep the White Knights under surveillance and in check while we quest."

Jacqui stared him down, but finally relented. Only someone who knew her as well as I did would've seen her discreetly wipe tears of frustration from her eyes. "You all had better find out what is going on and stop it. I'm trusting you. For Raye's sake."

All of us were silent for a moment as the princess's words hit home. It was more than just Jacqui's plea; there were many more lives at stake than just Raye's. It felt like if we let the White Knight's power grab go unchecked, if we allowed them to keep their messages playing on every mirror in town, the Apple's very soul was at stake.

Ravenna cleared her throat. "I know I'm the new kid on the block here, but how exactly are we planning on approaching this? No one has ever made it more than a day or two's journey into the Afterwoods and come back to tell the tale."

Antoine and Cade both started to speak at the same time, and then glared at each other. Antoine gritted his teeth and nodded to the taller man.

"We move quickly," Cade said. "Journey into the Afterwoods at dawn, when most of the nasties will be slinking back to their dens. Use the sunlight to get as far as we can. When the sun starts going down, we turn back around, so we can get back to the Apple safely before nightfall."

"What if we don't find it?" I say, my nervous thoughts forcing their way through my lips. "What if we go all that way just to have to turn around empty handed?"

No one spoke for a moment, and the stale smell of despair started to drown out the scent of cheap coffee.

Good Grimms, I thought to myself, *nice display of leadership, Bri.*

Alice finally spoke up, a bit of hope sparking in her voice. "What if you find the source twenty feet past the borders of the Apple? All we can tell from Linden's collar is the direction, right? So for all we know, it might not even take you until lunchtime."

My eyes rolled, but I still tried to latch on to the bit of hope Alice offered. "Sure, I mean, Joseph Campbell would be pretty disappointed in our heroic journey, but I guess that's possible."

"Alice is right," Jacqui said resolutely. "We have to try."

I looked to each of my friends and smiled at the faith I saw reflected back at me. It wasn't the best plan. It wasn't the safest plan. But if it meant we might stop the princesses from their torturous nightmares and cut off the White Knights from getting more support, we had to try.

I got three bars into the opening number from "Into The Woods" before Jacqui hit me with a pillow.

THE POISONED APPLE HAS many containers and buildings larger on the inside than they are on the outside. We've got Bags of Holding, Totes of Holding, even Fanny Packs of Holding. A man with hooves for feet often lures tourists out of Liars' Square into an "escape room experience" that seems to fit inside a burnt wooden puzzle box he always handles with gloves. Recently, someone claiming to be Baba Yaga started advertising properties that look like huts on the outside but are luxury condos on the inside. The condos were currently penned up in the Furrier's Quarter, strutting around on their giant chicken legs and waiting for yuppies to put in an offer.

But any of these magical contrivances would fall short when compared to my closet. I somehow managed to fit a hundred cubic feet of random junk into a simple three-foot square. And buried somewhere in its depths was my camping gear.

I was about to give up after I discovered a second ukulele that I had no ability or intention to play, but I heard a quick rap on my door.

"Knock knock," Antoine said as I opened it for him.

"Who's there?" I said immediately. He blinked his deep brown eyes, obviously startled.

"Oh, I—uh, didn't have a joke prepared. I just wanted to let you know I was at your door."

"C'mon," I teased. "You've traveled all around the world perfecting the art of butt kicking, but you don't know a single knock knock joke?"

Antoine chuckled and relented. "Fine."

"So who's there?" I repeated.

"Rapunzel."

"Rapunzel who?"

"Rapunzel only work if your audience is familiar with Egyptian gods and likes bad jokes."

I'll admit it took me a second of repeating it out loud before I gave somewhere between a laugh and a groan. "That's terrible."

"You asked for it," Antoine said, politely sitting on the arm of my desk chair, since most other horizontal surfaces in my room were covered in the detritus from my closet. "How are your preparations going?" He rolled up the sleeves of his light blue linen shirt; it had been unseasonably hot for the fall, so Antoine had felt scandalous enough to wear his finest khaki dress shorts on our excursions around the city today.

"I anticipate finding everything I need very shortly," I managed with a straight face.

"I told you, I've got plenty of extra hiking gear—"

"But your stuff is probably all fancy and stodgy. Can't I have my craptastic camping gear my dad got me in high school?"

Antoine smiled, indulging me as usual. It made me realize how far he'd come in the short time I'd known him, from a rigid

Knight Bachelor up on his high horse to someone who could appreciate my… um, let's go with "quirks."

I decided to push my luck. "Have you given any thoughts to our quest's playlist?"

"How about 'Silence' by the band 'We're Going to Be Surrounded By Monsters.'"

I felt my face light up with a smile. Antoine was actually pretty funny when he relaxed. "I'll add it in."

"We're having a playlist? This is a quest, Briar, not a road trip."

"I mean, quests are pretty much the Poisoned Apple equivalent to a road trip, right? I know I plan on eating crappy food and asking, 'are we there yet?' a lot. And my playlist heavily features the soundtrack to the movie Crossroads."

Antoine shook his head. "I'm sure Ravenna will sing along with you."

There was a split-second pause, and that was all it took for the friendly atmosphere of banter between us to drain away, replaced with the moldy-gym-sock odor of questions unasked.

"Ravenna seems nice," I say lamely. It's true. She did seem like a genuinely cool person, but somehow her presence was throwing into relief whatever dynamic existed between Antoine and I in a way that made my skin itch. "How did you two meet?"

"She consulted with me on a few of my first jobs as a freshly trained Knight," he said. "She really is quite incredible. Pretty soon she was my go-to resource for anything magical that came up in my work."

"A knight and a magic-user teaming up, having adventures," I said before I thought better of it. "Kind of sounds like us."

Antoine shifted his perch on the chair, causing it to spin and him to almost fall on his ass. He caught himself and used the momentum to fold into a casual lean on my desk, but he was fooling no one. It was a remarkably ungraceful movement for someone I'd seen use his rapier to spear an apricot that was thrown at him (yes, I was the one who threw it, and yes, he deserved it).

"I mean, she was more of a contact than a partner," he said, a subtle flush of color invading his cheeks. "And, full disclosure, we were—um, together, for a while."

"Cool," I said. My mind was completely empty of talking words. "Cool," I repeated for more emphasis.

We caught each other's eyes, and somehow the sheer tension made us both laugh. Antoine smiled and ran his hands through his chestnut hair. "Sorry, I just thought you should know—I didn't mean to make you uncomfortable. I don't have a good track record with that."

I quirked my head to the side as my chuckles subsided. "What the elf do you mean by that?"

Antoine gestured vaguely, apparently finding this conversation as difficult as I was. "You know… that one time… I made a fool of myself."

I swallowed. "You mean the kiss?" Without meaning to, my eyes went to the flat line of his lips, soft and vulnerable amidst the slight stubble that dotted his chin.

Antoine scrunched his face up and looked down at his feet. "Yeah, that. I appreciate you haven't held that against me."

My partner was one of the most specific and direct communicators I knew, so this stumbling version of him was almost as shocking to see as the words he was saying. "Hold it against you? What—you didn't do anything wrong, Antoine."

"I mean, obviously I misread things," he said, still not meeting my eyes. "I had thought—but it's fine. You weren't interested, and I respect that. I'm just glad we've still been able to work together. And be friends, I hope."

I sat down hard on my bed, trying to piece together what I was hearing. "Antoine, I was never... *not* interested. I just thought—I dunno, you were just trying that out. Then when nothing else happened, when you didn't make another move, I thought you just wanted to be friends. Or I'd done something weird with my teeth or something."

Antoine's head shot up, and his dark brown eyes found mine. "I thought when *you* didn't make another move, you weren't interested." His gaze scrutinized me like he was seeing me for the first time. He took a somewhat shaky breath in, and I noticed his chest rising against the linen of his shirt, not too far from me. "But you're saying that's not the case?"

"Antoine, I—the more I've gotten to know you, the more I get thoroughly confused about what I want. The thing is—"

"Cade," Antoine finished my thought for me. There wasn't an accusation in his voice, but I smelled the hurt behind his carefully controlled tone.

Now it was my turn to lower my gaze. "I'm sorry—there's just so much going on, and I care about both of you so much, that I just know I'm going to do something stupid and hurt you." The looping swirls of my floorboards became blurry as I fought against tears.

I felt a gentle pressure on my chin, and Antoine's warm fingers guided my head back upwards, so I was looking into his face. I was close enough I could see the fringe of his eyelashes, their tips turning a tawny brown from the summer sun. "Briar, you have nothing to apologize for."

My mouth went dry, and his hand lingered on my jawline before flicking away. But his gaze still held mine as my brain's speech center flatlined.

"It seems to me," Antoine stared, a small smile playing at his lips, "that we're not doing a particularly good job of communicating when it comes to all of this."

I nodded. "Yup."

At least I didn't say "cool" again.

"We should really just discuss this, like rational adults, and clear the air."

I nodded mutely,

"Really make sure we preserve our working relationship."

Our eyes met. His were so close I could see his pupils dilate, the deep brown reflecting my face back at me.

I couldn't tell who moved first, but our lips met in the charged space we'd left between us. My nostrils flared as I inhaled in shock, the honey-and-molasses smell of his desire mixing with the minty taste of his lips. My brain reeled, trying to catch up with the decision my body had made, and I started to feel almost lightheaded, the room slipping away as only Antoine's lips felt real.

I steadied myself on his solid arm, my hands clutching them as he shifted himself onto the foot of the bed next to me. Sensing how precarious my perch had become, Antoine snaked his arm around my waist, leaning forward as the kiss got deeper, and slower for a moment. My fingers brushed the broad plane of his shoulders and snaked underneath his collar, bracing themselves against the nape of his neck. I felt confused and comforted all at once; this was Antoine, someone I felt like I knew so well, and yet the feeling of his body underneath my hands was alien and exotic. He was always so composed, so polished and reserved, so I found myself surprised at the warmth of his skin, the blood I could feel pumping through his veins as he angled his body against mine, poised so I was between him and the mattress.

Despite my quick moan of protest, he pulled his mouth away from mine. "Is this okay?" he gasped out, voice ragged.

"Yeah," I said, sucking in some much-needed oxygen. "Thanks for asking. Now come back here."

I could feel his smile as he kissed me again, the stubble on his upper lip tickling against my skin. Antoine leaned back and pulled me across him, so I was on his lap, straddling him with his hands curving tantalizingly around my waist. I pushed my palms against his chest, exploring the taut muscles underneath his thin shirt. In response, he threaded his fingers through the back of my hair, angling my head to the side and planting a string of kisses up the hollow of my neck, chuckling a bit as I gave an involuntary shudder of pleasure.

I could smell the whirl of emotions around me, too many, and at such an intensity I had no hope to separate or identify them or figure out where mine ended and Antoine's began. Instead, I pressed myself against him again, our bodies melding into each other, limbs tangling, a desperate push towards unity, until we fell to the bed with a—

CLANG.

I sprang up from Antoine's embrace, nearly overbalancing and tumbling off the bed as he said a series of very unknightly words while clutching his head. Scrambling through the pile of clothes and junk from my closet, my hands finally found the mace that Antoine had just banged his skull into.

"Simurgh on a stick," I swore. "I am *so* sorry—"

Antoine put a hand up to stop me while he inspected his head for damage. When it was clear he wasn't bleeding, he unscrunched his eyes and gave me a look, half mirth and half pain.

We both started laughing.

I chucked the mace to the floor and collapsed next to him until our giggles subsided. He grabbed my hand in his and pressed a gentle kiss against my fingers. "I was not expecting that," he purred. His tone was different, lower and sharper somehow, the voice of the private Antoine that I'd only seen in flashes in the time we'd known each other.

"The mace or the make out?" I said, my breath still coming quick. I rested my hand against his chest, feeling his heart still racing. I gave it a quick squeeze, willing my fingers to be gentle enough with it, to hold it warmly without clutching too tight.

"Both," Antoine said, quirking his lips into a surprisingly wicked smile.

I felt my lips stretch to echo his smile back at him. "Not an unpleasant surprise, I hope?"

"Definitely not," he said. "Well, the mace was."

"Sorry about that. Marie Kondo never told me where to store my blunt weapons." I took a breath in.

His hands came up to my face, his earlier enthusiasm having simmered to the softest touch as he pushed a strand of hair behind my ear, his fingertips tracing a lazy river down my neck. "It's okay. I know you didn't mean to hurt me."

His words hung heavier in the air than perhaps he'd meant, and I took a deep breath in. "Antoine, I, uh, obviously enjoyed that and all, but—"

"—but," Antoine said, giving my hand a squeeze as he effortlessly predicted where my mind was going, "we still haven't had that Big Mature Adult Conversation about where this leaves us."

I sighed and nodded. "Yeah, we should probably do that."

Antoine closed his eyes, as if steeling himself to do something he didn't want to do. I was treated to the sight of his angular face at peace for a moment before his thick eyelashes fluttered open. "Then I should probably go," he said, sitting up and adjusting his very off-kilter shirt.

There was an unpleasant kick in my stomach as his hands disentangled from mine, and suddenly the bed felt very cold without his body heat radiating from next to me. "Ugh, why does being an adult suck sometimes?"

Antoine laughed and leaned back, his hands nervously smoothing out the nonexistent wrinkles in his shorts as he hovered near my doorway. "I know. I feel the same way." Then his eyes caught mine, piercing into me with the kind of eye contact I usually only make with cats and store mannequins. "But I'm willing to wait for you if it means we do this the healthy way and get a chance at something more."

I audibly gulped and nodded, my words running away again. The butterflies in my stomach had metamorphosed into a whole swarm of sparkly pixies, and a less than lucid voice within me wondered if I was going to puke fairy dust. Is this what these feelings felt like when I wasn't the one dishing them out?

Antoine smiled, as if he knew the effect he was still having on me from across the room. "How about we table this conversation until we come back from our possibly fatal mission to the Afterwoods? Hopefully we'll be in a more stable place to address it."

A memory of my very similar proposition from Cade rose unbidden to my mind, but I pushed it back. "Right. I'm all for that. And hey, maybe we'll get lucky and get devoured and never have to deal with it."

Antoine's laugh was rich and inviting as he got up to go to the door. "Try to finish tearing your room apart soon and get some sleep. We leave tomorrow before dawn."

As soon as the door closed, I gave my mace a dirty look and flung myself backwards onto the bed. My head had almost stopped spinning, and I spent a moment just soaking in the feeling of a soft mattress underneath me. As much as a I joked, there was no guarantee I'd be making it back to my comfy bed tomorrow. I was suddenly overwhelmed with the fear that I might never get to explore whatever had just happened with Antoine any further.

I turned on my bedside lamp, and the spell inside it projected soft, afternoon light that seemed to come through a curtain of orange leaves. In a few short hours, I'd be out in an actual forest, trying to track down the source of a magical anomaly strong enough to rip across multiple dimensions.

My worried frown turned to a smile, however, when my vantage point on the bed revealed my old hiking boots sitting forgotten on the top of my armoire, their aged leather heel catching a glint of autumnal sunlight.

If I was going to be eaten alive, I'd least I'd have good arch support.

I WOKE UP, BIZARRELY, before my alarm, and the nerves in my stomach meant there was no way I was going back to sleep. I begrudgingly pulled off my warm covers and put on my slippers—the heat from yesterday had finally dissipated, leaving a delicious chill in the early morning air. I opened my bay window and looked out at the Apple; the shrieks seemed to have become just background noise in the time we'd been living with the princesses. But as I sat there, breathing in the first cool morning of the fall, the screams hit me like they had the first time. I'd been mentally turning them off, tuning them out instead of actually recognizing all the pain behind them. Curse or not, the princesses were trapped in torment, and we'd all just grown to accept it. It was easier to put our headphones in and turn the volume up than listen to the world scream. And that scared me, almost more than the creatures of the Afterwoods. How easy it was to turn widespread human suffering into background noise.

I let out the breath I'd been holding in, and a curl of steam escaped with it. For better or worse, we were going to get some answers today, and I just hoped Raye and all of the other princesses could hold on a little bit longer.

After the bustle of the last few days, I was thrilled to find that no one was awake downstairs. I love my friends, I love being around people, but I had just about reached my limit. Linden was asleep on the couch, his eyes flitting underneath his lids. Poor guy. Even in his dreams, he didn't get the chance to be alone.

I made a cup of tea as quietly as I could, indulging in the little pleasures of watching the milk swirl into the mug, marble veins amongst the brown. Cradling my honey-soaked little treasure, I eased the French doors to our backyard open and slipped into the pre-dawn air.

My bags were packed, our supplies were ready, so I felt nothing but contentment as I stole this quiet moment before we embarked. The first sip of my warm English Breakfast trickled down my throat, sending tingles as it pushed away the crisp chill. I breathed the cold air in low into my belly and pushed it back out again, feeling some of the tension leak from my shoulders. The nerves that had been dogging me since I'd awakened took a break, but I could almost feel them lurking in the bushes, waiting for another chance to pounce.

But not right now.

As my breathing deepened, I could smell the earthy scent of my own calm rising to my nostrils. Normally I can only smell myself when I've been too busy to shower for a second day in a row, but this smell was much more reassuring than my B.O. My eyelids drooped but stayed open a crack, and I felt my muscles loosen as I cupped my tea reverently in my lap.

A streak of sunlight moved slowly across the garden, painting the hundreds of rose blooms a light pink, as if they'd all let go of their mismatched colors and relaxed with me into a single harmonious hue. My breath almost caught, afraid that if I breathed out too forcefully, the beautiful sight in front of me would pop like an iridescent soap bubble.

On my exhale, the blooms all turned a tropical seafoam, and I realized it wasn't the sun changing their colors. It was me.

I'd started having issues with my powers getting away from me and affecting roses I wasn't touching during the Grimmour kidnapping case. Still, I lost control sometimes, like I had visiting my dad, and my powers seemed to burst out from me uncontrolled. It scared me, the thought of my already chaotic power venturing out of me, crossing the boundaries of my skin to do who knows what.

But this was different. This felt measured, harmonious. A pleasant blurring of the lines I'd wrapped so tightly around myself, separating me from the world around me. It was almost as if I could feel what the scent of the roses was trying to tell me, scratch the surface of their deep contentment as they lived their quiet lives, each day soaking up the nutrients and moisture from the earth around them and growing immeasurably closer to the sun.

I made the slightest effort, and the roses all started to pulse in waves of color emanating out from me, a tie-dyed cornucopia in motion, centered on me and my breath. It reminded me of the intricate details of a mandala I'd seen a group of Buddhist monks make in Blue Fairy Park one afternoon, only to have it blown away by the wind when they were finished. My eyes were moist, but I couldn't for the life of me explain what emotions my tears contained.

Was it in my head, or had the screaming of the princesses died down as well?

Inside, I heard the footsteps of my friends coming to life as dawn beckoned. I gave one more exhale, returning the roses to their usual colors with a thought. Soon, we'd be on a path deep into the woods, and I'd have no time to myself. So I held onto this moment, to this feeling, a little while longer.

Then I sighed, finished my tea, and went back inside to prepare for my journey.

I WAS RIGHT; OUR departure passed in a hectic blur of packing and goodbyes. Alice and Jacqui woke up to see us off, Alice looking remarkably somber despite her pink Sailor Moon PJs. After hugging me, Jacqui looked deep into my eyes, and it was all I could do to nod back at her. She was trusting us with her sister's life, and it wasn't a burden I took lightly.

Before I knew it, Antoine, Cade, Linden, Ravenna, and I were walking into one of the Red Hoods' trailheads near the Academy of the Iron Wand that led into the Afterwoods. It didn't become the deep, dark woods instantly. The fringes of the forest were quite pleasant, with lightly spaced trees and waving fields of grass. People still thought the outskirts were safe enough to send their children through to visit their grandparents, even though the city had put out a great series of PSAs warning against it. The latest one even starred Betty White.

The autumn seemed to have come sooner to the woods than the rest of the Apple, but it was still in the early stages. The treetops were kissed with yellow and orange, with only a few tinges of brown and red. Here and there our boots crunched the odd fallen leaf as we walked reverently through the morning mist. Perhaps it was the early hour that kept us all silent, or the gravity of the task ahead of us, but the five of us didn't speak for the first hour of the journey, besides Cade pointing out a multitude of poisonous and/or carnivorous plants.

We adjusted our route every twenty minutes or so, pausing to let Linden use his collar under Ravenna's watchful eye. He led us into a slightly hillier part of the forest; it was still not heavily forested, but the sunlight here was dimmer and our path became more vertical than a flat horizontal. We wound around a large tree at the foot of the hill, its roots exposed by erosion to create a small shelf big enough for a hobbit to hide.

My body moved before I was consciously aware of anything; a prickly *something* on the back of my neck made me think I was being watched. My head whipped to the side, but a scan of the woods around us revealed nothing. Maybe all the silence and the constant threat of the forest was getting to me, but I doubted it.

I reached forward to squeeze Antoine's shoulder, and silently pointed up at the trees behind us. As soon as the two of us slowed down, everyone snapped to attention, forming a circle, facing outwards to watch as much of the forest as we could. I drew Prick and held it out in front of me. The woods were silent except for a light breeze that made the leaves dance. We held our collective breath for a long, tense moment, and I wondered if my instincts had been wrong.

A tree to my left suddenly moved upwards, as if something very large had leaped nimbly off of it, releasing a scattering of yellow leaves. Before they hit the ground, a creature the size of a stretch Hummer landed behind us, and I caught a glance of something grey and furry shooting towards us before Cade was lifted off his feet and thrown on his back ten feet away. The creature leapt with impossible agility back into the trees, this time scampering through the leaves, circling us.

I risked a quick dash to Cade's side and caught sight of a dozen or so pawprints in the mud. They were unlike any tracks I'd ever seen, a variety of sizes from the span of my hand to a trashcan lid, all laid into the dirt helter-skelter, with no repetition or rhyme. These nonsensical observations barely had time to register in my panic-soaked brain before I reached Cade.

He was already struggling to sit up, bruised but unbroken. A quartet of claw marks made red rings around his bicep, but the damage was surprisingly minimal.

The fear in his eyes, however, gave me pause. I could see the whites all around his greyish-green irises.

"Briar," he wheezed. The air must've been knocked out of his lungs. "It's a Cattywampus."

I heard a creak in the canopy of leaves above me, and a large branch groaned as the weight on it bent it down. It felt like I was turning in slow motion, but I saw just in time as the Cattywampus came into view.

It was lithe and serpentine, with cloudy grey fur that seemed at times silver-white and others the dull rust of oxidized metal. There was no pattern as comforting as stripes or spots, just waves and patches that seemed to shift as I looked at them, like shadows shifting in storm clouds. It had a scattering of dozens of legs along its body, all different sizes and lengths, like a housecat crossed with a mutated millipede. But its head was all feline, with a dark grey nose and a Cheshire grin full of too many teeth. As I looked up at it, its jade eyes widened, the pupils growing until its eyes were almost all black.

Good Grimms. It was *playing* with us.

Its fluffy tail swished once, like a smoke plume in a heavy wind, and that was the only warning before it was soaring from its tree branch towards us. Cade scrambled, and I yanked his arm with all my weight, and together we were able to tumble just away from the point of impact of its three frontmost paws. Our other companions scattered, Ravenna hustling Linden into the hollow underneath the giant tree's roots. Antoine sprinted forward, waving his arms in an attempt to attract the beast's attention. With a quick resonant *"MROWR"* of interest, the

Cattywampus changed direction at a sixty-degree angle, its earth-shaking weight turning on a dime. Antoine barely had time to sink into an *en garde* position before the giant cat/caterpillar was flying at his face.

A scream was already leaving my throat when Antoine spun, twirling out of the way of the giant missile of claws and fur. He swept his rapier in a wide arc, tracing a line of red across the Cattywampus's side. The kamikaze kitty seemed to overbalance while twisting away from his sword and landed heavily on the side of hill in front of us.

For a second, the creature blinked, as if registering the pain of Antoine's attack. Its confusion quickly turned to pain, which turned to white-hot rage at a speed that only cats can accomplish. It fixed Antoine with a death-stare, its pupils narrowed to nothing more than vertical slits. Opening its mouth of irregular, shark-like teeth, the Cattywampus hissed, spittle flying out onto the forest floor.

Playtime was over.

I still couldn't get used to the speed the thing moved with; in an instant it had encircled Antoine, weaving a complete circle around him like a catlike Ouroboros. I couldn't see what it was doing inside, but I heard Antoine grunt as the clang of claw and metal sounded above the patter of the Cattywampus's many paws.

He'd be cut to ribbons if we left him in that whirlwind (more like *purr*-lwind, my somewhat addled brain corrected). Cade and I staggered forward, our weapons seeming so small in the face of the creature's giant flanks. But before we could close the distance between us, a flash from the other side of the valley caught all of our attention.

Ravenna stood with her arms bent in front of her, a curved rune floating between her palms. It glowed like a supernova, purple and gold waves of energy oscillating out from it that made my eyes hurt, but I couldn't look away. The shimmering light was hypnotic, even as my eyes watered with pain. As it pulsed, a sound echoed off the hills almost like… crumpling paper?

She was trying to draw the animal away from Antoine by luring it to her.

My adrenaline must have given me almost catlike reflexes because a split second after the Cattywampus had taken off towards Ravenna, my right hand flung out towards them, a rose from my boot hovering up and following the arc of my arm. Its petals turned an ectoplasmic Beetlejuice green, and the bloom deformed to resemble an arrow as the flower flew towards the Cattywampus.

But too late.

A giant paw swept Ravenna aside like a rag doll, and the Cattywampus cocked its head as it passed through the rune with no effect. Like a magical laser pointer, the rune floated idly while the Cattywampus tried swatting it again.

After the monster's third swing, my rose arrow found its target.

Somehow, instinctively, I knew my rose would have little effect on the creature itself. Size matters, at least when it comes to my magic, and the largest animal I'd ever been able to affect was a very snooty talking horse.

Instead, my rose sunk into Ravenna's rune, the petals racing along its curves and ligatures. The spell seemed to collapse in on itself, my Free Spell weirdness overloading the precise calculations of the Academy magic. It formed a tiny sphere the size of my fist, and then—

BAM, the spell exploded like a gunshot, reverberating throughout the little valley we were in. The green of my rose had turned into smoke that drifted from the detonation. Even thirty feet away, I felt the reverberations of the emotion I'd sent out: the same fear, shock, and adrenaline that the Cattywampus had inspired in me.

Also, somehow, I included the anxiety-producing sound of a vacuum cleaner, because, you know. Cats.

The Cattywampus shot straight up in the air, its elongated spine forming a perfect semi-circle. With a mangled yelp, it scrabbled onto a nearby tree, gave one frightened look back at us, and then bolted, all the hair on its tail standing on end. The sounds of its departure faded, and I imagined it would find some place to cuddle up and lick its figurative and literal wounds.

A quick look to both Cade and Antoine showed they were nursing scratches, but nothing seemed life threatening. My stomach lurched when I saw Ravenna; she hadn't moved from the hillside where she'd landed, her feather-trimmed black traveling cloak spread out around her like a burial shroud. Antoine got to her first, just as her eyelids fluttered and she started to sit up.

"Hey, hey," Antoine said soothingly, "don't try to move." He slid to his knees and started looking her over. She held her right arm clutched against her chest, and Antoine gingerly took it to inspect. She winced and swore impressively as he turned it over.

"Looks like a break, Rav," Antoine said, frowning.

"Good thing I'm left-handed," Ravenna said, her voice tight. She was obviously in a lot of pain and trying to mask it with devil-may-care humor.

Selkies on a stick, we *were* a lot alike.

Antoine had the patience of a saint as he got out our first aid kit and made a makeshift sling for Ravenna, all while enduring her pained teasing. His voice had gone smooth and soft, and a very hurt part of me recognized it as the same gentle tone he'd used with me last night in my bedroom.

Ravenna had just been smacked by a two-ton cat while saving Antoine's life, and I was getting *jealous*?

Linden snapped me out of my reverie, offering me a granola bar from his pack. "That shit was crazy," he said, taking a big bite of his own bar and talking with his mouth full. "I'm never going to be able to look at the cat bus from *My Neighbor Totoro* the same way again."

I nodded my thanks and took the food. "They say Miyazaki still visits the Apple every year in the spring. Maybe he saw a Cattywampus one time."

"If he did, I'm not sure how he survived. I'm not sure how *we* would've survived if Ravenna hadn't cast that spell."

It felt like poor taste to mention that my rose had been what had actually scared the beast off, but I sure as hell thought it.

Cade joined us, patting the bandages he'd just applied to his claw wounds. "This sucks to say, but we need to keep moving. We've only got a few more hours until we need to turn around if we're going to make it back before nightfall."

Antoine laid Ravenna down gingerly and got up, wiping the knees of his chinos. "Should we think about heading back? We could get Ravenna an actual healer, try again another day—"

"Ogreshit," Ravenna swore, her voice back to its normal sultry edge. She braced her good arm on the ground and got to her feet without too much grunting. "I'll be fine. We need to keep pressing forward."

"What if you and I went back and we got you help?" Antoine asked.

Ravenna snorted. "I'm good, Boy Scout. I can still cast with my left hand. And I need to be here to keep track of the collar. If the grounding rune gets even a little smudged, the whole thing could catch fire in two seconds."

"Sorry, what?" Linden said, looking up from an apple he was now munching on.

"We've made it this far, we've taken some licks, but we're not stopping now," Ravenna said, planting her feet and pointing a finger at Antoine.

"There's no use fighting you on this, is there?" Antoine sighed. His voice sounded exasperated, but I saw the hint of a smile on his lips.

"Absolutely not," Ravenna said.

We all started grabbing our gear and getting ready to move out. "Hey, can we circle back to the part about the collar I'm wearing being highly flammable?" Linden said over the din.

"You'll be fine," Ravenna said bluntly. "That barely ever happens with untested enchantments. And it's a wonder what they're doing with eyebrow regrowing potions these days."

I tried not to laugh at Linden's flabbergasted face as we walked out of the valley.

WE WERE MORE CAUTIOUS after the Cattywampus attack. In the next few hours, we covered more ground than we had in the morning, taking readings from Linden's collar to guide us through the increasingly dark forest. The land we now traveled through was thick pine forest, with craggy limestone outcroppings and gnarled old trees: less of a "beautiful early autumn stroll through upstate New York" and more of a "soggy scramble through the Pacific Northwest."

Each of us took turns walking with Ravenna, keeping an eye on her as she hiked the winding paths and stepped over fallen logs. Her balance was a little off, and I wondered if maybe she'd gotten a concussion to go along with the broken arm.

"You really don't need to hover," Ravenna said kindly as I steadied her steps along a dry, rocky creek bed.

"It's self-serving," I promised. "I want to be closest to our fireball cannon if more monsters attack."

Ravenna snorted. "You were pretty handy with that rose against the Cattywampus."

"I got lucky. I wasn't sure how my magic would interact with yours, but fortunately it exploded in a good way this time."

Ravenna pulled back a tree branch that blocked our way so I could walk through. "There's been some interesting research into the interaction between Free Spell magic and academy runes."

"My research into the subject involved getting stalked by a disgraced Academy lecturer who combined his wizardry with Free Spell smoke magic," I said.

"Ah, Elias Clewd, right?"

"Yup. Not fun," I answered. "That was my first adventure with Antoine."

A delicate silence followed the mention of his name, and we took a few steps without saying anything. "You and he make a good team," Ravenna finally said, but I could tell she was fishing for something diplomatic to fill the void.

"Well, he speaks very highly of you," I rushed to say.

Ravenna smiled. "Antoine is good people. And if he likes you as much as he seems to, that makes me think you must be pretty special yourself."

I felt heat rising to my face as we entered more uncomfortable emotional territory; I would much rather take a punch than a compliment. "Thanks for what you did back there. Luring the Cattywampus away from him. He's good, but there's no way he would've lasted much longer fighting that thing on his own."

She shrugged. "I am one-hundred-percent sure he would've done the same for me. I don't know many people who I can say that about."

I looked ahead, to where Antoine and Cade were walking with Linden. "I know what you mean. When you find those people, you stick with them."

"And you definitely don't let them get eaten by giant sociopathic cats," Ravenna said.

Her eyes were twinkling as she looked at me, and I found myself smiling. "Sociopathic cats? Redundant much?"

She chuckled, and then scrunched her face up, like whatever she was about to say tasted terrible. "Listen, Briar, I'm not always good at lady bonding, but I feel like I should make it clear, there's nothing going on between Antoine and me now. We're just good friends. His runway is clear, if you know what I mean."

My mouth felt suddenly dry, and I couldn't come up with anything pithy and clever to say, so I just nodded. "Gotcha."

"Sorry if that was crossing a line," Ravenna said. "I did receive a large blow to the head this morning. But yeah, I care about him, I'll always care about him, but we've put things to rest. You know what I mean?"

As if summoned by our words, Cade walked back to join us. I looked at Ravenna and muttered, "I wish."

"It's about time," Cade said sadly. "We're going to start losing daylight soon, and if we're going to get back to the Apple before—"

A screeching sound filled the air, and Cade whirled, his axe in his hand before I could process what was happening. All I saw was a dark cloud coming towards us, flapping—

"Bats?" I said, whirling my cloak up and over my face. The forest around us became dark as hundreds of the rodents descended on us. I braced for an attack, a bite, but the air just vibrated as they flapped past us. One got caught in the drape of my cloak for a second, but I was able to gently push him up to fly and rejoin his friends.

Once the sound of their wings had died out, I uncovered my face. "What the flying Fisher King was that?" I grumbled to no one in particular, my heart still racing.

"I'm no biologist," Ravenna said, standing shakily from where she'd dropped to avoid the swarm, "but aren't bats supposed to come out at night?" I wondered if that was part of the reason I'd been so shocked. Something about seeing all those flying, furry creatures in the afternoon sunshine just felt... wrong.

Cade nodded. "I didn't want to say anything, but I was a little confused by the Cattywampus attack. They're known to be crepuscular."

"Their muscles are made out of French pancakes?" I asked.

Linden rolled his eyes. "They're usually active around twilight." We all turned to look at him, and he shrugged angrily. "What? I use Word of the Day toilet paper. Don't act so flummoxed."

"So what?" I said. "These animals were out at a different time of day. Maybe there was a predator or something."

"I spend a lot of time in these woods," Cade said. "Animals don't just change up their schedules for fun. Their behavior is life or death—"

"The Dream Slip," Ravenna said, her voice distant. I could see her mind working at lightning speed behind her mascaraed eyes. "Maybe whatever is causing the princesses to scream is disrupting the sleep schedules of the wildlife around here."

"That could mean we're getting close!" I said. "We haven't noticed anything like that affecting the Apple, so the effects must be getting stronger the closer we get to the source."

"We need to head back," Cade said, shaking his head. "If all the nocturnal animals that prowl these woods could be active at any time, the sun won't keep us safe—"

"No," I retorted. "Not when we're this close. For all we know, just around the next bend could be the source of all of this."

"Cade is right," Antoine sighed. He was even classy enough not to sound bitter about having to say it. "Maybe learning this can help Tamsin and Ravenna get a more accurate tracking device, and we can come back—"

Ravenna looked at Antoine, and then back at me. "We have to try to end this. The longer it goes on, the longer the White Knights have a blank check to run rampant over the Apple."

"Getting devoured by whatever nocturnal monsters might be wandering the woods isn't going to help anyone—" Cade rumbled.

"All I'm asking for is one more hour—" Ravenna snapped back.

"You're hurt," Antoine said, joining the fray. "If we keep pushing you, your arm could be permanently damaged—"

"*Our city* is going to be permanently damaged, Antoine!" Ravenna all but shouted.

"Hey!" I said, trying desperately to be heard over the tumult. "Arguing isn't going to solve anything. We've got two of us who want to continue on, and two of us who want to head back. But we've got one more vote."

We all turned to Linden, who paused in the middle of adjusting his wedgie. "Oh. *Oh.* You mean me. Um, pass? I don't like being put on the spot."

"I get it, Linden," I said as kindly as I could. "But this decision affects all of us. Nobody can stand on the sidelines."

"We'll accept whatever you decide," Antoine chimed in.

Linden inhaled shakily and ran his hands through his messy hair. His eyes closed for a second, and he took a second breath, and the tension seemed to ooze out of him. When he opened his eyes, they met mine.

"We keep going," Linden said quietly. "I saw the part of the Dream Slip where the princesses are being kept. I can't imagine what that's like, being trapped in there, but… some of those girls were only thirteen or fourteen. And all they can do is *scream*. So I'm going to listen to what Briar and Ravenna have to say. We keep going. For the princesses."

No one spoke after Linden finished, but we all nodded our agreement. I think I even saw Cade wipe at his eyes discreetly. I mouthed a *thank you* at Linden.

"We move forward, then. One more hour," Antoine said softly.

"One more hour," I echoed. I just hoped it was enough.

IT WASN'T. ANOTHER HOUR of pushing ourselves as fast as we could safely go. Another hour of Ravenna shushing any of our concern for her, even when I could tell each step jostled her broken arm. Another hour of the shadows lengthening, and we still hadn't found anything out of the ordinary. Or at least out of the ordinary for the Apple. We did run across a talking badger in a waistcoat who told us he'd been having terrible insomnia the past few weeks, but that was it.

I knew our gamble hadn't paid off. I knew Ravenna and I had talked everyone into taking this risk, and now we had to find our way back to the Apple in the waning light, beset by who knows what flavor of Things That Formerly Went Bump In The Night.

I knew all of that, but I wasn't ready to hear it.

So when Antoine turned to me and cleared his throat, I shot him a *look*. "One more hill," I got out through gritted teeth.

"Briar—"

"One. More. Hill."

He knew better than to try to stop me, but he also didn't follow as I clomped up the rocky ridge ahead of us. My eyes stung and my teeth jangled with the force of my footsteps, but I couldn't bear turning around. Not yet.

We'd lost a whole day in our fight against the White Knights. Every day they got more prominent, more of their banners popped up around town, more of their patrols circled the neighborhoods of Commontown (because in their eyes, of course, whatever was causing the princesses' plight couldn't be coming from Castle Fortnight or the wealthier neighborhoods around it).

My boots slammed into the last few steps harder than was strictly necessary. After I'd stomped the last few steps to the top, my breath caught.

"Briar," Cade called from below me. "I'm sorry, but we've got to turn around."

I turned to them, knowing my smile was so wide I probably looked like a feral Cheshire Cat. "Don't you guys want to see this house first?"

It was a sprawling wood and stone construction with the aesthetic of a rustic cabin and the square footage of a small chateau. It seemed to be built into the landscape around it, flowing amongst the rocks and trees in a way that would've made Frank Lloyd Wright break down and cry. A small brook flowed under the far wing of the structure, and the house lifted over it in an elegant enclosed bridge resplendent with stained-glass windows.

It was beautiful, and there was no way it should exist.

"Holy nixie nuts," Linden swore when the others joined me on the ridge.

"This—this can't be real," Cade said. "The only structures the Red Hoods have found in the woods are much closer to town, just abandoned ruins."

"Someone or something is keeping this place in spotless condition," Antoine observed.

While the rest of us gaped like idiots, Ravenna had taken out a small, six-inch telescope and was peering through it. She rattled off information as she twisted the various runed bands circling her spyglass. "It's not an illusion," she muttered. "No major wards protecting it. There's a lot of magic floating around, but it seems like mostly preservation spells. I'm not picking up any hostile enchantments."

We all looked at each other. My head was a buzz of excitement, fear, and confusion. "We need to check it out," I stammered.

"It is literally a mysterious cabin in the woods," Linden said. "Have you seen any movie ever?"

"Try your collar, then," I countered. "Maybe it's the source."

Linden grimaced but did as I asked. He turned in a wide circle, but his crystal didn't light up until he was facing the large structure.

"That only shows the direction," he complained. "Maybe what we're looking for is farther past it." Even he sounded doubtful.

"This is a risk," Antoine said, but I could tell from his voice he knew we were going to do it.

I nodded. "Then we do it smart. We stick together, check for traps, all that Dungeons & Dragons shit."

Cade raised a dark blonde eyebrow at me. "The only time I played D&D with you, you got our entire party killed."

"How was I supposed to know kobolds take offense that easily? They're not even real."

Here I was, mouthing off in the face of uncertainty and danger. I'm nothing if not consistent.

We made our way down the hill as quietly as we could. Going in the grand double doors at the center of the complex seemed conspicuous, but we found a small entrance in one of the stone sections out back. After a thorough inspection by Antoine and Ravenna, we found nothing dangerous about the door.

And it was unlocked.

Taking a breath, Antoine opened it seamlessly, and we huddled into a large kitchen. Wooden counters ran along the outside of the room, and a massive set of stone stoves took up the entire far wall. Pots, pans, and other kitchen utensils hung along the walls, but nothing was rusted or damaged; it all looked like whoever lived here had just stepped out for a moment.

We all spread out silently to search the room, and then I realized what was making my hackles rise about this room: everything was about twenty percent larger than normal. I'm tall, but these counters went up to my armpits, and the knives were the size of my forearms. Someone would have to be a good seven feet tall to use this kitchen comfortably.

Whoever or whatever built this house, I did not want to run into them.

Antoine gestured us all over to the stoves. "Still warm," he whispered. A handful of bowls with cracked eggshells sat to the side of the oven, the remnants of someone's breakfast.

"Okay," Linden said, "hopefully whoever lives here just eats eggs. And not, you know, humans."

"There is a bit of a precedence when it comes to mysterious houses in the wood," I allowed. "But I licked the door on the way in and it was most definitely not made of candy."

Antoine raised his eyebrows but didn't comment on my hygienically questionable choices. "All right, any ideas on how to track these people down before they find us?"

"*Memoriae vestigiis*," Ravenna intoned, making a gesture with her good hand, and a flash of purple lit up the floor, forming into a mess of footprints. She crossed her arms and gave Antoine a satisfied smirk.

"That'll do," Antoine said, impressed.

I just hoped whatever we were tracking didn't use its legs to move as fast as the Cattywampus.

As we walked forward, Ravenna's spell conjured more steps; they looked about the size of the average shoe, but as they moved away from the stoves, I noticed they seemed to move in an odd clump of three. They lead us up out of the kitchen and through a long, stone servant's hallway to a small staircase. Our three-legged quarry made even more confusing progress up the stairs, which opened into the circular main foyer we'd seen from outside.

Whoever or whatever had built this place, they still had a Downton Abbey, upstairs / downstairs aesthetic, because this room couldn't have been more different from the utilitarian area we'd been in previously. Dark oak paneling covered the lower half of the walls, while the upper half and ceiling were a light cream-colored stone; it looked like sandstone but was smooth to the touch and shot through with gold veins like marble. The wood panels were carved in a mess of knotty, looping designs, all irregular but harmonious with each other. Something like a chandelier hung in the middle of massive hall, but it was made out of pure magic—it looked as if someone had frozen a firework in mid burst and left it to decorate their entrance hall. If I listened closely, it seemed to ring faintly, like the crystalline sound of fingers being run along a wine glass.

It says something about the opulence of the room that it took me a second to notice the dragon's head mounted above the far doorway.

Cade's jaw dropped and he immediately went to the trophy; its iridescent scales looked freshly polished, its mouth pulled back in a very lifelike snarl.

"Flippin' fairies," he muttered, "this must've been a fifty-footer, at least. And look at those horns! We haven't seen anything like this in the Apple since the twenties."

I jerked my head towards the glowing footprints, which were leading us towards the other wing of the mansion. "C'mon. If whoever lives here doesn't disembowel us, you can come back and take a selfie later."

I swear, the six-foot-four, muscular woodsman *pouted* as I pulled him away from the dragon's head and into another hallway.

The sound of a trickling brook reminded me that we were heading towards the bridge I'd spotted from outside. This gloomy part of the hallway had no windows, and there was only the faint light from the magic chandelier behind us. As it faded, we had to rely on the purple glow of the shining footsteps in front of us to light the way.

We turned a corner, and the floor before us rose into wide stone steps. The sound of water echoed throughout the whole structure, and I knew we were right above the brook. Vaulting arches spanned the room, subdividing the ceiling into arcs of pristine stone.

At the top of the staircase, the rows of stained-glass windows shimmered with a brilliance that overwhelmed my eyes at first. As I adjusted, a myriad of prismatic shapes came into view. Transfixed, I walked up to take a closer look.

"Briar!" Ravenna hissed, pointing at the stairs I'd just walked up. The footsteps stopped midway, and in my peripheral vision I noticed a pair of shapes lurking in the arches midway up the stairs.

Before I could react, a ridiculously large greatsword arced out of the shadows, aiming for my neck. I stumbled back, hitting the back of my feet on the step above me and landing painfully on my butt. But the sword stopped to hover less than a foot away from my face as its owner stepped out of the shadows.

She was wearing a simple peasant blouse and shorts, but it was clear she was no farmer; the woman was built like a brick house, power written into every sinew of her scar-crossed forearms. Her wispy blonde hair was tied back in a simple braid, and her eyes were narrowed in a look of extreme focus. While massive, the swordswoman still didn't fit the absurd scale of the house.

I goggled as the woman held the weighty sword in front of her, unwavering as it pointed at my throat. "We don't want any trouble," she rumbled, her voice clear in the echoing chamber. "We'll give you what rations we can spare, but if you're here to rob us, not all of you will leave alive."

The sound of a bowstring being pulled back punctuated her sentence, and another woman stepped into view. She was slight of frame with light brown skin and a dark green head scarf. Her simple dress belied her powerful bearing as she stared down my four companions, letting the arrowhead in her longbow point at each of them in turn.

Antoine spread his hands wide and stepped forward, and the archer swiveled to keep him in her sights. "We apologize for the intrusion," Antoine said smoothly. "We stumbled across your house by accident."

"And decided to let yourselves in?" the smaller woman said. Her voice lacked the booming resonance of her friend's, but it carried easily through the hallway.

"We're on a quest," Antoine explained. "But I swear to the Blue Fairy we mean you no harm."

The two women exchanged looks. An oath like that wasn't something a denizen of the Apple takes lightly. Whatever silent exchange took place between them, they lowered their weapons but didn't put them away.

"You from the Apple?" the swordswoman said. Antoine nodded, but I saw a look of confusion briefly wash over his face.

Where else would we be from?

"Then you'll be peckish, I imagine," she continued gruffly. "Come along, then." She sheathed her sword in a scabbard strapped along her back and started to walk further into the hallway. Something about the way she spoke struck my ears oddly, but I was just happy not to have a sword pointed in my face. As she moved, I noticed her right leg was prosthetic, an older leather model that didn't seem to slow her down in the slightest.

That explained why only three feet showed up from Ravenna's magic.

The archer put her arrow back in the quiver but peered uneasily at us with keen eyes in her heart-shaped face. She pointed the way, so that we'd be walking between the two of them, I assume to keep us in her sights in case we tried anything.

They didn't say much as they led us to a conservatory off the back of the house. Large glass panes showed the late-afternoon woods around us, and in the center of the round room a makeshift sitting area had been constructed, with roughly carved chairs and a table, all made to a comfortable human size (although the lady with the sword was probably an inch or two taller than Cade). It was a stark contrast to the opulent, oversized furnishings of the rest of the house. Something about the cozy, casual décor and the gently dancing trees outside put me at ease.

Antoine introduced us as the larger woman got us tea. "This is Aya," she said, gesturing to the slender woman. She'd taken up a seat in the corner, her bow still laid across her laps. "And I'm Grav," the swordswoman said, placing an entire tray of biscuits down in front of us with one hand.

"Like Grav the Barbarian?" Linden asked. I smiled, remembering the stories of Grav from the 1920s, a buxom warrior who fought the Germans in World War I before returning home to have a series of high-profile adventures. Sort of a fey Wonder Woman, always ready to fight for the little guy. In a time when women were barely encouraged to leave the house, Grav took up her sword and won over the hearts of the Apple. Her last adventure had involved her fighting a dragon over the rooftops of Castle Fortnight, and not long after she retired and disappeared from the public spotlight.

Something about her… losing a leg?

"Wait," I stammered, "you're *the* Grav the Barbarian?"

She grinned sheepishly. "Just Grav is fine."

"But that's not possible," I said. "You would have to be like a hundred and ten years old."

"You hear that, hun?" Grav said to the other woman. "We're centenarians!" I looked at them both as Grav chuckled and Aya smirked faintly. They couldn't be past fifty.

"What year is it in the Apple these days?" Aya asked nonchalantly, like she was asking what the weather was like in the Hamptons.

"Nobody has heard about Grav since the thirties," Antoine said. "About ninety years ago."

"Being this far out in the woods," Ravenna muttered, "they must be living in a Van Winkle. Time for them has gone at a different rate than the Apple." Antoine and I had lost half a day in a Van Winkle once, but the idea of time becoming this unhinged made me queasy. When we finally made it back to the Apple, how much time would have gone by?

I took a breath and tried to push the panic aside. On the list of things I had no control over, the vagaries of extradimensional time dilations seemed pretty high up there.

"What brought you here, if you don't mind my asking?" I said, trying to steer the conversation back from contemplations of the time-space continuum. "I've heard stories about Grav the Barbarian, but nobody ever knew what happened to you."

"That was sort of the point," Aya said, the ghost of a smile on her lips. The lithe woman seemed to be letting her guard down the longer we all sat around drinking tea.

"It sounds like you've heard the standard stories about me. Escaping the Hag of Hell's Kitchen. Winning the Battle of the Borogoves. Punching Lucky Luciano in his little rat face. Things were going well until after I returned from the Great War," Grav recounted.

I realized these women probably didn't know what had happened in the decades they'd been gone: the end of World War II, the founding of the Multiarchy in the Apple, the Beatles breaking up. Or the Beatles forming, for that matter.

"I was living in Commontown at the time," Aya said. "My mother was third in line for the throne of Zerzura before we came to the Apple, but none of the African dynasties were recognized by the Royals there. My title was all but worthless. But no one told that to the orc brigands who abducted me."

"I just heard that a princess had been kidnapped," Grav said. She locked eyes with Aya. "By the time I got to their hideout, this one had wriggled loose and had a knife to the orc leader's throat." They shared a smile that warmed their entire faces. Even Aya looked relaxed and serene. It almost felt like we were intruding; they were telling this story more for each other than the rest of us.

"After that everything changed," Aya murmured, her voice barely above a whisper.

"We knew we couldn't stay in the Apple. There was too much... We needed to be on our own. We knew the Afterwoods might kill us, but it was the only place we could see a life together." Grav seemed to be almost talking to herself now, lost in the memories from long ago. "We walked, and we walked, and it felt like maybe the night would fall and the woods would claim us, but then we stumbled on this house.”

“It saved us,” Aya said simply.

“I know we could go back,” Grav continued. “We’ve had other visitors; we know things have gotten better since our time in the Apple. We’ve heard about the progress made, the long fight for a more tolerant world. But at the end of the day, we love our lives out here, and the forest has always accepted us.”

“I thought you said you hadn’t heard from people in the Apple in a while,” Ravenna said.

“From the Apple? No, not for a decade or two, I think. But we had a nice couple from Shangri-La last year, and every few years some knights from Avalon come looking for the Holy Grail,” Grav explained.

“Grav always challenges them to a duel, and they get all huffy when she wins,” Aya said with a wry smile.

My companions and I all looked at each other dumbfounded.

“Sorry,” I said slowly, “I think I misunderstood you. You mean these people came from the Apple through the Afterwoods, but were from other World Slips?”

“Nope,” Grav said. “They came here directly from all those places. They don’t call it the Afterwoods there—sometimes they said they’ve been in Arcadia, or the Cedar Forest, or Myrkviðr.”

Ravenna bolted up out of her chair and began pacing. “But—but—that doesn’t make any sense. You can’t just go from one World Slip to another without passing through Earth.”

She was right. The wizards of the Apple believed the World Slips were all individual realms tethered to Earth. Each one was a discrete Otherworld, bounded by some impassable natural feature, like a forest, or mountains, or an ocean.

“We even got a few lovely gentlemen from Atlantis. They said they washed ashore a few miles from here.” Grav took a big gulp of tea to hide her smile. She did seem to get a smug satisfaction out of completely shaking our world view. I didn't blame her.

This was big.

"Then where are we?" Ravenna blurted out. "Where is here? And who built this house?"

Grav drained the end of her mug and stood up from the table. "We're not sure. But we're happy to share what we know. Follow me."

We didn't talk much as she guided us back into the raised hallway, to the stained-glass windows that had intrigued me so much before. I'd kind of forgotten them in the process of having a greatsword drawn on me and meeting one of my childhood heroes. Now that I could finally examine them without any sharp implements being pointed at me, I was awestruck.

The room was awash with color; the setting sun must have been just right to make the windows on the west side of the room glow like that. It was like nothing I'd ever seen before. The glass had so much depth and texture… the robes of a wizard draped over him like something out of an El Greco, while I swear the brilliant emerald leaves of a tree appeared to sparkle and move in an imaginary wind.

When I'd finally gotten over the sheer artistry of the panels, I started to take in the imagery and the story they seemed to tell. The first window showed a sort of Edenic woodland scene, with humans in scraps of homespun wool and leather sitting around a campfire. A swirl of riotous color emerged from their open mouths, and within it were dozens of familiar creatures: fairies, dragons, skeletons, goblins. The colorful design continued into the next scene, where strange, tall figures stood in the trees—I didn't even spot them at first, as they seemed almost treelike themselves, with long, thin arms and textured brownish-grey skin. Whatever they were, they plucked the monsters and spirits from the air, gathering them like farm animals. The next window showed them erecting standing stones that glowed with a greenish light. A pair of humans were shown passing through them, into some sort of mystical realm of bright colors and magical creatures. The final scene showed the humans settling into this fantasy land, building castles in a lush valley filled with griffins and unicorns.

I studied the panels, over and over again. We'd all fallen into a reverent silence that seemed befitting the sight in front of us.

"Holy hellhounds," I muttered after an appropriate amount of time. "Is this... the creation of the World Slips?"

Ravenna nodded behind me. "Certainly seems like it."

"And who are these *Ancient Aliens*-looking assholes in the trees?"

"We don't know," Grav said. "But we imagine whoever they are, they're also the ones who built this house. Who else could build a house this far out in the woods in a fluctuating time stream?"

"Doc Brown?" I muttered, without a lot of hope.

"This... this has always been one of the questions of the Apple," Antoine said. It seemed like more of an inner monologue he was too shocked to keep inside. "Which came first, the stories or the World Slips? How did the folklore of our ancestors become the worlds we live in today?"

"It seems like these... *things* heard those stories, the first stories we told to each other around some ancient campfire, and made them a reality," Ravenna said, tracing a finger along the swirling colors of the stained glass.

"But who were they?" I asked no one in particular. "Where did they go?"

"Are they going to be mad we've been squatting in their mansion for so long?" Aya asked wryly. At least someone was fulfilling my usual role of wiseass in the midst of our shared existential crisis.

"Wait," I said, an idea striking me, "have we checked Linden's collar since we got here?" In the midst of the mystery of Grav, Aya, and this house, we'd forgotten to see if this house contained what we were looking for.

I explained the basics of our quest to Grav and Aya while Linden conducted his all-too-familiar spin. The crystal lit up as he was facing the wall on the far side of the hall.

"Is there anything in the house that way?" I asked, but my gut already knew the answer.

"Nope," Grav said. "Just about twenty feet of clearing and then more forest."

I swore as my shoulders slumped. "Then we're screwed. What we're looking for is *even deeper* into the time travel forest and there's no way we're going to make it back to the Apple before sundown."

Aya and Grav exchanged a look, and Aya gave a slight nod. "Would it help if you guys camped out here tonight?" Grav said cautiously. "We've got plenty of extra rooms."

The prismatic sunlight streaming through the stained glass was already getting dimmer. It seemed like we didn't have much choice. And at least this way we wouldn't be going back to the Apple empty handed. We'd find whatever was hurting the princesses.

Or disappear into the forest trying.

GRAV CHATTED JOVIALLY AS she led us upstairs to a hall of well-appointed rooms. Whatever magic was still active within the building kept the unused rooms spotless and the linens smelling like lavender. I set my pack at the foot of a giant bed that could easily fit two California Kings within it.

"What you all were saying makes a lot of sense. I was just telling Aya that some of the beasties around here have been acting weird," Grav said as she threw a blanket onto the bed. "A few days ago I saw a pair of baku out in one of the marshes I was hunting in. In the middle of the morning, bold as you please. What would they be hunting in the daytime?"

I nodded and stretched, the day's events finally catching up with me. Making small talk with a Prohibition-era Apple celebrity wasn't even the weirdest thing to have happened since breakfast.

"You all right, sweetheart? It seemed like your group was already a little weary when you got here. And our whole surprise attack on you couldn't have helped," Grav said, perching on the corner of the massive bed. "Sorry about that, by the by."

I shrugged. "Just a little quested out. I'm sure you know the feeling."

Her laugh was deep and warm, and made me relax a little as I bent to unbuckle my boots. "The quests were the parts I loved. I could be on the road for weeks, away from everyone. I'd take fighting a hundred ettins over walking down Looking Glass Lane and seeing everyone snickering at my sword and armor."

"Really? In my time everyone talks about you like you were universally beloved."

"I had my admirers, it's true. Had to turn down about a dozen marriage proposals, if you'll believe it. But I was always more of an oddity. The girl with the sword. It was exhausting." She shook her massive head and unbuckled her prosthesis, giving her thigh muscles a quick massage.

"Exhausting how?" I asked.

"I had to keep beating them. I could never slip up. Any other hero, he had his highs and lows. But I always felt like the instant I took a fall, that'd be it. Everyone would say, 'I told you so. Women shouldn't be warriors.'"

"That can't have been easy."

Grav's brow furrowed as she seemed deep in thought, but she snapped out of it and broke into a grin. "But things seem better now. You're the leader of your own quest!"

"Me? Leader? Hardly. We're more of a democracy. I just talk a lot."

She shook her head as she put her leg back on and got up. "Sorry, I don't buy it. Every time something new came up in our conversation, everyone in that group looked to you."

"They were probably afraid I was going to make a pun."

"There's a lot of different types of leadership, my friend. And whatever you're doing is working."

I felt my face get hot. "I guess? Responsibility makes my stomach hurt."

"Of course it does. I was nauseous for probably eight out of ten daring rescues. But you get used to it. And I think the people who start to get too comfortable bossing people around are the ones who we need to worry about."

I thought of Baron Landgreaves and his irritatingly white veneers. "Sadly, I know the type. Although I'm sure what we're dealing with in the Apple now can't compare to how things were for you in the 1920s."

The towering woman walked over to the door. "No matter how long I stay in this forest, there are always going to be assholes. As long as you're not letting them win, you'll be fine."

"Hell no." I looked up at her, silhouetted in the doorway by the golden light of the hallway. "Hey Grav? Thanks. For the advice and… for everything you did. You were one of my heroes growing up and… my story feels a little easier because I heard yours."

The barbarian's smile lit the night. "Anytime, darling. Get some sleep. Your fight's not over."

THE MORNING LIGHT DRIFTED sluggishly through the trees, weaving through the post-dawn mist. Compared to the woods we'd been traveling through, this area wasn't anywhere near as threatening. The path was wide, the trees were spaced widely enough to let in the sunlight, and the only noises filtering through the chill air were snatches of birdsong.

I heard a sigh of satisfaction from behind me, and turned to see Linden sipping a LaCroix. "Good morning, starshine," he said with a grin.

"Wait, where did you find LaCroix in the middle of the woods?" I said. There was a nagging feeling of confusion in my mind.

"Wait for it…" Linden crossed his arms and leaned forward with anticipation.

Oh, duh.

"This is a dream," I said. I realized I had no memory of leaving the mansion, and neither of us had our packs with us.

"Nailed it in one," Linden said cheerfully as he sauntered along the path.

"Whose dream?" I said as I followed behind. If I was going to have to face someone's subconscious, it'd be nice to at least be prepared.

"Not sure!" he chirped from the small hill he'd just skipped up. "Isn't that fun?" I sighed as a I followed behind.

Looking into the next valley, I saw a vast, stone structure, overtaken by the natural world around it. Vines crept up the columns of what looked to be some sort of rustic woodland temple.

The stone base supported a thatched roof that had mostly fallen in on the right side, but somehow the general impression was one of a pleasant, beautiful decay.

"Shall we explore?" Linden said, twirling his hand in front of him like a Royal herald.

"I dunno. This still seems pretty invasive," I said. "I feel weird going through my friends' heads."

"Hey, I didn't ask for this power. I'm just going with the flow."

"I used some of the same excuses with my magic," I said flatly. "Especially when I knew what I was doing was questionable."

"I mean the only other option is to sit quietly and do nothing until the dream ends. We're not hurting anything by looking around. Besides, I'm usually stuck in the Dream Slip by myself... it's nice to have a dream buddy."

His earnest tone won me over, and I relented. "Fine. We can at least peek inside."

One of the large wooden doors was conveniently off its hinges, so it was easy for us to enter the temple. (How come Lara Croft always makes archaeology look so strenuous?) The interior was dim, but the partially missing roof let in enough light. Leaves and sticks covered most of the floor, along with a few broken pews and torn tapestries. The focal point of the room, however, was the altar on the far end and the statue looming over it.

It was larger than life, about ten feet high, but the woman it depicted had the lanky proportions of someone tall. She wasn't beautiful, not by the Apple standards of nymphs and princesses, but striking, with a strong jaw, sharp eyes, and a hint of a smirk on her full lips. The simple cloak she wore billowed behind her as if she were in motion, her right foot drawn forward, stepping forward with her chest thrown out. Her pose was majestic; she was a woman not afraid to put her foot down and stake a claim.

"Briar," Linden said quietly, "is that statue…you?"

There was no denying it.

The statue, the temple, the serene woodlands… suddenly I was very sure we were in Cade's head.

"Grimmsdammit, Linden," I muttered. "This is why I didn't want to go poking around."

But he'd already walked closer to the altar. "Um, Briar? It looks like someone has been here lately."

My curiosity got the better of me, and I walked slowly up the main aisle of the temple to the altar, crunchy brown leaves crinkling between my boots and the stone slab floor. The altar was cluttered with more leaves, a few broken vases, and rusted candlesticks, but someone had brushed off a part of the stone in the middle. A green cloth had been laid out, with a trio of small votive candles on top. The center candle was still lit, the end of the wick sputtering smoke in the morning air.

"I hadn't been here in years," Cade's voice said from behind me. I turned, and he was standing in the center of the temple. It was the Cade I knew from today, but seeing him brought me back to the teenager he'd been half a decade ago. I finally realized why I was getting so nostalgic: he was wearing the tuxedo he'd worn as my date to the Spring Ball our last year of high school. The night that I'd accidentally used my powers for the first time and enchanted him to love me. The night I'd screwed everything up between us.

He wouldn't show it, but he had been so excited to wear that deep maroon tuxedo. Cade had just been accepted into the Red Hood training program, and his tux was a perfect match to the cloak that would eventually become his uniform. Whatever dream logic applied here, the tuxedo still fit him like a glove, accommodating the powerful build he'd developed through years of training. The only thing that didn't match my memory of five years ago was a tear in his left lapel, right above his heart.

I recognized it as the place where I'd pinned the rose boutonnière that had enchanted him. It looked like he'd bunched the fabric up in his fist and ripped it off of him.

"I hadn't been here in years," Cade repeated, "but in the last few months… I dream about coming here. I'm remembering how things were. Between us."

I sucked in a breath, not sure what to say.

"I'm gonna go outside," Linden said quietly, before doing an exaggeratedly awkward shuffle out through one of the fallen sections of stone wall. A distracted part of me noticed he'd left his empty LaCroix on my altar.

"Cade, this is…" I gestured around to the temple. "Is this from the spell? Is this what my magic left in your head?"

He bowed his head and walked towards me, not making eye contact. "I think this place has been here since we were kids, in some form. Its meaning has changed throughout the years, but… you've always been important to me."

Even in a dream, I could feel the heat of his body from a few feet away, and I looked away. "And I've always cared about you, Cade. I always will."

He chuckled and gave me a half-smile. "I'm sure if things hadn't gotten so screwed up, if your magic hadn't put us through a loop, I would've realized what this place meant in good time."

"I'm sorry—"

"No, no apologies needed. It was never your fault. I know you didn't mean to use your magic like that. The timing really sucked, though. I was finally realizing how amazing you were. How amazing you are."

My body tensed. The things Cade was saying were what I had so desperately wanted him to say all those years ago. None of the cat-and-mouse games, the endless banter, or retreats from any "serious" conversations. Finally, he was saying all the right things.

…Then why did something inside me want to run straight out of the temple and into the woods?

"Amazing is one thing," I said quietly, my thoughts coalescing as I voiced them, "but Cade… you quite literally put me on a pedestal."

Cade caught my eye and gave me a roguish smile. "I mean, don't let it go to your head."

His sense of humor softened my resolve, and for a moment I felt myself relax into the fantasy of the two of us that I'd held on to for so long. I remembered seeing his face in the hallways of Witchdale High and feeling the rest of the world fall away until I couldn't see anyone else. I remembered sun-soaked walks through Central Park, our laughter rising up through the leaves as the late afternoon sun painted them gold. I remembered doodling "B.P + C.A." in hearts in my notebooks, thinking he would always be the generous, goofy jock, and I would always be the sarcastic loner who made him laugh.

Those dreams were still there, underneath the surface, the stickiest, gooiest, sugar-plum Taylor-Swift-song romantic notions of boy-meets-girl. Would it be so bad if our dreams finally matched?

I looked up at my massive stone doppelgänger, standing proud and strong, and I knew what I had to do. I just needed to find the words.

"But this, this hero worship… this was about high school Cade and high school Briar. That statue looks like me, but it's not who I am. It's just a picture you had in your head, frozen in time. And I get it. I did the same thing. I had this picture-perfect idea of what we would be like together, but that had nothing to do with who we actually were: flawed, flesh-and-blood people. It was a fairy tale.

"Even the drama, after my magic got involved, and the angst… it became part of a story that I told myself to feel better. It became familiar, something I held on to, something I could go back to when life was hard and moving forward was scary. But now, after repeating the same words for half a decade… I realize that story is holding us back."

Cade was quiet for a moment, and part of me worried he'd dream-glitched or something. But then I understood he was struggling to find his voice. "But Briar… I love you."

I broke into a smile even as tears began to trace their way down my cheeks. "And I love you too, ya big goof. Of course I do. And I always will."

Cade stared down at the stone floor, nodding. "I think that's always why we couldn't… say anything. I wanted to. I wanted to get this out in the open, find out how you felt. But I didn't want the story to end. I was so scared we'd be out of each other's lives for good."

I made some sort of disgusting snort-laugh sound that I was sure would haunt my dreams. "Well, that's not going to happen. This isn't an ending—think of it more like a next chapter. But we're going to have to figure out a way to be in each other's lives that is healthy."

Cade sighed, an equal mix of disappointment and relief flowing off of him. (Could I still smell emotions in dreams, or was I imagining it?) "So I should probably move out, then, huh?"

Hearing him say it felt like a gut punch. I didn't want him to leave. The change was too sudden, too much like a loss, but as soon as I heard him say it, I knew he was right. I nodded, surreptitiously wiped a tear from my check, and swallowed the lump in my throat. "But you better find a place in Havmercy. I am not going to put up with a long commute to go watch jousting with you."

He smiled too, and the rigid feeling between us finally crested and broke like a wave. "You hate jousting."

"Yeah, well. I'm a good friend."

He opened his arms, and I almost threw myself into a big bear hug. "You are," he murmured into my hair. I don't know how long I stood there, enveloped in my friend's arms, in the ruined temple that bore my likeness.

And then I woke up, or he woke up, and the dream was over. I was back alone in my bed. And after a short cry, I fell into a restful, dreamless sleep.

I WASN'T SURE IF Cade would remember his dream, or if what felt so real and lucid to me would have registered with him. But when I stumbled downstairs in the morning to the giant, oversized kitchen, he was waiting there with a mug of tea for me. And the warm but sad look in his eyes told me he remembered the dream we'd shared.

GRAV AND AYA LOADED us down with as many supplies as we could carry and explained the layout of the path ahead as best they could. They even applied some sort of poultice to Ravenna's broken arm that seemed to ease her pain immensely. It was a strange goodbye with these women we'd known for less than a full day, both parties uncertain of what the future would bring; perhaps we would complete our quest and return to them that evening to rest before triumphantly returning to the Apple. Maybe we'd be torn apart by monsters within the hour. Hard to tell. That's the adventurer's life for you.

Linden's collar pointed us downhill, into a soupy marsh with narrow pathways winding through a thick mist. Our pace slowed as we navigated around bogs and ponds, the air slick with a cold humidity. The trees above us drifted in and out of view, and I started to notice they lacked any consistency; one moment they'd be jagged black branches cutting through the fog, the next I'd see a tree full of spring cherry blossoms. Even their scale shifted as we made our way further into the swamp. I saw a towering oak tree with a trunk as wide as a redwood's and a small forest of weeping willows the scale of bonsai trees.

We didn't talk much, as if speaking would trigger the slightly foreboding atmosphere into attack mode. I couldn't help but notice Cade doing his best to stay away from me, and, honestly, I couldn't blame him. While he was scouting ahead, trying to keep us from sinking into the swamp like that horse from *The NeverEnding Story*, I ended up bringing up the rear with Antoine. He offered me an easy smile, and suddenly the air felt ten degrees warmer.

"You all right?" Antoine said, quietly enough that our companions ahead of us wouldn't hear.

"Yeah, I—I'm okay. I had a talk with Cade last night, is all."

"Oh?" Antoine's face shut down as he tried to hide his reaction, but the rush of apprehension that exuded from him almost made me sneeze.

"We, uh, settled things. Terminally. In a negative direction." Why was I explaining this like an SAT question? "He's going to move out," I clarified.

Antoine cocked his head to the side, still wary. "And is that what you want?"

Ah, the age-old question. The smile that came to my face surprised me as I nodded. "Yeah, I think it is. We were both stuck. It almost felt like we've been under a sleeping curse for the past five years, and maybe this is what will finally wake us up."

In the swirl of emotions I smelled coming from Antoine, there were definitely hints of elation and excitement. But the thing that came through most strongly, the thing that made my stomach drop and my heart flutter, was a feeling of concern. Of compassion and care, of wanting to make sure I was okay. He wasn't arrogant or smug that his rival had lost because Antoine didn't see me as a prize to be won.

The cacophony of feelings he was feeling as we looked at each other became almost overwhelming, and I felt my own emotions begin to rush ahead of themselves. Walls that I realized I'd put up to hold back the feelings I thought were too wild, too scary, too silly, too much, began to crack. A hazy, indistinct future where I dove headlong into those uncharted territories past my borders began to take shape. And in the end, it didn't feel so scary.

Because I knew I wouldn't be taking the leap alone.

I blinked a few times, willing my vision back from the slightly blurry haze that my emotional cornucopia had brought on. "Antoine," I said, my voice shockingly even, "thank you again, for waiting. For giving me time. I know I owe you a good, long talk when we're back."

In response, Antoine reached over, his smooth hand moving to cup the curve of my neck and give it the gentlest squeeze, the pads of his strong fingers pushing out all the stress and tension that seemed to permanently reside there. "You don't owe me anything, Bri. But if you want to talk, I'm here."

My eyes caught on something behind him, and my head started to spin for non-crush-related reasons. "Um, speaking of here… what is that?" I pointed past him, and I must have been speaking loudly, because everyone in our group turned to look.

The small pocket of marsh looked normal enough on first glance. Enclosed by a ring of rocky dirt and a few cattails, it seemed nonthreatening, if a little mucky. But the reflection in the water didn't show the willow tree arcing over it like a circus tent; it showed a desert under a purple sky, with series of strange ziggurats along the horizon. As we watched, storm clouds boiled in this other sky, bright lightning chaining between them like a war goddess's necklace. A strong wind seemed to ripple whatever body of water we were looking through, although everything on our side of the water was still.

Looking into the nearby ponds revealed a variety of other landscapes. Steam rose from the surface of a hot spring in a craggy frozen wasteland, where two monkeys wearing towels on their heads seemed deep in conversation. A neon jungle with glowing electric trees soared above an exhaust pipe pouring sludge into another mirror-lagoon. One of the other pools showed nothing but an inky darkness, until a slender, feminine arm broke the surface and proffered a sword. We all just looked at each other and awkwardly shuffled away.

My dad always said never take on a heroic destiny that didn't offer health insurance.

"So, right," I said, shaking my head. "What in the name of Galadriel's golden scrunchie is going on?" We all turned towards Ravenna, who gave us a very violent shrug.

"How the hell am I supposed to know?! I guess… from what Grav was saying… these are linked to other World Slips? But not any I've ever heard of."

"Did anyone else see the one that was just a constant, bloody war between giant armored puppets?" Linden said, a haunted glint in his eye.

"Motion to call these portals to other dimensions 'Worldpools?'" I asked. I got one "aye" from Linden and a lot of rolled eyes.

"We know time is wonky out this far in the woods," Ravenna muttered. Part of me was terrified that one of the Apple's most brilliant magical minds had been reduced to using words like "wonky" to describe our current situation. "So my guess is space is starting to break down as well. These are the holes that are poking through as reality stretches thinner."

"Okay, as someone who has only seen the trailer for *Interstellar*, what does that mean?" I said.

"I think whatever we're looking for might be at the edge of the world."

We all shared a collective breath while my mind repeated *holy shit* on loop.

"Ravenna," I said, "if nothing else, I do want to point out that what you just said was completely badass."

"Thanks," she said weakly.

"Do we… keep going?" Cade asked uncertainly.

I nodded. "As long as we can. We've come this far, and all we need to do is step carefully around the holes in the fabric of the space-time continuum."

"Um, Briar?" Linden said meekly. "Your boot is untied."

THE WORLD AROUND US continued to devolve, and it almost felt like we were heading back into one of Linden's dreamscapes. We meandered through a panoply of worlds reflected back at us from the other side of the swamps; peeking into the mountaintop towns, the moonlit forests, and desolate tundras felt like browsing through the fantasy section of the world's best library. A thick mist hovered around us, forming intricate geometric patterns illuminated by the glow of the luminescent Spanish moss growing on the branches above us. Its iridescent purples, blues, and greens made it look like the trees were getting ready for Coachella. If I hadn't known any better, I would've thought Grav and Aya cut our trail mix with mushrooms from a fairy ring.

The thing that really got to me, though, was the silence. No trickling brooks, no trilling songbirds, no patter of faun feet. The land felt dead and barren.

We stopped at a rise to check our orientation—we'd been doing our best to follow the signals from Linden's collar, but it wasn't easy considering the landscape's general topsy-turviness and the constant threat of tripping through a puddle into another world. Linden went through the ritual we were all familiar with, turning in a circle on top of the muddy knoll. But as he started facing over the hill, the crystal dangling from his collar flared with a fiery green light, so intense I had to turn away. Linden yelped and tugged the collar off, tossing it to the ground where it continued to sparkle and smolder.

He stood sputtering over it, startled but otherwise unharmed. "I guess that means we're close," he panted, looking back at the rest of us. Ravenna muttered a charm to deactivate the collar and threw it in her backpack, while the rest of us prepared ourselves to meet our journey's end.

We walked slowly down the incline in front of us, the mist so thick that we could barely find our footing in the loose grey soil. Finally, we reached level ground, and a silent wind seemed to pull the mist away from in front us with the theatrical flair of a stage magician.

I thought it was a tower in front of us at first, because its height rivaled the tallest spires of Castle Fortnight. But the craggy surface wasn't made of stone or brick, but bark, older and more gnarled than the surface of any tree I'd ever seen before.

We all gaped up into the sky at the massive tree above us, and I realized why a lingering feeling of wrongness permeated the whole spectacle. Besides the fact we were at the foot of a tree the size of the Empire State Building, I realized we were staring up at its root system. Where the trunk widened out to become branches, the tree plunged into the earth beneath us. If this perspective were right, all of the land we'd been walking through, the marshes and their portals to other worlds, was supported by the branches of this giant inverted tree.

"It's a World Tree," Ravenna muttered, a faraway tone in her voice. "Lots of mythologies place some cosmically significant tree in the middle of the universe. I just never thought the Poisoned Apple had one in its backyard."

"So this is what is making the princesses sick?" Antoine said. "Why? And why now? It looks like this thing has been around for a long time."

"The roots," I said, suddenly remembering. "From the Dream Slip, when Linden and I tried to get into Raye's dreams. The thorny root things attacking the princesses must've come from here."

"Does anyone else feel that?" Linden whispered. I began to ask him what he meant, but for once I shut my mouth and closed my eyes.

There.

It was like a pulse, a slow heartbeat emanating from the tree. An all-encompassing energy washed over me with a slightly uncomfortable tingling sensation that made me shudder.

"Oof," I said, opening my eyes and shaking my head. "It feels like licking a kitsune tail."

"When have you licked—" Cade started, then remembered. "Oh yeah, that one Halloween party in Bushwick."

Antoine, Cade, and Ravenna took a moment to reach out with their chakras or whatever. "I don't feel anything," Antoine said slowly. The other two shook their heads as well.

"Oh," I said, dumbfounded. "I don't like this at all."

"Is it a Free Spell thing?" Linden mused.

Ravenna had taken out her magic telescope and was scanning the giant tree. After a moment, she took the spyglass from her eye and blinked rapidly. "Well I don't know what that thing is, but it's definitely not Academy magic. It has an aura like a Mac screensaver on acid."

"So what… what do we do?" I asked no one in particular. "I was thinking there was going to be a perp with a motive. Someone we could stop with words or swords. I didn't think our enemy would be plant life."

"You know what I think?" Antoine said, a slight grin on his face. "I think you should try your magic on this thing."

"What? How am I supposed to give a tree a rose?"

"It seems like you and Linden are connected to this thing, whatever it is. And I've seen you pull off some pretty wild stunts with your magic before." The warmth in Antoine's voice was unmistakable, but I couldn't help but feel like his faith was misplaced. What could I do to a magical entity no one had ever heard of that was so powerful it could disrupt other planes of existence?

"I'm down to try," Linden said nonchalantly. "If it fries us, it saves us having to walk all the way back to the Apple."

"That's the spirit," I grumbled.

Ravenna patted me on the shoulder encouragingly. "If it makes you feel better, I didn't see anything overtly hostile in my magical analysis of the tree. Although at this point, I feel like an ant trying to solve calculus, so maybe take that with a grain of salt."

I swallowed the lump that was pressing its way up my throat. This was what we came here for. I was the one who stopped us from turning back, who pushed us, who said we had to see this thing through. The princesses of the Apple were counting on me.

No pressure, right?

"Shall we?" I said, offering Linden an arm with forced bravado. At least I wasn't on this fool's errand alone.

As we linked arms and approached the tree, the pulses from its bark grew more frequent and powerful. My hair started to blow back in the force emanating from the tree, like we were walking into a storm. But it still felt—if not good, then at least electric. Like the charge just before a storm breaks, when the humidity hanging in the air is almost ready to be released. Like the feeling of a crowd just before their favorite band takes the stage. Like the top of a roller coaster, just seconds before the world gets turned upside down.

As we got to the base of the tree, I wasn't even surprised as a rose wriggled out of my bag and floated into my hand, completely unbidden by any conscious part of me. I panicked quickly, trying to think what emotion I should give to an arboreal mystic beacon.

Another wave of that feeling pushed through me, and I realized it was a call and response. The tree was giving out the feeling of potential, of something new about to start, of coming up to the edge of a precipice.

So I conjured the emotion I could best think of as a complement to that: stepping off the ledge, diving into the unknown, welcoming change with open arms. Picking up destiny's call instead of letting it go to voicemail.

Usually my magic changes the color of a rose, but this time the cream-colored tea rose shuddered when my power reached it and started to fold in on itself, turning from a full blossom into a bud just beginning to open. A tiny, incipient light glowed from within it, the sparkling promise of new beginnings.

Linden watched wordlessly as I placed the rose stem-first into the knotty bark of the tree and turned it like a key. Instantly, a large, arched section of the bark glowed briefly with yellow light and opened inward as smoothly as any door.

There's a special sort of power that comes when you've stopped being surprised by all the things you can do.

The interior of the tree was dim, but a golden, honey-colored light seemed to faintly illuminate everything, although I couldn't see any discernible source. The trunk had been hollowed out inside, with a smooth wood floor marked with the irregular rings of a tree trunk, hundreds of feet across with what looked like thousands of rings. At the center of the tree, a spindly column wavered its way through the middle of the space (the tree's pith, according to some long-forgotten part of myself that had paid attention in high school biology class). The exterior walls looked mottled in bands of all sorts of dull colors, until I looked closer and realized the walls were actually shelves. And on those shelves, thousands and thousands of ancient-looking, leather-bound books.

A spider's web of curved staircases traced haphazardly up the walls, reaching up so high I couldn't see the tops of them. The waves of anticipation that had been flowing out from the bark weren't tangible here, but every few moments, the pith would glow with golden light as a scattering of runes raced up its surface towards the root system thousands of books and hundreds of stories above us.

You're not supposed to be here, a voice of some sort echoed through the space, or maybe it was just within my head. It had no discernible character or gender; instead, the words seemed to condense out of the air, like meaning carried on the crest of a wave or within the susurrus of wind through leaves.

Linden and I froze and looked around the room, just as a figure unfolded itself from a nearby desk I hadn't noticed while first looking around the space. The creature was tall, probably eight or nine feet high, and I immediately recognized it as one of the beings from the stained-glass windows in Grav and Aya's mansion. Its thin frame was stretched in a parody of human proportions, with double-jointed legs that came up to my armpits and ended in thick paws. The grey skin that had looked like bark in the illustrations looked softer and more malleable up close as its face twisted in a look of concern. Two black, almond-shaped eyes took up much of its heart-shaped face, and in place of hair, it had strange twists and tangles of branches that pushed back up off its face like braids.

The strangest thing was it was wearing a cardigan with arm pads and a pair of houndstooth trousers, like some stereotypical professor at Creepy Plant Alien University.

Don't get me wrong, it continued, *it's quite interesting to have visitors. It's been so many decades... but I'd be remiss if I didn't tell you how dangerous it is to have humans in The Tree.*

"Who—who are you?" I managed to stammer out in the face of all the weirdness.

Ah, yes. I'd forgotten your kind's insistence on names. As if a single word could contain the multitudes of even your identities, never mind mine. I don't cling to any such word to codify my existence. Quite simply, I am. It cocked its head to the side, and it seemed to smile a little, if I was reading the movements of its jagged, bark-covered mouth correctly. *That actually could work, considering. You may call me Iamb. And I understand this is where I should ask your names.*

It wasn't exactly a question, and I got the distinct feeling that Iamb didn't care in the least, but if it was making an effort to be polite, I figured I should return the favor. "I'm Briar. And this is Linden." Linden gave a little wave, but his eyes had the haunted look of someone having a bad pixie dust trip.

Questions tumbled all around in my head, and something came out of my mouth to the effect of, "What is—where are we?"

Iamb looked around, almost as if it were unsure itself. I noticed the massive wooden desk it was sitting behind before we entered; it looked like it had been grown in one piece from the ground, with twisting branches for legs and a smoothed trunk for a surface. On top of the desk was a book that seemed to match the thousands on the shelves around us, its pages half-covered in a strange, looping language I didn't recognize. It seems we'd interrupted a writing session when we barged into the tree.

I didn't want to think through the logistics of a race of tree people writing on paper.

This is an outpost. We listen, and we write, Iamb said, as if that explained a single damn thing. Linden and I paused for a moment, but it seemed like no other explanation was forthcoming.

Okay, we can work with this, I said to myself, trying to think through the whirlwind of feelings I had meeting a creature who might've been one of the creators of the Apple. *Iamb doesn't seem hostile. If nothing else, it seems like a bit of a stick in the mud.*

Part of me wondered if it was offensive to use that phrase about a creature seemingly made of wood.

"Iamb," I said, "maybe you can help us. We've been searching for some sort of magic that is hurting people in the Poisoned Apple. It seems to be coming from here."

Iamb cocked its head to the side for a moment, watching me with an unnervingly direct stare, like when a cat makes direct eye contact with you while using the litter box.

Ah, yes. I recall your world. What seems to be the problem?

Part of me shuddered to think that it took Iamb that long to remember which World Slip we were talking about. How many were there? And were they all connected by the branches of this tree?

"There are princesses in our world who are under sleeping spells, and whatever is happening to them is harming them in their dreams. They're screaming, and some of them have even started sleepwalking and trying to attack people."

Iamb bustled over to the pith at the center of the of the room, and Linden and I cautiously followed. It placed its long, thin fingers on the surface of the tree, and suddenly a rush of rainbow-colored runes started to swirl up and down the tree. It looked almost like a more colorful version of the code from the Matrix, except if it were programmed in some sort of proto-Elvish. The display danced in front of us, reflected in Iamb's dark eyes, until finally a single rune blazed brightly on the tree, and the others skittered away like frightened mice.

Here, Iamb said simply. *This is the Working that was sent out to your world.*

The symbol was symmetrical, and looked almost like a flower with swirling roots, but instead of a normal flower, there was a single eye that looked like it was just opening.

"What… what is it?" I asked. "What does it mean?"

Iamb said something that must have been in its own language, or however these beings communicated to each other. It felt like a crashing of static against my ears, a hundred conflicting sounds whispered on top of each other. But somehow, I could glean a vague understanding of it.

It means Awaken, Iamb confirmed.

"Great. Looks very nice. Can you, uh, turn it off? …Please?"

Oh man, I was really nailing this negotiation.

Iamb made a trickling, chortling sound that must have been a laugh. *I listen, and I record. This is the work of one of my siblings who is more... directly involved in your world. There's nothing I can do.*

"Could we speak with them? Maybe work something out?" I asked, desperately.

I have no idea who is responsible for this particular Working. The Tree is a place of coming and going, sending and receiving. But I listen—

"—and you record. Got it." Interrupting a sylvan demigod probably wasn't the smartest move, but if Iamb couldn't help us, we needed to get a move on. I drew Prick and held it out for the tall being to see. "Can you tell us anything about this?"

Iamb peered down at it. *How strange. You shouldn't have that. That's strictly for the use of the Fata.*

"And the Fata are—?"

My siblings and I. We are the Fata. It is a name given to us by early humans, and which we are burdened with.

I made a mental note, since all I was learning could completely upend everything the people of the Poisoned Apple knew about their world. "Someone sent it to me. Someone who has been interfering in my life, and in the Poisoned Apple. They call themselves the Arsenic Queens."

Iamb put a hand on its hip in a display of what might have been sass. *As I've mentioned, my siblings and I eschew names. But there are those in your world who are aware of us. Some even worship us as gods.*

Swear to Grimalkin, Iamb winked at me. Like it thought the idea of being worshipped was a big joke.

Now, if there's nothing else, I do have recording to get back to. Iamb bustled back to the desk, but I stepped forward.

"If you and the other Fata record what is happening in our world, can you tell us? We're not sure how long we've been gone."

I am really not supposed to—

"Please," I say, looking Iamb in its eye and hoping that whatever he was, he felt some sort of sympathy, that the powerful, ancient creatures that built my world at least had a sense of mercy.

There was a long moment, and finally Iamb relented with a creaking noise that must have been a sigh. *Oh, all right. Just this once, I can give you a very brief taste.*

It pulled a weathered green book off of the shelf and laid it open on the desk, tracing through the writing with one of its fingers. *Oh. Oh dear. Are you sure you want to know?*

"Yes, please," I said as Linden nodded. "I need to know what's happening to my town."

Iamb dropped the words like stones into a pool, almost completely without emotion. *Unrest. Rebellion. Conspiracy. Chaos.*

And we didn't know how long we'd been travelling in the temporally disconnected wilderness we'd found ourselves in. Was it days? Weeks? Months?

Years?

I shook my head and looked over at Linden. He looked as shaken as I felt at the Fata's words.

A sudden idea came to me. I pulled out my magic mirror and captured an image of the Awaken rune, still floating on the central spire of the tree. If nothing else, maybe it would mean something to Ravenna.

"Thank you for your help, Iamb," I said hurriedly, starting for the door we'd come in.

I am happy to help, little niece, Iamb said, already back to writing. *It has been centuries since I've met a member of the bloodline, never mind two.*

Linden and I nearly slammed into each other as we both stopped short and turned back to him. "Sorry, what?" I choked out.

It is faint, but I can hear the call of Fata blood in you both.

I could feel that blood throbbing in my ear drums as my vision started to tunnel. "But—how?"

Like I said, the tree being said with all the polite sass of the phrase "per my email," *some of my siblings are more directly involved in your world. And before you ask, no, I do not know anything more than that. It would be impossible to trace the Fata lineage across the centuries, through all the branches of The Tree.*

Linden's mouth was wide like a slightly nauseated fish out of water. His expression somewhat mirrored mine, but it was more than that; I had always noticed, but never really put my finger on the similarities between our faces, the same rich brown irises. Suddenly, the shared traits were hard to pick out, because my eyes were filling with tears.

I took two shaky steps forward and gave my cousin a hug.

MY MEMORIES OF LEAVING The Tree are as foggy as the forests we were in, as my mind was too ablaze with the revelations to have recorded much. I do recall Iamb looking up as we reached the door and saying with the most alien intonation, *Toodle. Oo.*

I'm similarly fuzzy about exactly what I said as I word vomited what we'd learned to our friends outside, shaking and clutching Cade's water flask like it was a lifeline. He'd handed it to me wordlessly as I shivered, and he didn't even look away as Antoine threw an arm around my shoulders, his firm grip anchoring me as my world continued to churn around me. We sat in a small circle of stumps, the mist around us floating by in eldritch patterns in the grey afternoon light.

After a while, my breathing started to steady, and my head stopped swimming. More than anything I just felt numb. I groggily tried to latch on to everything we'd learned. Everything besides the last part. I couldn't—I could process the rest of it. I just needed to focus.

"We need to get back to the Apple," I grated. Why was my voice hoarse? I had drained Cade's flask at some point in my chattering. "As quickly as possible. Whatever is going on in the Apple, we've been gone too long."

Ravenna was still peering at the image I'd caught in my magic mirror, frowning. "I… yeesh, this looks sort of like the spell that was in the thorn from the Dream Slip. I think if we got this to Tamsin, she might be able to… I don't know? Find a cure, a counter-spell, or some other way to disrupt it."

I tried to pull myself off of the stump I'd been sitting on with my still-shaking legs, but after my first try failed, Antoine put gentle pressure on my shoulder, holding me closer to his body. "We need to be smart," he said. "Let's eat something, then make our way back to the mansion for the night."

I shook my head woozily. "We don't know how quickly time is passing here. Every minute we spend here could be hours back in the Apple."

"Antoine's right," Cade rumbled. "It's going to be at least a two-day journey, and even traveling leisurely, we can still make it back to Grav and Aya's place before nightfall."

Ravenna cleared her throat quietly, but it spoke to how much we all respected the shit out of the wizardess that everyone immediately shut up. "I might have another way." She took a small vial out of her cloak and held it up in front of her. The liquid inside looked like quicksilver on steroids; the metallic liquid seemed to be reflecting Ravenna's face from several impossible angles, like someone had animated a cubist portrait and liquified it.

"I swiped this from one of the Worldpools earlier," she continued, giving the bottle a shake. "It seemed to lose its connection to the other World Slip as soon as it was away from the pool."

"You're telling me you went in and took a sample from one of those holes in reality?" Antoine growled protectively.

"I didn't go in personally, duh. I cast Mage Hand," Ravenna said rolling her eyes. "It's like you've never even played D&D."

I don't know why, but somehow the sound of smart people bickering made me feel more grounded and at home. These were my people. My acerbic, sarcastic people.

"You were saying about the water…" Cade prompted.

"Right. So if this stuff is some sort of… World Slip conduit, I think I could probably key it in to the Apple's frequency to make a short term link."

"You could jury rig us a portal back to the Apple?" I said. "Hell yes. Let's get that Stargate popping."

Ravenna smirked at my enthusiasm. "*I think*. It's hella risky. I'm not sure how long I can keep the portal open"

"Then we try it for one person," Antoine said. "That way we can at least get the picture of the rune back to the Apple."

"Then you go through, Ravenna," I said. "We need you to help Tamsin deconstruct the spell, and we'll follow on foot."

Ravenna shook her head, her onyx tresses waving with the movement. "I've got to stay on this side to anchor it."

Cade, Linden, and Antoine all looked at each other. "Sooo… we're sending Briar, right?" Linden asked. The other two looked at me and nodded sheepishly.

"What? Why me?" I stammered.

"Bri," Antoine said in the voice he always used to try to soothe me, "you're our best bet. You've gotten us this far. You can do this."

"How?" I said. "Ravenna's our magical expert. I'm basically a flower delivery girl with a big mouth."

"You know that's not true," Antoine said quietly, giving me a look.

"You're… resourceful," Cade said. "You figure shit out, you make things happen, and you don't back down."

"Your protagonist game is strong, girl," Linden added.

At another time, the kind things my friends were saying might have warmed my cold heart. But the thought of leaving them all in the forest, traveling through a soggy wormhole, and dealing with whatever chaos Iamb had warned me about on my own… the weariness that I'd been fighting off threatened to overwhelm me.

"You won't be alone," Antoine said, as if he were reading my mind. "Jacqui and Alice will be there, and Tamsin. Getting this symbol to them could be the final piece of the puzzle."

"*Could* be," I grumbled, but I knew they were right. Especially if this all had to do with the Fata.

My family.

Ravenna seemed to sense my beleaguered acquiescence, because she nodded and started gathering her things. "Give me fifteen minutes and I should be able to work something up. And, you know, advance our knowledge of applied magiphysics by decades."

The rest of us began reorganizing my packs, transferring everything outdoorsy that might be useful to them out of mine. I realized, with the weird time anomalies, I didn't know when I would see Linden, Cade, Antoine, and Ravenna again.

Or *if* I would see them again.

I pushed that thought back, my pragmatism reasserting itself. I couldn't give in to hopelessness. I couldn't break apart because I'd learned I was part alien stick person. Not yet.

I handed Linden my water flask. "In case you get tired of drinking dream LaCroix," I said with a smile.

"Never," he chuckled, but it was noticeably half-hearted. If anyone knew what I was going through, it was him.

"So yeah, I, uh, guess we figured out why I went along with you into those dreams," I tried awkwardly. Linden's shoulders lowered, and I could smell he was glad I'd broached the subject. There was no good social script for discovering your shared semidivine heritage.

"Guess so," Linden said flatly. "So are all Free Spells related?"

I shrugged. "I don't know. I hope not. I've met some real dicks."

"It'd be a hell of a reunion though." He didn't completely sell the nonchalance.

"Well, I guess we can start with the two of us, see if we want to invite anyone else," I smiled, and Linden looked up at me. "I've never had any biological family before."

"Mine was a mixed bag," Linden shrugged. "You've got a really low bar to live up to."

I snort laughed. "I'll do my best."

He grinned and somehow it felt... easy. Not nearly as hard as I thought it would be, finding out I had a cousin. I'd always been afraid to open the Pandora's box of my biological family, but even having it thrown open so dramatically... at least I wasn't going through it alone.

"Mind if I borrow her?" Antoine said, startling me. I had been so engrossed in my bag and my new relative that I hadn't heard him walk up. Linden nodded, and I took a deep breath in. We had about five minutes until Ravenna claimed her portal would be all systems go.

Antoine led me to a thick tree covered in moss, just out of sight of the others. After two straight days of near-death adventures, I felt my jaw unclench the minute we were alone. It had been a rough forty-eight hours. Or possible a rough forty-eight days, depending on how quickly we were burning through time in the Apple.

Antoine brought his hand up, gently squeezing more tension out of my shoulders. "You okay?" he asked in a low tone. He always asked in times like this, and I never knew what to say.

A sigh escaped my lips, and I lazily rubbed my cheek against the back of his hand. "No, but that's helping."

He smirked as his eyes found mine. "I wish I could go with you."

"Me too."

His other hand came up to my other shoulder, and he brought his forehead down to touch mine. The simple pressure nearly broke me, as everything came welling back up again. My hands shot out of their own accord, wrapping around his waist in an iron grip. I just knew I needed him close, needed something solid to keep from crumbling. The scent of Antoine's smile, rich like morning coffee, surrounded me as I pressed myself into the hollow of his throat, his arms moving up naturally to encompass me. I felt the slight grate of the stubble that was growing along his firm jawline, darker than the short chestnut curls of his hair. It gave his normal straight-laced charm a bit of an edge.

He shifted his grip to hold me closer, pressing a kiss onto the top of my head as I tried to silence my tears.

"You're going to be—" he started.

"Don't say I'm going to be fine," I squeaked out.

"I was going to say 'magnificent.'"

Despite myself, I laughed, breathing in the scent of his white poet shirt. "Okay, that's allowed."

I allowed myself a few shuddering breaths, drawing strength from the lazy, comforting circles Antoine traced across my shoulder blades.

"What do I do when I get back?" I asked no one in particular. "I thought we were going to get more answers. Helpful ones, not just incredibly overwhelming ones."

"You'll do what you always do," Antoine said softly, his soothing baritone rumbling through his chest like a cat's purr. "Adapt and find a way."

I pulled back just enough so I could see his face. "Even if a vengeful demigod who may or may not be related to me is behind all this?"

Antoine's deep doe eyes reflected my own back at me. "Demigod or not, my money is on you."

I swallowed. I could tell he was holding back, not wanting to overwhelm me. Giving me the space I needed.

I pressed a single, firm kiss on his lips, holding tight for a moment I wished could last forever. "Thank you," I murmured against them before stepping back and wiping my eyes.

The softness in his eyes had kindled into a smolder as he watched me compose myself. "I'm going to be there as soon as I can," he promised. "I think we promised ourselves a Very Adult Talk when this was all over."

I took his hand and squeezed it as I began to walk back to the others. "Guess I'll just have to hurry up and save the Apple then."

RAVENNA HAD CHOSEN A flat spot on the forest floor and laid out six small iron pyramids inlaid with glowing runes, all whirring like overheating computers. The metallic liquid she'd collected was suspended above them in a flat disc, rippling in the wind as it displayed trippy refractions of the woods around it. She stood across the circle from me, going over the instructions for a third time.

"As soon as you see the image of the Apple solidify, you've got to jump in," she repeated. It felt a little condescending, but given my current level of emotional fry, I wasn't against having things repeated for me.

"Got it," I said deadpan. "Thanks for *spelling* it out for me."

Ravenna rolled her eyes. "If this portal turns you into a frog, I blame that pun."

I grinned and shook my hands out, getting ready to throw myself, once more, into the unknown. Adrenaline ran like soda pop through my veins, tracing down my arm and making me exquisitely aware of my body. Just in time to hurl it into the magical goo hovering a foot off the ground in front of me.

I looked to Antoine, Cade, and Linden where they stood off to the side and gave them a salute. "See you all on the other side." Their anxious smiles didn't hide their apprehension about Ravenna's ritual.

Ravenna started to chant, the fingers of her unbroken arm swirling through a complicated series of patterns, leaving small purple contrails through the misty air. The disc of water shuddered, and the images reflected within it began to twist. Fuzzy, indistinct shapes began to form, and my heart sped up as I tried to identify them. How did I know when they were solid enough and I should make the leap?

The droning words coming out of Ravenna's mouth began to pick up speed, and with a jolt the grey silhouettes in the portal resolved into the most iconic image of the Apple I could imagine: the spires of Castle Fortnight, the First Skyscraper.

Home.

With an undignified grunt, I jumped feet first into the water, gasping as the cold liquid instantly soaked through my boots. Magic isn't normally so visceral, but I guess Ravenna was working with a somewhat slapdash improvised spell.

It felt my body sink more slowly than it normally would have in water, and I was treated to the shocked look on the guys' faces before my head plunged under. I was in a slate grey sea, with a diffuse light that pulsed around me, seemingly in time with my breath. A few bubbles pushed themselves up past me, each containing a tiny snow-globe view of another World Slip.

I looked around in a panic, seeing no sign of where I was supposed to go. The pressure all around me made me think this wasn't one of those magical liquids you could breathe like air.

Just as my tiny lizard brain started sounding the alarm that I was for sure going to drown, I looked down. Under my feet, the same image of Castle Fortnight glimmered like sunlight filtering through the water. I did an awkward half flip, orienting my head towards the glow. My lungs crumpled in on themselves like cheap paper as I frog-stroked as best I could, my cloak dragging behind me in the silver water. The pressure in my chest reached a breaking point as my last stroke left me just inches from what looked like the water's surface. I gave one more half kick, just breaching the surface and—

—falling face first into a small, shallow pool. I sputtered, pushing myself up so I could breathe sweet, sweet oxygen.

"Welcome to the Poisoned Apple, where every journey—" a voice began, before cawing in surprise. "Bilbo on a bike, what happened to you?"

I was in the small courtyard where Jacqui, Alice, and I had crossed through from Battery Park, the night we'd gone out in the Financial District, what felt like a lifetime ago. The tranquil, lily-pad-dotted water feature now had a metallic sheen where the Worldpool water washed off me. The giant raven in front of me was staring, a dog-eared Octavia E. Butler novel clutched in its claws. I realized I must look like hell, much different from the serene way I'd floated through the water on my first visit. Even in the torchlight—

I looked around. Though it had been early afternoon just moments before in the Afterwoods, it was full night here in the Apple. Stupid Van Winkles.

"Is the spell broken, ma'am? Because you're not supposed to belly flop like that—"

I got to my feet and waved away the raven's concerns. "It's fine. I kinda… hopped the turnstile, magically speaking." I shook my head in an attempt to clear it. Being back in the Apple all of a sudden, after two full days in the Afterwoods, was disorienting. Where were all the people?

"Oy, you there. It's after curfew. You got a permit?"

Two guards wearing chainmail emblazoned with the seal of the White Knights stepped into the courtyard. The one who'd spoken was shorter, with a swathe of unkempt blonde locks and a patchy attempt at facial hair. His partner peered at me cautiously with dark eyes, leaning on a large, iron-capped wooden staff. Neither of them wore helmets, making me think they were either lazy or off the clock and looking for trouble. The blonde blustered up towards me aggressively as my eyes narrowed in confusion.

"Curfew? Excuse me?" I said, trying to hide my frustration as well as I could. Fairy tale Otherworld or not, we were still in New York City, Grimmsdammit.

"Shoulda been home hours ago," the man spat with a wicked smile, clearly enjoying this. "You gonna make me hafta lock you up, sweetheart?"

A moment of shock easily transfigured itself to rage. The cacophony of experiences I'd had in the woods thrummed into a single chorus of fury.

I cracked my neck slowly. Honestly, I was going to enjoy this.

The rose sprang into my hand with a thought, sparks of angers already flowing down my left arm and into the rose. It flashed red and darted out of my hand, curving around the first guard and stabbing into an unprotected part of the second guard's thigh. My right hand reached across my body and drew Prick from its scabbard by my waist.

The second guard sagged, supporting himself with his staff as I felt the rose doing its work. I'd never tried administering my roses like a blow dart before, but something about it felt good. *Pricking pricks with roses before pricking them with Prick*, I thought with a grim smile.

Blondie turned to me, red-faced with surprise. "What did you do to him, you friggin' witch—"

The dark-eyed man's staff caught him in the back of the head, and the mouthy guard staggered forward. All the rage I'd put into the flower surged through the second guard's blow, as he brought the other end of the staff into the back of his partner's knees, arms pumping with deadly efficiency. With one more thwack to the side of the head, the blonde partner went down.

The raven greeter cawed and unleashed a string of expletives before flying away. Whatever they were paying him wasn't enough to get wrapped up in this.

After a quick glance down to make sure the other guard was unconscious, the tall guard's eyes found mine, cold fury unmistakable in their stare.

I had not thought this rage rose situation through completely.

He lunged forward, his staff coming down in a swift arc. I barely side-stepped it, stumbling a bit as I had to move even further to avoid the staff coming up into my face after its first miss. The man had all the advantages—with his long arms and a quarterstaff, his reach far outpaced my dagger's. But the magic making his blood boil kept him unbalanced, striking ferociously instead of penning me in and finishing me off.

I could beat him, but I had to be smart.

My legs blurred in a feint forward, drawing the guard into a sweeping strike at my head. I felt the wind of the blow whistle past my face as I threw myself backward, landing roughly on my ass. With a feral snarl, the man drew his staff back in a baseball windup and stepped forward, driving it with lethal force—

—into the wooden post of the raven's perch, which I'd just managed to retreat to in my fall. Both pieces of wood seemed to splinter with the force of the blow, but the White Knight was able to keep his grip on his weapon.

My hand reached behind me and found what I was looking for. With a strangled grunt, I threw the raven's tip jar as well as I could from the ground, right at the guard's Grimmsdamn face. My aim was a little off, but I still winged him in the shoulder with enough force to distract him. As his eyes followed the jar as it bounced off him and smashed to the ground, I threw myself forward onto my feet, using my momentum to aim Prick right into the back of his hand as it gripped his staff. He jerked out of the way, but I got what I needed: a shallow cut along his knuckles.

Instantly, the disenchantment charms stripped the rose-induced rage away from him, and I heard him breathe out in surprise and confusion. It was just enough time for me step inside his guard and bring Prick's hilt smashing into his temple.

The tall man swayed, obviously stunned, but not crumpling like an extra in an *James Bond* movie like I'd hoped.

Before he could regain his bearings, I aimed a kick at his midsection, leaning into the man with my full weight. Like a shitty fascist Jenga tower, the guard fell slowly, knocking his head painfully against the stone wall behind him before slumping into unconsciousness.

Looks like they should've worn their helmets, I quipped internally.

I shook as much water as I could from my clothes before grabbing my pack. The courtyard was a mess, but I put a twenty-dollar bill neatly on the pile of change I'd broken loose from the raven's tip jar and walked into the chilly Apple night.

AFTER A DISCONCERTING TRIP through the empty streets of Havmercy, I discovered Jacqui and Alice weren't at home, but I was correct in my first guess, and found them working by candlelight in the backroom of The Second Breakfast. I guess I wasn't the only one breaking curfew that night.

Alice almost knocked me off my feet as she ran to give me an excited greeting worthy of the perkiest Golden Lab. Jacqui looked like she might cry. She smiled, but it did little to hide the grey bags under her eyes.

They told me I'd been gone for just over two weeks. But the upside is the portal hadn't dumped me in some parallel universe or erased everyone's memories of me.

My best friends / bullies ganged up on me and made me tell my side of the story first while Flora made me a breakfast burrito. Recounting our adventures in the Afterwoods made me realize how unbelievable they were, even by our standards. I started with our fight with the Cattywampus, Ravenna's injury, and the discovery of the eerie mansion in the woods.

"Ogreshit," Jacqui swore as I continued. "You met Grav the friggin' Barbarian? And she ran off with another woman into the Afterwoods?" She shook her head. The two of us had traded worn paperbacks of Grav's adventures back and forth in elementary school, thrilling to the adventures of one of the Apple's first lady heroes. "That's so cool."

As I narrated our journey among the Worldpools and described entering the inverted tree, my voice started to shake. I was getting closer and closer to the parts I still hadn't wrapped my mind around. Seeing my distress, Jacqui and Alice sat next to me on the padded bench, in the candlelit room of our favorite brunch spot, and put their arms around me as I relayed all of what we learned from Iamb the Fata.

My jaw felt tight and my eyes burned with tears as I told them what I'd learned about myself, but finally saying the words, letting them out, felt good. My shoulders loosened, like I had finally let down a heavy load. I still cried a little, as Alice patted my hair and Jacqui squeezed my hands tight in hers, but the numbing pressure that had been following me since the World Tree released its grip on me, even just a little.

"Bri," Alice said quietly, after we'd all had time for a few deep breaths, "you know this doesn't change anything. Not really, right? You're still the same person you've always been."

I blew my nose into a napkin and shook my head. "But that's the thing—it almost fits too well. The thing that happens with my magic sometimes, when I feel like I can… rewrite people? That's not just a weird mood I get. That's who I am. Something inside me wants to open the floodgates and let my magic loose. Become less of a person and more of an… author. No matter who I might hurt in the process."

"And you think your parentage determines the kind of person you'll become?" Jacqui asked me, an eyebrow raised. "That sounds like something the White Knights would get onboard with."

"I mean, of course not," I said. "But we're talking about a different species, here. Unknown plant people with mysterious magic."

"Well, if I were going to choose someone to have some sort of cosmic power to change people, you'd probably make my top ten," Alice said with a smirk.

Jacqui nodded and grinned. "Top twenty at least."

I snorted, somewhere between laughing and sobbing, and mussed her hair. "All right, you jerks. I told you my story. Now spill. What has been going on in the two weeks we've been away from the Apple?"

The air in the room felt like it dropped ten degrees, and I smelled the perfume of their enjoyment instantly sour. Jacqui took in a long breath.

"It's been hard. The princesses kept sleepwalking and attacking people with their freaky super strength. It seemed totally random; some princesses barely ever stopped attacking, while some have had no episodes. But everyone was uneasy, and then—a handful of them all woke up at the same time, and Castle Fortnight went into lockdown. One of them threw a maid through a window on the top floor."

My hand went to my mouth in horror, but Alice was quick to jump in. "The maid was a sylph, so she just flew away. But people started panicking."

"That's when the White Knights made their move," Jacqui spat. "They said they wanted to move all of the princesses to the White Tower, for their protection and for everyone else's. But it was all…" Jacqui struggled to come up with a word.

"Shady?" Alice supplied.

"Super shady," Jacqui agreed. "The whole thing seemed very... off. There was no transparency, no public records of how many princesses they were gathering. Some Royals complied, but others barricaded their towers and said the White Knights had no right to take their daughters."

"And Raye?" I blurted out.

Jacqui gave a grim smile. "My parents and I don't see eye-to-eye on a lot, but none of us were willing to give her away to those fascist sword-jockeys.

"But the White Knights kept pushing, and there were clashes with the Royal Guard—it almost turned into a full-scale riot. The Knights have been growing in number, and their tough guy act keeps winning people over people as things get scarier. But to avoid total warfare with the Multiarchy, they came to a truce: they're only taking princesses who have had known violent sleepwalking episodes."

"After all the tension and unrest," Alice said, "they were able to get the Multiarchy to agree to a 'temporary curfew,' for our protection, supposedly. But their guards are... whatever idiots fell for their regressive rhetoric in the first place. They've been shaking people down, terrorizing the Gingerbread Tenements..."

I took a second to choke this all down. The fact that I was rooting for the Royals against these assholes said a lot. The Nobility and I don't get along well on the best of days, but even I didn't want to see their daughters ripped away from them.

"So, what are we doing to fight back?" I asked, confident my friends had a plan.

Jacqui smiled. "We're getting organized. We've got a mirror network set up so people can report where their patrols are, record them, and hold them accountable for the way they're treating people."

"I've been connecting with all the service staff in Castle Fortnight," Alice said, "trying to make sure they intercept any reports of sleepwalking princesses before anyone blabs to the White Knights. It's a war of attrition, but so far they've only been able to grab a few dozen." My stomach twitched. *A few dozen?* Any number of princesses in the hands of the White Knights was too many.

"Mostly we've just been gathering information, trying to figure out what their endgame is," Jacqui sighed. "I know, I just *know*, there's something more to this. So far, they've been establishing power, presenting themselves as these saviors of the Apple, but I know there's a reason behind everything they've been doing. They're up to something in the White Tower. We're going to find out what, and we're going to stop them," she finished, determination straightening her spine.

"The secret is in their blood," I muttered, thinking aloud. "That's what the Baron said to me, in his dream." A thought hit me. "Do you think he's looking for people with Fata blood?"

Alice frowned thoughtfully. "Why would they go after princesses then? Most Free Spells are commoners, from what I understood."

"Maybe it's not all about you, Bri," Jacqui said teasingly. I could tell she was trying to pull me back from my own obsessive merry-go-round of Fata thoughts. My Fata-l Attraction, if you will.

I tried to glower at her menacingly, but I was interrupted by a yawn so powerful I tweaked something in my back. Suddenly I was very aware of how much the trip through the Afterwoods had taken out of me.

"All right, tomorrow we need to check in with Tamsin and get her working on disrupting... whatever the Fata are broadcasting," I said. "But for now, Briar needs sleep. Briar needs sleep badly."

I WASN'T LYING. I slept for a solid twelve hours, happy to be back in my own bed. If the entire fate of the Apple didn't hinge on me (again, ugh), I could've probably rolled back over and gotten another five or six hours.

Tamsin was delighted to see us, although the professor also looked a little rough around the edges. Judging from the number of dirty teacups scattered around her office, she'd been spending almost all of her time at the Academy. The walls were papered in lists of runes, handwritten notes, and scrolls like some unhinged TV detective's murder board, except every so often a piece of paper would glow and make faint barking sounds.

I told Tamsin the entire story, again. A palm reader in Liars' Square once told me we gain power over our life stories as soon as we learn how to tell them to others. If so, I tried to think of this as another free hour of therapy. It did feel easier, and it was honestly heartwarming to see the older woman light up at all of Ravenna's triumphs, and, at one point, whoop with pride in her former student.

She was predictably ecstatic to learn there was a cadre of tree people living out in the woods using super-magic, and I did my best to answer her barrage of questions about what we'd seen there. The rune that was responsible for the princesses' plight seemed to present a delightful challenge to her, and she enlarged it onto a mirror hanging above her fireplace, poring over each line and curl with greedy eyes.

Jacqui and I got up to leave her to it, but I noticed the great difficulty with which she tore her eyes from the magical mystery in front of her.

"Briar," she said, stopping us before we got out the door. My stomach lurched, and I pictured her asking me to stay for some sort of experiment. I could just imagine what discoveries she could make combing through the blood of a Fata-human hybrid. But when she cleared her throat nervously, I saw only concern in her eyes. "If you ever want to talk about any of that… if you want me to help you figure out anything about your family, or your magic… I'm here for you. And I will use my utmost discretion with what you've told me."

I blinked. Here she was, in a basement office of a mostly deserted department of the Academy, sitting on some of the most earth-shattering revelations the magical community has ever come across. And she wanted to make sure I was doing okay?

"I—thanks, Tamsin. Really. But wouldn't you want to tell people about this? Spread the knowledge of the Fata? Of how the Apple was made? For the sake of knowledge?"

"Eventually, yes, of course. But this isn't something you just run out into the streets screaming. The Apple is already unstable enough as it is before we introduce a whole change to our cosmology," Tamsin said matter-of-factly. "Plus, there's more research to be done, of course, and peer review—no offense, but until we have some corroborating evidence, there's still the very real possibility you got dosed with pixie dust and this was all a very fanciful hallucination."

I laughed. "Quite right. You're a true woman of science, Tamsin. And… thank you. For being cool about this."

She nodded as Jacqui checked her magic mirror, which was chirping urgently. I looked over just in time to see her face fall.

"It's my mom," she said, as I was about to ask. "There are White Knights at their tower—they're trying to take Raye."

JACQUI TRACED THE BROOMVROOM sigil on her mirror, and by the time we got upstairs to the entrance of the Magiphysics Department, there was a witch on a broomstick waiting for us to climb aboard. My stomach lurched as the young woman kicked off the ground and we whirled into the sky. It was partly the flying and partly the anxiety of what we'd find when we got to our destination. Our broom zipped through the towers of Castle Fortnight, barely slowing as we came to the bridge-strewn spiderwebs of the Aeries.

I barely had time to throw an excessive tip to the witch and thank her before Jacqui had hopped off and run in the door of the D'Lucien Ardor tower. There were no guards at the entrance, which I'd never seen before in all my years as a kid playing around the castle grounds with Jacqui. We bolted up the carpeted foyer stairs inside, still not seeing anyone. After we got a few floors up the spiral staircase at the center of the tower, things started to feel… wrong, is the best way I could put it. The edges of the torchlight seemed sharper, the contrast more painful to the eye. It felt like someone had taken the world and applied an Instagram filter from hell.

Jacqui must have noticed it too, and we slowed as we got to the family's private quarters, the pressure laden in the air forcing us to move as if we were walking through jello. It felt like there was a constant thrum, a ringing in my ears that drowned out the noise of my boots on the stone steps. But within that ear-rending sound, a faint, high-pitched wail traced its way to my ears.

The word came to me with a flash of dread. *Keening.*

There was no doubt that the source of whatever was happening was in the conservatory at the end of the hall. It took all my willpower to force my legs those last few yards, step by step, until we finally got through the door.

The glass-walled room must have been lovely at one point, a partial dome on the side of the tower, far enough up that it let in the sunlight and gave lovely views of the Aeries' vaulted turrets and Drake Mountain in the distance. At one point, I imagined all of the ferns, orchids, and succulents in the room were meticulously pruned and cared for.

But no longer.

Spiderweb cracks formed along all the glass panels of the walls and ceilings, the tremulous vibration in the room still shaking the broken shards. All of the plants had wilted, their dead stalks twisted and charred like they'd been planted in soil samples from Chernobyl. A few potted trees had dropped their leaves to the ground and become twisted, thorns sprouting from their branches in extremely unbotanical ways. What was once a charming oasis in the city looked like the charred remains of a wicked fairy's garden.

In the center of the checkerboard-tiled floor, a single maroon fainting couch stood, the eye of the storm still raging throughout the tower. Reclined upon it, Lady Aurelle D'Lucien Ardor writhed in agony, her eyes open and full of tears. It shook me to see the similarities between her and Raye in that moment. Her yellow taffeta dress was frayed and shredded, like a bomb had gone off in the ballroom scene in *Beauty and the Beast*. Kneeling by her side, blood streaking down from his ears, Jacqui's father Marchall clung to his wife's hand as she sobbed and gnashed her teeth.

As soon as Aurelle looked up and saw Jacqui, the force bubbling within the air lessened, and I realized it was the pure strength of her Largesse. Far from getting birds to do her laundry, Aurelle's Royal magic, mixed with her grief, had turned two floors of the tower into a waking nightmare.

"J-Jacquinetta?" she muttered, still not completely lucid.

"I'm here, Mom." Jacqui's voice was choked with emotion, but she took the opportunity to run forward to her mother's side and take her other hand. "What happened? Where's Raye?"

At the sound of her daughter's name, Aurelle squeezed her eyes tight, and a rush of power surged out from her. "They—they took her, honey. They took Raye!"

"I don't understand," I said, gritting my teeth as Aurelle's Largesse buffeted us. "Was she sleepwalking?"

"No!" Marchall barked. "She didn't. I told them, I tried to stop them, but—they brought so many Knights. Usually they've been coming in small groups, four or five at most, but they had at least two dozen of them. The trained ones, not the yokels they've been recruiting."

"They—they put her in a coffin," Aurelle cried, "A glass coffin."

I had forgotten how morbid some of the classic tales could be.

The browned and tattered stalks of the dying plants around us began to sway again, and I could feel Aurelle's control slipping. "Briar," Jacqui said, her voice brittle with barely concealed tension, "do you think you could help my mother calm down?"

Anxiety roiled through me, and I hesitated, thinking through the morality of giving Aurelle a rose, never mind the possible repercussions of our magics interacting.

"Yes, please, "Aurelle said. "I just—I can't think clearly. Could you give me something?"

That clinched it, and I just hoped I wouldn't somehow trigger her Largesse going off like a Disneyland nuclear bomb and turning us all into singing woodland creatures. Luckily, my roses hadn't wilted like the plants of the conservatory, and I chose a gentle purple French rose that reminded me of the dress Aurelle had been wearing the last time I'd seen her.

I thought of sinking into crisp, clean bedsheets after a long day and curling up in a quilt. I thought of deep breaths, so deep they fill the lungs with a pleasurable pressure. I thought of sitting on a deserted beach in the early morning, the year Jacqui and I had gone to Cape Cod for a weekend on the off season, the waves rolling out with a rhythm that broke down any sort of stress or tension with their comforting regularity. I breathed all this calm down into the small bloom, watching as it lightened to a dainty lilac.

"This will help, if you want it," I said softly, proffering the rose to the Royal.

Her face was still twisted with pain as she reached out to take it but slackened once she took the rose in her perfectly manicured fingers. Aurelle exhaled, and the entire room drained of the tension. More than that, I saw a few drooping lilies start to perk up, green slowly tracing its way up their wilted socks. I figured it was only a matter of time before Aurelle's magic caused friendly raccoons to start repotting the plants.

Aurelle fixed me with her wide eyes and took another deep breath. "Thank you. Thank you, I was just feeling so—I'm ever so sorry if I caused you any trouble."

"It's fine, Mom. It's okay," Jacqui said, giving her mother's hand a squeeze. "You just relax. I'm going to go talk to Mar—to Dad, okay?"

Her mother nodded, and I hoped the peace I'd put into the rose would help her get through… whatever had happened.

Marchall took us into his study, an oak-paneled display of intense wealth and questionable taste. I sunk into one of the leather armchairs facing his desk, my legs still weak from the exertion of resisting Aurelle's magic.

"Dad, what happened? Why did they take Raye?" Jacqui sputtered, the calm front she'd put on for her mom's benefit gone.

Marchall sunk his head into his hands, his muted plaid suit almost falling off of him from the rips and tears. "The White Knights just showed up—they moved so quickly. Started marching in, pushing our guards around. I yelled at them, I said it must be a mistake, I threatened, I offered bribes—nothing. They said to take the matter up with Baron Landgreaves."

Jacqui shook her head. "I don't understand. The White Knights had reached an agreement with the Royals. They said they'd only take princesses who had been violent sleepwalkers. Why would they violate the cease fire?"

"I can only imagine," the Earl grumbled. "Maybe one of the servants said something, spread lies about Raye as revenge for some petty slight—"

The glance Jacqui gave her father could have shattered the glass of the conservatory all over again. "No, Dad. Alice and I have been monitoring all the communication going to the White Knights. Especially about Raye. We would have heard something if it had come from any of your staff. Don't blame your servants for what the White Knights did."

"You said earlier," I interjected, trying to guide the two back to more helpful topics, "that they brought a big contingent of Knights. More than they have been using to grab other princesses. Any idea why?"

"None whatsoever. I would understand if they had brought backup to raid one of the more warlike Noble houses. But neither the D'Luciens nor the Ardors have any real military force in the Multiarchy. What kind of monsters bring two dozen men to kidnap a little girl?"

His words hit home. If Jacqui's family was a relatively easy target, why would they expend so many resources to guarantee Raye's capture?

The only logical answer I could think of was that Raye, among all the other princesses in the Apple, was so valuable that the White Knights were willing to put their entire conspiracy at risk to get their hands on her.

"IT'S MY FAULT," JACQUI said, anguish dripping from every word. We'd convened a meeting at the Second Breakfast in the afternoon, trying to figure out if there was something we could do to respond to Raye's kidnapping. Tarris and Rick showed up, both haggard but delighted to see me safe. Thankfully, Alice had filled them in on all of the relevant details from my trip, and I was spared having to repeat my story for the third time in twenty-four hours.

"They must know that I've been organizing against them," Jacqui continued. "They grabbed Raye as leverage to use against me. I must've screwed up somewhere along the way, tipped them off to what we've been doing—"

"Hey wait," I chimed in, "have you received some sort of blackmail message that we're unaware of?"

She shook her head.

"And has Raye's abduction made you want to give up fighting?"

"Of course not. I'm mad as a fire troll on bath salts, and I want to burn their shit to the ground."

"Then I think we can safely say that, if their goal was to take you out of the fight, they've failed dramatically," I said.

Jacqui hesitated before nodding, a steely resolution crystalizing in her gaze.

I smiled at my friend. "So what are we going to do, General?" I asked.

Jacqui rolled her eyes but turned to the table where the map of the Apple had been laid out since before I left for the Afterwoods. A scattering of stone chess pieces had been placed around the map, both white and black representing the White Knight patrols and strongholds they'd taken throughout the city.

My heart sank as I saw the checkerboard vise around the city I loved.

"We've been watching them for weeks, trying to learn something that could tip the balance in our favor," Jacqui said. "For all the messages we've intercepted, for all the missions we've observed, we still don't know what they're planning."

"Well," Rick said, his voice even and reasonable, "let's start with what you do know."

Alice walked over and pointed to the empty cake stand that stood for the White Tower. "The Knights have taken over the ground floors of the White Tower, using that as their base of operations and storing the captured princesses there as well. As far as we know, the rest of the Tower is still housing the usual prisoners; we think they worked out some sort of deal with the gaolers."

Jacqui's finger traced a string of pawns coming to the cake stand from the rest of the map. "There's a constant string of guards and wizards coming into the Tower. It was an impenetrable prison before; now it's even more heavily guarded."

"Hang on," I said. "What are the wizards for?"

"Officially, they're trying to cure the princesses. But I can't imagine that's really it. The White Tower was already warded up the wazoo, so we reckon whatever their plan is, they need a pretty constant stream of wizards from the Academy to implement it."

"I put little pointy hats on these rooks to make them wizards," Alice said with solemn pride.

The stirrings of an idea formed in the back of my mind. "So we just need to figure out a way to get in there, find out what the White Knights are up to, and expose them to the rest of the Apple for the regressive despots they are."

Alice's already fair face paled. "Briar, we've been casing their movements for weeks now. I don't think there's any of their outposts we could breach, never mind *the White freakin' Tower*. Nobody has ever gotten through their security."

She was right. In a town full of stories, there wasn't a single tale of someone breaking out of the highest-security prison in the Apple.

Jacqui looked at me, clearly noticing the cogs whirling behind my eyes. "Do you think we could do it?" she asked, unrestrained hope hidden behind every word.

"It's too soon," Alice interjected. "We're just getting our feet under ourselves in this new order. We can't be sure—"

"We'll never be sure," I said, my voice firm. "There's always a risk when you stand up to assholes who want to take us back to the dark ages. But I know if we stand on the sidelines, if we let people get accustomed to curfews and raids, we're going to lose the one advantage we have."

"What's that?" Tarris asked.

"The people who support us. The people who are outraged that these bullies have strong-armed their way into power and know deep down that it's wrong. If we can't catalyze that, if we can't lead them into taking action *soon*, they'll lose hope. And then we lose everything."

I looked around to everyone's faces, worried they would be looking at me like I was out of my mind. But even Alice seemed to have shed her doubts and looked ready to throw down.

"All right, Rick, you were an Art History major, right? We're going to need art supplies. Lots of them."

"Actually, my focus was more on neoclassical architecture—" Rick started, then saw my glare. "Art supplies. Got it. What for?"

"We've got more signs to make."

IT TOOK US TWO days to set up the protest, all of the organizing and connections that my friends had been working on finally coming to fruition. Once the word was out, it spread like wildfire to all corners of the Poisoned Apple. I had been right. People were mad, scared, angry, frustrated, anxious—but without an outlet for their emotions, they had become frozen and inert. With just a slight nudge, my idea began to take on a life of its own.

There was no news of Antoine and the others in the woods. I had to keep reminding myself that if the time distortion worked the same way it did on our trip out there, they could be gone a full two weeks. It wasn't because they ran into something horrible in the forest, they were just caught in a Van Winkle.

I just… had to believe that.

The morning of the rally, there was an electric current in the air, like something between a thunderstorm and a national holiday. The streets were weirdly silent, the normal commuters on a Thursday morning suspiciously absent.

I had just picked up Tamsin at the Academy, and she was shifting anxiously as we walked towards the White Tower through the almost deserted streets of the Gingerbread Tenements. The delightful smells of the frosting-iced fire escapes did nothing to lighten her mood as we made our way briskly through the fall morning chill, the screams of the princesses still floating through the empty neighborhood. She jumped at a movement on the other side of the street: a group of dryads, bundled up in thick wool hats pulled over their vine-like hair, turned onto the main road. I relaxed as I noted the protest signs clutched in their hands and gave them a cheerful wave.

"You sure you're okay with the plan?" I asked Tamsin for the fifth time. She wasn't my first choice for this role, but she was the best wizard we had, and while Ravenna would've been a little more comfortable with the deception involved in our plan, she still wasn't back from the Afterwoods.

"I'll be fine." Tamsin blanched, and I knew behind her reassurances, she was white knuckling it. I hated that I had to ask this of her, hated that I was clearly throwing her into a situation that terrified her and that could end very badly for us. But all I could do was stand by her side and try to guide us both to a happy ending. Or at least a happy-ish one.

The alleys of the Gingerbread Tenements opened out to Chopper's Green, the large natural amphitheater where Kings and Queens once made displays of public executions, and where revolutionaries returned the favor to more than one monarch. A sizeable crowd was already gathered at the base of the muddy, grass hill, milling about expectantly and casting determined glances up at the Tower. The Knights had set up a series of cordons around all of the entrances, a brittle tension hanging in the air as they looked down at the amassing crowd.

Following the plan, Tamsin turned off to a stone staircase, guarded by two restless Knights with halberds. Her navy Academy of the Iron Wand cloak billowed behind her impressively, and she barely slowed her pace as the guards waved us up the stairs. I was in the shorter, less-impressive black cloak of an Academy apprentice, so I did my best to look obsequious and mild as I scurried after in Tamsin's wake, despite having almost a foot in height on the Welshwoman. As we summited the hill, the throng of protestors began to swell, and three figures walked to a small stone dais halfway up the hill, still marred with rust-brown stains from its previous use. Tarris and Alice walked solemnly behind Jacqui, who looked striking in a tan trench-coat with glinting gold accents. She had been angry to be kept on this side of the Tower walls, but we all agreed that her presence, her voice, could do more to support our plan than anyone else's.

The trio settled on the stone platform, and Jacqui raised a brass horn to her lips, like something from an old-timey gramophone. As she spoke, it started to glow with auburn runes, amplifying her voice so it resounded around the Green.

"Good morning. My name is Jacqui D'Lucien Ardor, and first I want to thank you all for being here today. I know how hard recent events have been for our city, for our community, and it means a lot that, in a world that seems to be drowned out in screams, you are ready to make your voices heard.

"My sister Raye loves the fall; when we were younger, she and I would always head out on the weekends to Treantley Orchards for a hayride and caramel apples. But this fall, instead of watching the leaves change outside her window, my sister sits inside White Tower, after being torn from her bed by the dangerous, unregulated paramilitary organization calling themselves the White Knights. For weeks, these armored strongmen have done as they please, trampling on the rights of all of us in the Poisoned Apple, under the guise of keeping us safe." Jacqui paused, letting her gaze trace across the protestors. "Well, I think it's time the White Knights realized that, unlike the young women they have been unlawfully kidnapping, we aren't asleep. Our eyes are open, and we see them for exactly what they are: tyrants."

The crowd surged with cheers and applause, and I felt my eyes start to water. She was crushing it like the Grimmsdamn rock star she was, and my heart surged with pride for my best friend.

"Identification papers," a Knight grumbled from in front of us as we summited the stairs. I tried to hide my surprise at the face of a young woman about my age staring out at us from beneath her helm. How could she not only support the Knights, but voluntarily join them? It was only a matter of circumstance that kept her outside the White Tower with an axe while princesses her age were held captive inside.

"Of course," Tamsin said, handing over her Academy badge, a slight edge in her voice starting to crack through her confident façade. My hands jerked to the rose hidden in my belt, but my mind swirled with questions. It was easy to think of the Knights as these masked, inhuman stormtroopers, but the woman expectantly waiting for my papers could've been a face I'd see next to me on karaoke night at the Woodsman's Log. What happened? Was the world so scary she'd clung to the easy answers the Knights provided? Was the stability of tradition worth a worldview where princesses were inert pawns for the Knights to manipulate?

"And yours?" the young woman turned expectantly to me. Tamsin kept her reaction in check, but when she gave me a sidelong look, I could see the panic in her eyes. Me freezing up wasn't part of the plan.

But none of the feelings storming within my brain would be useful if I put them in a rose right now. Confusion, frustration, and a mounting panic would only escalate the situation. Where was the cool disinterest that I'd planned on giving the guard?

"Yes, yes of course," I said, making a big show of patting down my pockets as my mind whirred. I took a ragged breath, trying to buy myself time to calm down.

Meanwhile, the Knight was looking through a large scroll, frowning. "Professor Davies, right? I'm not seeing your name on our list for the day—"

"Really?" Tamsin sputtered faintly. "How—how odd!"

"I'm going to need to mirror my lieutenant," she said, a groan not quite hidden in her voice. It reminded me of a million other service workers who were tired of their role. I remembered my high school summer job at Vagabond Vale, the Apple's version of Coney Island, selling churro wands to tourists. Fielding a million complaints and issues when I was just trying to get through the day.

I didn't agree with this woman. Her choices repulsed me. She was helping the people who had taken my best friend's sister. But I realized until I knew her motivations, until I could see her as anything more than a walking suit of White Knight armor, I would always have questions. Granted, I'd still fight like hell to take down her and her friends, but I recognized I was just as ignorant of the circumstances surrounding her choices as she was of the reasons I was making mine.

A huge breath filled my lungs, almost without my conscious thought. I drew the rose to my lips and blew, the pink leaves turning a mix of pastel hues. The rainbow cloud fluttered around the Knight's face, and she took a step back as the petals infused their magic within her.

I'd given her the emotion I'd just experienced: the feeling of recognition, of seeing bits of ourselves in others. Of acknowledging the same universal humanity in the person across from us, despite our many differences.

While she reeled from my magic, I dove headlong into the only gambit I had. "Hi, sorry, my name is Lily. Lily d'Lis. What's yours?" I said, stepping forward to talk to her apart from Tamsin.

"Uh, Breahan," the young woman said, blinking rapidly as she stared at me with fresh eyes.

"It's nice to meet you, Breahan. Listen, this is all my fault; I was supposed to mirror ahead to confirm my boss's name and mine on the list, but with all the protestors, my commute was totally bonkers."

Breahan nodded hesitantly. "Yeah, the trolleys weren't running from SoLArca—I guess the drivers went on strike."

"Ugh," I said, jumping on this shared experience, even if it was feigned. We were all New Yorkers, and we'd all had public transit bite us in the unmentionables. "So listen, if you could just let us go inside and explain things to the Head Magister, I'll make sure to come back out with the proper documentation and give you the all clear."

She took a breath before saying, "We're really not supposed to…" but I could feel the magic working on her.

"Please," I said, clutching my fists in front of me in a somewhat desperate display of submission, "we won't tell anyone."

I'm sure there was no way this would've worked under normal circumstances, but with the roar of the crowd in her ears and my magic pumping through her veins, Breahan cracked a smile and shrugged. "Okay, just this once. But hurry back out with those papers."

"Will do," I said, nodding to Tamsin as Breahan opened the door for us. "And Breahan? Thank you."

To my own surprise, I meant it.

ONCE WE WERE INSIDE, the Academy cloaks were all we needed to pass normally through the nerve center of the White Knights. Maybe it was the protestors outside, or the general malaise of the Apple, but everyone bustled around us, heads down, not giving a shit about who we were or what we were doing. Armored Knights patrolled, robed Wizards carried large stacks of books, and slick-looking propagandists dictated as they walked, their words recorded by enchanted quills and parchments that floated along behind them.

"—and the Knights have been successful in keeping crime rates low, sorry, scratch that out, *the lowest possible* ever recorded, since implementing the curfew," a round-faced woman said as she passed by us in the corridor. I was glad the collar of my cloak hid what was my probably record-breaking eye roll.

This floor of the White Tower seemed to have always been more administrative in function, and we passed a variety of offices and storage rooms, loosely following the flow of wizards in their navy cloaks. Soon, we reached a stairwell that went down into a large, subterranean vault, the size of eight Manhattan restaurants put together, or one suburban Applebee's. Large wooden worktables were distributed throughout the room, filled with heavy tomes, bubbling beakers, and intricate alembics, one of which vaulted through the entire room, a spanning arch of glass spheres through which dripped and bubbled a multitude of colored liquids, like a very studious-looking lava lamp. Dozens of wizards and apprentices bustled around, measuring, recording, and casting spells in small, table-top pentagrams.

"Tamsin!" a tall, olive-skinned man in his forties said from a nearby table. "Things must be bad if they're plumbing the depths of the Magiphysics department."

Tamsin's eyes widened as she plastered a shallow grin on her face. "Hello, Arthur. I shouldn't be surprised to see you here, I suppose. This is my apprentice, Lily." We went over and stood by the man's table and he swept off a pair of griffin-skin gloves and offered his hand to me. I attempted to hide my distaste for him as he smiled with too-white teeth.

"Charmed, Lily. If you ever get sick of the little leagues and want to come work in Evocations, you look me up."

If my grip caused a few of his joints to crack, he hid it from his blandly handsome face. After a moment, he let go and turned back to Tamsin.

"So you think you can crack it, eh, Davies? Think you'll be able to earn that big grant they're dangling in front of us all?"

"Not one to shy away from a challenge, Arthur," Tamsin said brittlely. "How's your research been going?"

I could smell the smug satisfaction wafting from the other wizard as he began to boast. "Swimmingly, swimmingly. My work into sub-runic displacements has shown so much promise that they've trusted me with a fresh sample that they seemed to have high hopes for." With a flourish, he produced an ornate ceramic bottle, gleaming with golden curlicues like something a 1920s Hollywood starlet would keep her perfume in. Jarringly, it had a piece of masking tape stuck diagonally on it, and someone had written the day's date, and the initials R.D.A.

Raye D'Lucien Ardor.

I knew what was coming as he tipped the fanciful bottle out into one of his beakers, but I was still shocked as the coppery smell of blood hit my nostrils. The edges of my vision became tattered and dark as three large drops of glittering garnet plopped into the solution in Arthur's vial, lightening to a vibrant berry color as it diffused.

I was going to be sick. It was one thing to hear the Baron's mysterious plans had something to do with blood. It was quite another to see some jerk with tenure carrying around a vial of Raye's blood like it was cheap cologne. I was glad all the roses I was carrying were concealed, because I'm sure the rage that pounded through my temples was making them go haywire.

Tamsin kept her head better than I was able to, still subtly playing on her colleague's ego to try to pump him for more information. "And so you're using sub-runic displacements to break down the sample's thaumaturgic resonances. My guess is with a solution of banshee essence and a repeated incantation of Auromir's Alarming Articulation. Quite brilliant."

Arthur waggled his black eyebrows. "Bless the Blue Fairy's knickers, you still remember your Evocations. Who knew? And yes, still getting the titration right, but ideally we'll be able to suss out what we're looking for, and even isolate it and replicate the condition in other subjects."

If I hadn't been standing so close to Tamsin, I don't think I would've seen her back straighten with sudden tension. I took a whiff of the perfect mixture of satisfaction and horror that was coming from her.

She must've figured something out, and it terrified her.

"That's the hope, right? Well, I'll leave you to it, Arthur. Nice to see you!" she rambled quickly, grabbing my arm and leading me back up the stairs we'd entered from. My heart raced as she pulled me into a side hall off the main corridor and hissed in my ear.

"It's Largesse. That's what they're trying to find in the princesses' blood. That's the reason they stole Raye—her mother has the most powerful Largesse of any Royal left alive. They want to figure out what makes Royal magic work and—"

"—and give it to the people they think are worthy," I finished, the pieces falling into place. Largesse was one of the few things the Nobility could still point to as a sign of their fitness to rule, the power that once upon a time was believed to be proof of their divinely appointed place at the top of the Poisoned Apple. No matter how much wealth a merchant accumulated, or how famous a hero became, no one could possess the subtle, elegant magic of Largesse.

Until now.

If the Baron used his hired gun wizards to crack the code in the princesses' blood, he'd not only have a powerful new tool to advance his cause, but he could dangle the offer of power to new recruits. Create new bloodlines of his followers, magically elevated over the rest of us. It was like fairy tale eugenics.

"We've got to go," I managed to get out. "We need to get this out. People need to know."

Tamsin nodded, running a hand along her golden spectacles. For a second, the runes she'd put there gleamed—they had been recording everything she'd seen since we entered the Tower, and all we needed to do was get them to a magic mirror and we could have the Knights' secret blood laboratory broadcast on every reflective surface in the Apple.

I turned to re-enter the main hallway and pulled back, almost trampled by a squad of armored Knights jogging towards the main gate. The hall was thick with tension and traffic, and I strained to hear a voice coming from one of the side offices over the clank of metal boots.

"—the Baron's carriage, sir. It was delayed, the protestors were blocking the road, and—and our boys got a little heated and drew their swords. There was a skirmish and—oh wait, hold on."

My mind lurched immediately to Jacqui, Tarris, and Alice. What was happening outside?

Across from the hallway we'd ducked into, in the main entranceway of the tower, a large pair of wooden doors opened up and a unit of armored guardsman poured in, scattered and panting. Out of their midst, Baron Landgreaves stood to his full height, a single cut under his right eye matching the blood red of his doublet. His night-black jodhpurs were dirty and torn, and he took a moment to straighten himself out before stepping in front of his soldiers.

"Well done, lads. We made it," he said nonchalantly, as if he were announcing a pleasant quarterly report instead of discussing armed conflict. "Now get back out there and show those enemies of the Apple what the White Knights stand for!"

It was all so over-the-top cliché I couldn't stand it, but the guards roared and began drawing their swords, but not before the Baron gave one final command.

"But first, bring the prisoner to me."

Two of the largest guards dragged her forward, and for having just led the Apple in open rebellion, Jacqui looked radiant.

Pure hatred simmered off her as she shook off the Knights holding her and stood tall before the Baron.

"I'm a Grimmsdamn princess, you idiot," she said, glowering at the soldiers around her. "You might have been able to spin a tale about why you are holding the screaming princesses, but I'm awake. Do you know what's going to happen when the rest of the Royals hear about this? You've essentially united the Multiarchy against you."

The first sound I heard was quiet, a scoff under the Baron's breath that still managed to reach me where I was, perhaps because disdain echoes. The second sound was the back of the Baron's hand connecting with Jacqui's face.

Prick was in my hand before I knew it, and it was only Tamsin throwing her arms around me and using her entire weight that stopped me from charging out into the middle of the armed guards and trying to gut the bastard right there. My pulse pounded, my vision turned red, but Tamsin was able to muffle my grunts of rage with her hand and keep me from charging to my death.

Jacqui reacted much more coolly, remaining on her feet and straightening back to her impressive height. The angry welt on her cheek did nothing to mar the beautiful, boiling anger pouring out from her.

"I remember you, you know," the Baron said. "You and your smug parents, who thought they were too good to marry into the Landgreaves. Who thought their daughter was too precious to put under a curse. There's something downright poetic about you and your sister being the key to all this. I don't give a damn about the Multiarchy. Let them come. Pretty soon they'll be coming to me on their knees."

Jacqui rolled her eyes. "I've seen more convincing performances in high school theatre." She turned to the guards around her. "Is this sad excuse for a two-bit dictator really worth getting killed over?"

No one met her eye, but I saw a few exchange glances with their fellow guards as her words sunk in.

"Enough. Take her upstairs to a cell. I'll be up to deal with her soon enough," the Baron huffed, turning on the heel of his boots and stalking off as Jacqui was carted away. Tamsin pulled me back farther into the side hallway we were in.

"Briar, are you okay?" Tamsin asked shakily. I could see she'd teared up at what we'd just seen as well.

I took a shaky breath and nodded. We didn't have time to fall apart. Jacqui needed us.

"All right, you need to get out and get those recordings to Tarris and Alice," I said. Tamsin started to object but I put my hand up. "I know, but that's more important than any of us. I can't go after Jacqui knowing I'm putting the Apple at risk."

Tamsin bit her lip. A few hours ago, I was worried she couldn't handle some light espionage, and now she was volunteering for a prison break. "All right. But I'm going to do as much damage as I can on my way out," the professor said resolutely. I cocked my eyebrow, and she summoned a faint smile. "I don't know about you, but I noticed a distinct lack of safety standards in that laboratory they set up. But what will you do, Briar?"

The hallways around us still bustled with activity, but safely inside their walls, the White Knights weren't paying much attention to each other.

I looked back at Tamsin and set my shoulders. "Get Jacqui and get out. I'll see you on the other side, okay?"

Just after I figured out how to break out of a supposedly escape-proof magical prison.

The upper floors of the Tower were a series of mazes, by design. I'd switched cloaks with Tamsin, so I only encountered a few glances as I tried to walk purposefully through the winding halls. Luckily I'd pilfered a clipboard from the first floor, so no one asked me any questions.

It's amazing the places you can walk into with confidence and a clipboard.

The white stonework did little to brighten the windowless corridors, kept just bright enough with scanty torchlight. I did my best to look inconspicuously into the various cells I was passing, but most were dim, lit by small slit windows barely large enough to fit a scroll through.

In one cell I passed, afternoon light filtered off a jutting cheekbone, and for a second my heart leapt that I'd found Jacqui so quickly. But as I rushed to the small, barred opening in the door, I saw the dark hair lying stringy and unkempt from the girl's head.

Raye.

She was hanging from her arms, chained to the wall of the cell with heavy manacles. The slight young girl was still wearing a shift nightgown in the cold tower. As I watched, she shifted in her sleep, crying out as her arms moved against the chains holding her. Red runes glowed along the bindings, some sort of reinforcement. Still, her unconscious movement tore bits of mortar and loose stone from the wall to which she was tethered.

Whatever strength had been empowering the rest of the princesses was in Raye now too.

A distinctly assholeish voice echoed from down the hall, and I hid around a corner just before the Baron and two of his guards made their way to the cell three down from Raye's.

"What took you so long, Baron? Needed to change your pants after pissing yourself in the commotion outside?" The sound of Jacqui's voice from the cell, even as biting as it was, made the tension in my shoulders unknot, even just a little bit. At least now I knew where she was.

The Baron shifted uncomfortably, and I noticed he'd changed into a pair of dark slacks. I really hoped Jacqui was right.

"Get me a sample," Landgreaves said dismissively to his guards.

The door creaked open, and armor clanked as the Knights entered Jacqui's cell. "Hey, what are you—*stop!*" I heard a brief struggle, then Jacqui cried out once before they got a hand over her mouth.

"Good, that should be enough for the wizards," the Baron continued. "Now let's see how the princess likes shutting up and listening for a change—"

The ground beneath me shook as a massive explosion echoed from the floor below us. I grabbed hold of the stonework, my fingers finding purchase between the mortar as I fought to avoid stumbling into view as the Tower seemed to groan beneath us. What weak light filtered through the prisoners' windows around me turned dark blue in a cloud of smoke.

Good job, Tamsin, I thought smugly.

"What in the Billy Goats Gruff was that? Give me a status report!" the Baron shouted, I assumed into a mirror. "Leave the girl," he said, and I heard them close the door and hurry off the way they came.

It's almost like we planned it.

As soon as I was sure they were gone, I raced around the corner to Jacqui's cell. She was tied to a chair inside, a gag over her mouth. I could see a trickle of blood on her forearm, from where the Knights had taken their sample. Her eyes widened with relief when I stuck my face in the window.

"Hang tight, Jacqs," I whispered. "I'm going to get you out."

The average spellock is a fairly simple affair, using a combination of a regular locking mechanism and a basic rune to prevent anyone without the key from opening it. Prick can usually fry them in ten seconds, tops. The heavy-duty spellock on the door to Jacqui's cell took a minute or two, but eventually the disenchantment charms infused into Prick won out, and it opened with a fizzle of blue smoke.

It took me much less time to get the non-magical bindings off of Jacqui, and the gag out of her mouth. "Thank the stars you're here," Jacqui said as we embraced. "I knew you wouldn't leave me behind."

"Not a chance," I said with a smile. "We're just lucky I happened to be breaking and entering nearby."

"You always were a good skulker."

I gave a quick laugh before the seriousness of our situation sunk back in. It only took a few minutes to fill Jacqui in on what we'd discovered in the labs, and the Knights' plan to manufacture Largesse. "Tamsin made some sort of explosion downstairs, but it probably won't distract them for long—"

Jacqui's clear blue eyes caught mine. "Briar, we need to get Raye."

"I—Jacqui, we have enough dirt on the Knights now. We are gonna get *everyone* out, soon—"

"You know how you would never leave me behind? I can't leave her behind to have her blood taken by these monsters. I won't."

I nodded. "Of course. We'll get her." I tried to keep my mind from picturing what kind of *Weekend At Bernie's* shenanigans we would have to do to get a sleeping princess out of a high security prison. "The good thing is she's right down the hall."

I turned and stepped out of the cell, only to find a different hallway than the one we'd left. Where Raye's cell had been just a few minutes before was now a staircase leading upwards.

I swore under my breath. "Uh, scratch that. Disabling the spellock must've activated a Daedalus Charm. Everything has shifted."

Jacqui groaned. "Oh man, these are obnoxious. Remember when Macey's used to use these in their lingerie section, and you couldn't get out until you bought something?"

I threw Prick up in the air with a flourish, caught the handle underhanded, and jammed the blade straight into the wall to our right. The stone flickered, and then disappeared. Whatever industrial-grade illusion and/or spatial displacement magic was in this place, it was still no match for Prick.

"C'mon," I said, "I don't have time for any *Labyrinth* bullshit unless it involves David Bowie in those tights."

We covered decent ground, but even with Prick's help, it was slow going. The hallways before us twisted and rearranged themselves, the Daedalus Charm unraveling as I cut through more and more of it. Finally, I recognized the hallway where I'd hid from the Baron while he taunted Jacqui.

"That means…" I muttered, running through my mental map in my mind. "There! That one is Raye's cell."

Just as Jacqui made it to the little barred window, a group of Knights clomped up a nearby stairwell, shouting at us to surrender like they were all competing to be featured extras.

"Grimmsdammit," I swore, handing Prick to Jacqui. "You get the spellock open, I'll hold them off."

For once, even Jacqui was rattled. "Uh, Briar? Don't you need your weapon to fight?"

I smiled, turned to the guards, and pushed all the air out of my lungs. On the inhale, a half-dozen roses floated up from where I'd secreted themselves in my boots, belt, and sleeves. They rose up around me, and I could feel them trailing behind me, like floral wings sprouting from my shoulders.

A part of me was scared how easy this was getting. But hey, there had to be a few perks to finding out you were not completely human.

The guards were only a few yards away, but when I exhaled, all my roses shot forward, becoming swirling comets of petals, each striking a different guard. I hadn't had time to carefully select and curate the emotion blasts.

One guard dropped his sword as he was overcome with the existential dread of all birthdays after twenty-one.

Another got the tension of needing to cry but feeling emotionally constipated.

Two more got the feeling of panic when you can't find your wallet and keys, respectively.

A yellow bloom burst on a tall Knight's face, giving him the feeling of entering a room and pausing, unsure of what he'd come in for.

The last guard slumped against the wall with a satisfied grumble, as he got the best of the bunch. His rose's feeling was just that of a Saturday afternoon nap.

Not my best work, but most of those were bound to keep the guards reeling for at least the time we needed to get Raye and make our escape. Besides, if most of these whackjobs were as emotionally repressed as I suspected, they'd be caught in their feels for much longer.

The door to Raye's cell swung open, and Jacqui and I ran inside. Those bespelled manacles were going to be tricky, but so far Prick was batting a hundred when it came to overcoming the spells in this place.

Maybe the three of us would be the first people in the history of the Poisoned Apple to make it out of the White Tower.

Jacqui kept watch while I gingerly finagled Prick into the keyholes on Raye's manacles. I felt like I was moving slower than Goldilocks at a Golden Corral buffet, but I really didn't want to slip and make Jacqui's sister lose more blood. Luckily, the spells in Raye's bindings seemed more about keeping her from tearing down the walls than securing her cuffs, and I was able to get the second one off, sheathe Prick, and grab Raye, picking up the thin teenager without managing to stab her or myself.

As we made it back into the hallway, Jacqui grabbed a sword from one of the spell-shocked guards and we booked it in the opposite direction. The Daedalus charm seemed to have broken down completely, as no Escheresque mindbending happened as we ran towards the back staircase I'd used to get up here.

We were doing it. We were going to make it out.

No sooner had the thought crossed my mind than we turned the last corner. At the end of the hall, an arched window backlit the Baron and five more guards with crossbows as he waited at the top of the stairwell I had thought would lead us to safety. I gulped as the crossbow bolts pointed directly at us.

"How stupid do you have to be," the Baron drawled smugly, "to think that disabling half the security spells of the Apple's most sophisticated detention facility wouldn't alert us to your presence?"

My pulse quickened, but if he was still interested in gloating, I was going to indulge his James-Bond-villain impulses.

"Not as stupid as thinking the people of the Apple wouldn't find out about your illegal blood magic experiments on unconscious young girls," I snapped back. A few more of the crossbow bolts pointed at me, but I knew they wouldn't fire without the Baron's approval.

I was just hoping Jacqui and Raye's blood was too valuable to spill.

"The people of the Apple believe what I tell them to believe," the Baron spat, a glint in his eye. "They want to believe. People keep coming back to the stories I tell because they need them. Knights rescuing princesses and getting a happily ever after. That's all they want."

My mind raced, turning over the situation this way and that, trying to think of a way out. I was down to one rose, and even if I could get it charged and fired off with Raye in my arms, it wouldn't affect the whole lot of them. And precious blood or not, if I started slinging spells, I couldn't guarantee that the Knights wouldn't start firing.

"You have no idea what people want," Jacqui said. "They're not going to settle for old stories coming from cheap conmen. Not anymore. People are starting to wake up."

"If only the same could be said for your poor sister," he said with mock sympathy before turning his heartless eyes to mine. "Now, drop your weapons and give us the girl."

"No," Jacqui said, her voice hollow. "You can't have her."

"It wasn't a request." The Baron raised his hand, and the Knights readied their crossbows.

My eyes darted, from Jacqui, to the Baron, to Raye's sleeping form, before finally settling on the cruel, steel points of the crossbow bolts.

We were out of time.

"I'm sorry," I mouthed to Jacqui as I stepped forward, Raye squirming in my arms. One of the crossbowmen secured his crossbow to his back holster and stepped forward to take her.

"No!" Jacqui shouted, her voice ragged as I held her back. "Get the hell away from my sister, you bastards!"

"Such language from a young woman," Landgreaves said with a smile. "Now shut your mouth, before I decide I only need one source of D'Lucien Ardor blood."

Jacqui let out a choked sob of rage and threw her sword to the stone floor. The emotions I could smell radiating out from her were the same ones I was feeling.

This couldn't be it. This couldn't be the end. They couldn't win.

The guards put their crossbows away and swarmed us, three on each of us. They shoved me face first into the stone wall with enough force to knock the air out of my lungs. My head twisted awkwardly to the side as they yanked my arms behind me to put bespelled manacles on my wrists.

An eerie detachment settled over me as I caught a glimpse of the Apple outside the window. Somewhere out there, Tamsin was getting the recordings of the Baron's lab out into the world, and I knew my friends were going to fight like hell to bring the Knights down.

I just hoped I would be alive to see it.

Thinking of my friends brought me a strange, defeated sort of peace. Jacqui was right: people were starting to wake up, and soon the Apple would know the truth about the Knights. What I didn't know was whether enough of them were brave enough to stand up for that truth.

Tears started to cloud my vision of the Apple's skyline, the towers, the cottages, all the things I loved so much about my fantastic, incomprehensible city. The treeline of the Afterwoods danced in my vision, and I pictured Antoine, Cade, and the others trekking through, just as determined to set things right. To wake the Apple up.

I could see my house from here. And more than that, I could… feel my house.

The guards finished getting the manacles around my wrist and pulled me back from the wall. I locked eyes with Jacqui and gave her a quick nod. Her bewildered expression held a question, but I smiled at my friend.

It was going to be all right.

I inhaled, and with a pulling in my stomach, I felt the blossoms in the garden behind my house respond. The miles between us disappeared, and I caught a whiff of the sweet scent of their blooms as they lifted off their stems. As the blossoms took flight, a sense of weightlessness overtook me, brushing away the tension in my shoulders and the ache in my manacled arms.

"Get them down to the lab and tell the wizards to start taking samples," the Baron was saying to the guards who held Jacqui and me. "I especially want to figure out what that little flower witch's magic does."

I stood rooted to the spot, even as the Knight manhandling me pulled at my elbow. My eyes caught the Baron's, and when I spoke, I found my voice strong and unwavering. "I don't think you'll have to wait that long."

Landgreaves scowled. "What do you—"

Then he was yelling.

An explosion of petals flowed into the room, filling the space with the riotous colors of a circus tent. The guards all shouted, flailing about in the technicolor floral onslaught, but I just stood, watching the beauty of the flowers as they continued to pour into the room like multicolored sunbeams.

Soon, the blossoms did what they came for, and flowed out just as easily as they came. My awareness followed as the cloud of rose petals split, flying around the Apple, tracing the lines of towers and thatched roofs, soaring next to witches on their brooms, and dancing along the streetlights with the will-o-wisps. They visited the highest tower in the Aeries and the dingiest pub on Drury Lane, going wherever they were needed. As each cloud of flowers discharged its duty, the magic left it and it dissolved into a normal pile of petals once more, bringing a touch of color back to my city.

As the last of the petals came to a stop, I found myself back in my body, my head swirling. The Knights all checked themselves, surprised and confused. Landgreaves's scowl of confusion slowly resolved into a wicked grin.

"All that for nothing? Guess your magic isn't anything to worry about."

I grinned at him, baring my teeth so wide he took a step back. "Oh, honey. That spell wasn't for you."

Raye gave a theatrical yawn, her eyes fluttering open in pure princessly naivete. I could still feel the buzz of my magic within her and within all the others my petals had awoken from sleeping curses throughout the Apple. It had been easy, somehow. Just like I'd figured out what the complimentary emotion was to enter the World Tree in the forest, I knew what could awaken the princesses.

It was the feeling of being utterly, incredibly, heart-poundingly alive, so aware of the blood pumping through your heart that you could burst. It was extra-loud technicolor, a hum you could feel pulsing through everything always, as strange and unpredictable as anything I'd seen wandering the After-woods or the Dream Slip. It was good and bad, hilarious and heartbreaking, usually all at once. There was no way to feel that awake and still feel the grip of sleep, magical or not. Nobody who is alive, truly alive, will ever keep their eyes closed forever.

Raye's smile of contentment turned sour when she saw the Knight holding her. She squirmed in his arms, and he yelped and pushed her away from his chest. Twisting like a cat in mid-air, she landed on her feet and stumbled forward. The guard went for her, trying to scoop her up again, and in desperation Raye drew her elbow back into his chest. The blow landed like a jack-hammer, and the guard flew ten feet down the hallway, collapsing to the floor in a grinding sound of metal armor on the stone floor. Everyone stopped what they were doing to stare.

I guess my magic woke the princesses up but didn't take away their strength.

Raye barely had time to react before another guard, a tall, meaty half-orc who could've played linebacker, launched himself at her. But Jacqui shouted a warning, and her lithe sister got her hands up in time to grab the front of the Knight's armor, using his own momentum to swing him around and send him careening into the Baron and the rest of his honor guard, knocking them aside like bowling pins.

After breaking the laws of physics and probably at least a few bigots' bones, Raye shook her head, still waking up, and ambled over to us. "Jacqui? Briar? What's—where are we?"

"We're in the White Tower," Jacqui said, looking down at her manacles. "Do you mind—?"

"Oh, yeah," Raye said, still a little groggy. "Where are the keys?"

"I don't think you need one, kiddo," Jacqui said, a fierce smile shaping her words. "You've gone full Captain Marvel."

"Oh. Right."

With two strong yanks, Raye separated our manacles more easily than I open envelopes. We still had some badass metal armbands with chains around our wrists, but at least our hands were free.

The guards started to stir on the ground, and for the second time, I handed Prick over to Jacqui. "Get the rest of the prin-cesses out. If I'm not back in five minutes, take them to safety."

"Bri, what are you talking about?" Her voice was layered with misgiving, but Jacqui still took the dagger.

"The Baron. He ran up those stairs while the guards were still turtled on their backs in their armor."

"Bri, wait—"

I pulled out my last rose. "Don't worry, I got him."

Jacqui huffed her disapproval, but turned to start unlocking the nearest princess's cell. Raye went over to a guard who was trying to flip his heavy suit of armor onto his front and gave him a swift kick to the head. It looked like the D'Lucien-Ardor sisters had things well in hand.

My boots slapped the stone steps as I took them two at a time. I had seen the Baron take a nasty spill when Raye hammer-tossed that half-orc, so I hoped he hadn't gotten far. When I reached the top of the landing, I saw him slumped ten feet away, cradling one hand against his chest and fumbling with his mirror in the other.

I held the rose out in front of me, the emotions crackling around it like a Tesla coil. Landgreaves looked up, a sweaty sheen on his face. Whatever had happened to him in his fall, he was not feeling great.

"Go on," he spat, pushing himself up against the wall and letting his hand drop to his side. "You've got me right where you want me. End it."

"And turn you into a martyr for all the knuckleheads you've got following you?" I shook my head. "When all this settles down, prepare for a very dull, very drawn out, very public trial. I'm gonna make a tee shirt with your tax returns on it."

The Baron's body started to shake, but what I thought for a second was some sort of fit turned into a dry, bitter laugh. "You think I'll be the last? You think I'm the only one who is going to fight for a return to the way the Apple was? There will always be more of me."

Then the nasty son of a bitch spat at my feet.

Once I controlled my gag reflex, I recalled my magic back into my fingertips and put away my rose. "You're right, Your Lordship. There will always be more cockroaches trying to drag us back to the past. But there will also be more of me. And they'll have heard this story. They'll know that they can win."

The Baron bit back a response and shook his head, finally shutting his Grimmsdamn mouth. I smiled and drank in the silence for a moment before I heard Jacqui's voice calling my name from down the stairs.

It was when I took my eyes off of him that things seemed to start happening in slow motion, even though they took almost no time at all.

While I was distracted, the Baron's arm shot up, and I got the quickest flash of a small, sleek hand-crossbow as he readied to pull the trigger. As my world tunneled into a hyper focus, I saw the barbed tip, splattered with something green and toxic, point directly at my throat.

My legs buckled beneath me as I tried to drop to the floor, but I knew the bolt would travel the two feet between us faster than I could move. A deep, primal fear clenched deep within me as the resonant thrum of the crossbow's string propelled my death toward me.

I crumpled to the floor, my mind blank. Numb fingers I wasn't even sure were my own clutched at my neck and face, trying to find where the bolt had struck. I must have been in shock, because it felt like I was… fine?

Confused, I looked up to see an arm had snaked out of the cell behind Landgreaves and grabbed his arm. I looked and saw that the crossbow bolt had gone wide, having clattered to the floor down the hall.

With impressive strength, the thin arm grabbed the Baron violently by the forehead and jerked his head back into the bars.

The crack of his skull on metal made my stomach lurch, but I wasn't complaining as the asshole crumpled to the ground unconscious, his crossbow skittering harmlessly out of his hands.

My limbs were still jelly, but I somehow used their noodly consistency to push myself to my feet and peer into the cell.

"Hey girl." Miranda Grimmour's deadpan voice was instantly recognizable, but the girl in the cell barely resembled the glamorous princess I'd apprehended six months ago. Deep, dark circles slashed under her eyes, and she had the sickly pallor of a chicken cutlet.

"M-Miranda?" I stuttered. "I thought your dad sent you to some sort of high security boarding school."

"He did," she smiled, putting her slender face between the bars and watching me with the intensity of a caged tiger. "I kept escaping, so he pulled some strings to have me put in here under a fake name. He thinks it will teach me a lesson." She gave a fierce, hungry smile that made me think the things she was learning in that cell were not what her father intended.

"Um, thanks for, uh…" I trailed off lamely and gestured to the crumpled form of the Baron at her feet. "Thank you."

"Don't mention it. Guy seems like a piece of griffin shit."

"He is. He truly is," I said, and suddenly I was faced with the task of making small talk with the woman who had almost gotten me eaten by mountain giants. I cleared my throat.

"How's my brother?" Miranda asked, a little of the warmth I remembered present in her voice.

"He's good. He's been really happy with Rick," I said tersely. When I mentioned Rick's name, the boy she'd had kidnapped to try to start a war within the Multiarchy, she flinched. Her mask slid back into place and I was looking at the feral inmate once more. I decided to push my luck. "He's obsessed with finding the Arsenic Queens. Any leads you want me to send his way?"

Miranda rolled her bright blue eyes, still breathtaking despite the crappy lighting in her cell. "They were very cloak and dagger. We mostly communicated through coded messages and dead drops. They were bankrolling me with goons and magic, so I didn't look the gift basilisk in the mouth. But I know they had killer magic. I had never seen anything like it until…"

"Until what?"

"Until I saw you unleash your powers on top of Grimmour Tower."

We both paused, the scent of remembrance heavy in the hallway like incense. I remember threatening Miranda with a rose, promising to tear her apart and rewrite her very personality. Shame filled me, and my face went red.

"I'm… sorry, Miranda. I'm sorry things played out like they did. I know you were trying to help the Apple, in your own way, but… the things you did were wrong. I couldn't let them stand."

Miranda leaned in close, her slender fingers clinging around the bars. Instinctively, I mirrored her and got close as her voice got low and dangerous. "Briar, you can take your apology and shove it where a palantír can't see it. The only difference between you and me is that I know I'm in a cage. And neither of us will be free until it all falls down around us."

I stepped back, her words shaking me almost as much as the Baron's attempted murder. At that moment, Jacqui, Raye, and a gaggle of princesses started streaming up the steps, and Miranda gave me one more wicked smile before fading back into the darkness of her cell.

"Nice chatting with you, Bri," she said mockingly. "See you soon."

TWO WEEKS LATER, I was sitting in the rustic headquarters of the Red Hoods, tapping my leg as I spread out on a threadbare couch in their operations room. I stared at the large, enchanted map of the Apple hanging from the log cabin's wall, watching hundreds of red pins move themselves around the edges of the Afterwoods. Each one represented a Red Hood combing the forest for any sign of Cade, Ravenna, Linden, and Antoine.

Cade's squad mate Scuff McCorryn offered me a steaming mug of herbal tea, and I nodded my thanks as I took it. His instincts for hospitality were almost as strong as his cousin Flora's. Concern was written on his usually carefree face; the medic was just as concerned about Cade as I was. But until someone found something, all we could do was wait.

The rest of the Apple, on the other hand, felt like it was moving at high speed. After everything that went down at the White Tower, the public had turned on the Baron and his followers; many of them were now filling the cells of the prison they had been running a handful of days prior, awaiting the trial I'd promised. Their supporters were still voicing their support for Landgreaves, claiming the evidence of his misdeeds had been planted, or that the White Knights were the ones truly responsible for waking the princesses. Thankfully, these idiots were in the minority, and a small part of me was incredibly grateful that the average citizen of the Apple still hadn't hit that level of bonkers.

Part of the distrust of the "official" story was my fault. I'd asked Tamsin to cover for me and claim that she had been the one to wake the princesses. It took some convincing, but eventually we agreed it was better to have the public believe in the pedantic power of Academy magic than to tell them a descendant of all-powerful tree beings did it. I was still wrapping my mind around the truth myself, and in the meantime, I didn't need that kind of target on my back.

But the question that still plagued everyone, myself included, was: why? Why did someone want to give the princesses nightmares and at the same time empower them with magical strength?

I was going to find out. I was going to track down the Fata that was responsible and get some answers. But first, I needed my friends to come home.

"You know, you can wait at home," Scuff said gently. The Little Person had been watching over me in the days I'd been waiting for our friends' return, standing up to his Red Hood bosses to let me stay in their HQ. "I promise I will mirror you the instant we hear anything."

I shook my head violently; I couldn't go back to my house, couldn't handle sitting around waiting for the mirror to twinkle. Jacqui was staying in a guest room in her parents' tower, helping Raye adjust, and Alice had been working tirelessly to support the other princesses as they reacclimated to society. I'd mended fences with Tarris over a delicious lunch at the Second Breakfast, but he was still fixated on tracking down the Arsenic Queens, so he wasn't the best company at the moment. And I was pretty sure sitting alone in my living room with nothing but our ticking grandfather clock would break me.

Scuff's ocean-blue eyes lingered on me as my leg-tapping intensified. "Bri… Cade is the most skilled Red Hood I've ever worked with. I'm sure they will be back any second."

My throat scratched as I swallowed, trying to arrange my face into an expression of stoic positivity. Scuff wasn't necessarily wrong; with all the temporal weirdness we'd encountered in the fringes of the Afterwoods, this was well within the realm of possibility.

Then why was my intuition screaming that something was wrong?

With a swish of her maroon cloak, Anya Koronik stalked into the room, giving me an imperious look before she perched on a table to clean her crossbow. While I had little love for the third member of Cade's Red Hood squad, in his absence we'd managed to keep our feud to a simmer. "Caught another group of White Knight rebels in the caves near Hag's Pass," she said nonchalantly, waxing the string of her weapon. Their forces broken, many of the White Knights were whispering of open rebellion. But without the funding and legitimacy that the Baron provided, they were just a scattering of weirdos with swords.

Scuff wrinkled his nose in disgust. "Make sure we keep them in the outer holding cells. If they were hiding in the caves around Hag's Pass... most of the mushroom species around there are potent laxatives."

A ghost of a smirk graced my face, but my heart wasn't in it. Even thinking of the White Knights turning their uniforms brown wasn't enough to lift my spirits.

Anya's calloused hands paused, and the brunette swiveled her muscular body around with a predatory grace that still scared me. "Wait a tick," she said, her intensity barely muted by her droll British accent.

I followed her glance to where a cluster of red pins was forming on the map. As I watched, more and more pins seemed to converge on the same point. Anya had her mirror in her hand in a flash, punching in a series of runes to connect her to the nearest squad leader.

"Muzzy, what are you—" She paused, listening to the voice on the other line. "Roger that, and they're not injured?" Even Anya's perma-scowl thawed when the Hood on the other end of the line confirmed that my friends were okay.

I was already on my feet, although I didn't remember getting up. "Where are they?"

My eyes traced the map from where the Red Hoods were gathering into the Apple. They were right outside Havmercy. Specifically, about half a mile from my own backyard.

"Well," Scuff said as we all grabbed our coats, "looks like you could've stayed home after all."

AN EARLY OCTOBER CHILL tingled in the air as our BroomVroom zoomed towards Havmercy. The endless leaves of the Afterwoods stretched towards the horizon, riddled with the yellow and orange hues teasing the autumnal fireworks to come. Anya had stayed behind at the Red Hoods HQ, so I was currently sandwiched between Scuff and a very burly witch with an impressive beard. He guided the broom down onto my front yard and let us off.

"Remember to rate me five pentagrams!" he called out, hitching his striped stockings up and pushing off from the ground, but I was already running around the back of our cottage towards the woods.

My backyard was awash in the crimson cloaks of the Red Hoods. I hadn't been back here much in the weeks since I'd used the entire garden's worth of petals to wake the princesses; the empty stalks and browning thorns were gloomy reminders of the approaching winter. I scanned desperately through the crowd. There was Ravenna, with a pair of healers putting a cast on her broken arm. Linden sat on my favorite bench, curled up under one of those blankets they give to people in shock while he badgered a Red Hood into getting him a LaCroix. It took me longer to find Cade, as he blended in with the other Hoods so well, but I eventually spotted him huddled over a map with other squad leaders, charting out the course they'd taken back to the Apple.

I looked back through the crowd.

I looked again.

I could feel my heart stop.

Antoine was nowhere to be found.

By this point, the others had noticed me, and Cade, Linden, and Ravenna came rushing forward. I took a step back, panic starting to clench my ribs like a vice.

No. No no no nononono—

"He's alive," Ravenna said, but the tension and heartbreak in her tone did little to assuage my terror. Linden and Cade's faces caved in sympathy, and I was filled with the irrational desire to strike out at them, to shake them until they told me where Antoine was.

"What happened? Where is he?" I shouted. The Red Hoods around us turned to look, but I didn't care. My awareness of the world was narrowing to the three people in front of me.

"He—I—I made a mistake," Ravenna said, hanging her head. Although she couldn't meet my eyes, I smelled the saltwater tears beginning to overspill her long lashes.

Improbably, the theme song from Knight Rider started playing from my pocket. It took me a second to realize that was the ringtone I'd given to Antoine, a reference to some stupid inside joke I didn't even remember. I tore the mirror out of my pocket, the barest feelings of relief blooming in my stomach when I saw Antoine's face in the frame.

"Let's give her some space," Cade said, his voice booming throughout the yard. The Hoods moved quickly and efficiently at his command; Linden lingered near me, his eyes silently asking if he should stay. I shook my head and tried to swallow the bad taste my panic had left in my mouth.

In a few moments I was alone in my ravaged garden, looking into Antoine's soft brown eyes as I accepted the call. Instantly, the mirror rose out of my hand, spilling sparks of soft blue light—I'd forgotten I'd let Tarris enchant my mirror with that ridiculous SparkleCast spell. It seems he'd had it set to full blast, because my mirror kept barfing twinkling lights until an entire life-size version of Antoine stood in front of me, just under the arched trellis in the center of my yard.

"Briar? Ravenna let me know they just made it back." For all the theatrics of the special effects creating his image, his voice was his own, measured and melodic.

The motes of energy that made up his form blurred as my eyes filled with tears. "Antoine? Where are you? Why aren't you here?"

He smiled, sad and sweet. "I'm fine. I'm safe. I'm just... not able to get back to the Apple right now."

"What happened?" I could tell he was trying to ease me into it, but I just needed to hear the truth, to find some footing after everything had been torn out from under me.

"It was just after you left—Ravenna thought she had enough strength to create another portal back to the Apple. Well, that's not completely true. After I saw you disappear, I begged her to try again, to send me after you. She wasn't sure, but she tried it, she tried to channel another gate through the water of the Worldpools and... I got stuck."

"Stuck where?" I asked hoarsely.

"Not sure yet," Antoine said with a sad smile, still staring at me like I was a cozy coffee shop on a rainy day. "It's a World Slip, but a little more... abstract. Ravenna thinks it's the aetheric space we use to communicate between mirrors. The good news is I don't seem to get hungry here, or need to sleep..."

"...and the bad news is we can't get you out?"

"Ravenna's been trying. That's why I didn't want to say anything until they got back, in case she was able to fix it and I wouldn't have to worry you. But she's been working on a way to get me out, and now that she's back and can use the Academy's resources, hopefully I'll be out in no time."

"Hopefully?" I said. I still felt like the ground beneath me was constantly shifting, like I was a chess piece on a board in the hold of the Titanic.

"Briar," Antoine said, his voice breaking for the first time. "I'll come back to you. I promise."

"You can't—"

"*I promise*," he said. Even through the mirror I felt the strength of his words, the thrum of magic that accompanies all oaths in the Apple, but I still couldn't help thinking it was a vow he might not be able to keep.

I spent a good long moment trying not to cry, trying to be strong for him. He was the one stuck in some bullshit Matrix dimension; I shouldn't be the one breaking down. But I clearly wasn't doing a good job, because I could see the heartbreak in his face.

In unison, we both said, "I'm sorry" and stopped. Antoine took the initiative. "I'm sorry we won't be able to have our Very Adult Talk for a little while longer. I… don't want to force you to wait for me."

A pained smile found its way to my face. "DuCarr, you couldn't force me to do anything if you tried."

Antoine gave a quick chuckle. "I know, but—"

"I'm waiting. That's that. We'll do this long distance until then."

"Between dimensions is a very long distance—"

"Then I'll expect a call every night."

Antoine raised his head, looking me deep in the eyes. Even though he was made of glittering motes of illusion magic, it was the realest thing I'd felt in weeks. Slowly, he extended his hand, cupping my cheek with his long fingers. It felt like the kiss of a butterfly's wings.

"This wasn't how I expected our story to go," I said quietly.

"Me neither," he said, his voice deep and husky. "But then again, you've always been better at forging ahead with new plots."

I leaned into his hand, the tears threatening to overspill my eyes again. For now, it was enough to just stand like this in my ruined garden, together and yet so, so far apart.

"ONE GINGER ALE PLEASE, Josie."

Josefina Campbell raised a perfectly arched eyebrow at me. I hadn't been able to stay in my house, hadn't been able to face Ravenna and the rest of them, so I'd snuck out to the Woodsman's Log for a drink. Only my stomach was still in knots after Antoine and I had finally hung up, his starry form dissolving into a few stray sparks on the wind. So the thought of adding mead to my sour, emotion-scorched digestive tract seemed terrible.

Josefina flipped her long turquoise braid behind her shoulder and filled a pint glass with sparkling soda from a small wooden keg behind the bar. I offered her a five as she slid it over, but she turned my money away. "You okay, hun?" she said, her usually barbed voice smooth and low. It was a slow night, and the wood-paneled bar was mostly empty.

"Do you ever feel like no matter what you do, no matter how hard you try, your life's story is a largely plotless cosmic joke?"

Josefine took a step back, considering my words. She was dressed down, for her, in a navy-checked Bavarian dress like she was a barmaid at Oktoberfest. Her bright green wig was twisted to the side in an elegant braid that hung down to her waist and her elegantly manicured lilac nails clicked as she poured herself a shot of aqua vitae and downed it in a flash.

"All right, continue," she said, leaning in and fixing me with a sympathetic look from under the cover of her smoky eye.

"I…" I didn't know where to start. "I thought I was doing everything right. I put myself out there, I made a scary choice and did the mature thing for the first time ever, thinking that would lead me to something wonderful. And even after all that, I still got the stuffing kicked out of me."

Josefina nodded sagely, tapping her nails on the bar as she considered my words. "Do you regret it?"

"Yeah, everything has gone completely pear-shaped—"

"Right, but do you regret putting yourself out there?"

The ginger ale bubbles burst against my tongue as I took a gulp to give me time to think. "I… guess not."

"I get it. We all wish the world rained down riches on us when we did the right thing, or made a hard choice, but a lot of the time the only reward is more tough choices and more shit to go through," Josefina said. "Maybe your life didn't change, or it even got worse. But if you changed, if you learned something… I'd call that a win. I mean think of those princesses under the curse."

"What about them?"

"Those chicks went through hell. First, their families give them magical chloroform and trap them for who knows how long, then they're tormented by some still unknown magical assailant, before the wizards finally cook up some way to break all of the sleeping curses in the Apple."

I nodded along like I wasn't culpable. It was a skill I'd developed over the years.

"And after all that, the confusion, the suffering, they wake up to a world that's changed and find out they have Grimmsdamn super strength. Again, no explanation, no clear cause and effect, no direction of where to go from here. It's up to them to figure out how they're going to move through the world now, and honestly, I'm excited to see what happens. Just last night, one of them was in here, and this younger girl was getting hassled by a White Knight. The princess bent his sword into a pretzel and spanked him with it until he ran out. *It was awesome*." Josefina continued wiping down the bar as she spoke, her voice more grounded and human than the performative tone she used when calling out trivia answers.

"That reminds me," I said, still processing her advice. "I was here for trivia night, that day the princesses started screaming. We never got to finish, but you asked that question, about destiny or something?"

Her violet lips broke into a toothy grin. "The quote from Dante! That's right, you never heard the answer. I love that one—the full thought is, 'Do not be afraid; our fate cannot be taken from us; it is a gift'."

My ginger ale fizzed as I swirled it absent-mindedly in the glass. Antoine, the princesses, the Fata, my powers… sometimes I wished it could all be taken from me. I dreamed I could get a cosmic mulligan and start over, spend my life doing hot yoga and data entry. I didn't choose any of this.

If I were to believe Dante—who, let's be real, was best known for writing biblical fanfic—all the bullshit in my life was a gift. If I were to believe Josefina—better choice—the chaos I'd dealt with was making me strong, preparing me to deal with even more bullshit.

I guess the million-dollar question was, what fresh bullshit was coming my way?

THREE GINGER ALES LATER, I made it to my bedroom without running into any of my friends; whether this was a result of stealth on my part or respect for boundaries on theirs, I couldn't tell. But after pouring my heart out to Josefina, and at least knowing Antoine was alive, I fell asleep more quickly than I had in weeks.

So when I awoke back in the Afterwoods, in the strange, mist-soaked clearing near the base of the World Tree, I knew I was dreaming. Linden had gone to stay with some friends in the Cast-Iron District, so I hadn't been having any dreams this… vivid. The loamy scent of the earth beneath me, the chill of the dew on the leaves under my butt all felt completely authentic. I sat up in the moss and looked around for my cousin.

"Linden?" I called out, my voice hollow in the uncanny silence of the forest. The swirling mist gave no answer. A dull, languid light suffused the entire scene, either a sluggish morning glow or the tired afternoon sun, I couldn't be sure. The clearing around me looked exactly as I remembered it, making me wonder whose dream I was invading—it felt too distinct to be my own jumbled subconscious.

With nothing better to do, I walked towards the massive trunk in front of me. Even within the dream, I felt the pulses of emotion echoing out from it, just as I had in the real world.

"It's our way of calling to those who belong with us," a voice said from behind me. I whirled around, but all I could see was mist. The voice reminded me a bit of the soundless, almost telepathic way that Iamb communicated, but there were more identifiably human tones underneath it, a syrupy, feminine tone that vibrated the air around me.

As I scanned the mist, I realized the familiar weight of Prick was suddenly in my hand. The unseen voice noticed too. "Nice trick. I'm glad to see you've grown attached to my gift."

I shook my head, trying to clear it as the dreamscape whirled around me. "I'd love to thank you in person. What's your name?"

"Names, names, names. You should be careful, Briar Pryce, with whom you share your name. You met our ancestor…what name did it give you? Iamb? Very cute. Why don't you call me… Caesura."

A movement out of the corner of my eye captured my attention, and I saw a figure emerge from the shadow of the tree. I understood now why she hadn't been visible before; her skin was the same pale grey of the bark, and she wore a sleeveless flowing gown, just a few shades darker than her skin. While Iamb was distinctly alien, a creature made in a vague resemblance to humanity, the woman who approached me was a beautiful human made uncanny with her strange, plantlike features and obsidian-black eyes. The voluminous hair she'd swept off her face was the tangled brown of living roots, dotted here and there with brilliant orange leaves.

"As you can guess, we're related," Caesura deadpanned. "I lost track of the lineage, sometime around the Renaissance, but 'cousins' is probably as good a word as any to describe us."

"Would calling you great-great-grandma make you feel too old?" I said, my smart mouth the only part of me that wasn't in panic mode at the creature in front of me.

"I was one of the first hybrids of human and Fata. I was there when the Poisoned Apple was spun from stories and spiderwebs. I do not fear the passage of time as you do. That being said, call me 'grandma' at your own peril."

Was that a small twitch at the corner of her mouth? I couldn't tell.

"Well, Cousin Caesura, what am I doing here?"

"I thought it was time we finally met. I've been watching you for decades now, and I think you're ready to hear me out."

I gripped the handle of Prick tighter. She was so casual as she threw out the idea that she'd been stalking me for years, and I found that nonchalance terrifying. "So you're responsible for sending me Prick? And cursing Jacqui, helping Miranda almost overthrow the Apple… you're the head of the Arsenic Queens?"

She inclined her head casually. "You're a smart girl, cousin."

Even in this strange Dream Slip, I felt the blood pounding in my veins. "Why?"

"Our bloodline is thinning out, Briar. People like you and Linden come along maybe once in a generation, if that. So I took it on myself to shepherd you into your powers, giving you that weapon, throwing obstacles in your way so the magic pumping through your veins would find its full expression. I wanted you to become the force of nature I see before me, to be worthy of taking a place at my side."

"You…" I stammered, actually lost for words. "You turned my best friend into a cat *to help me build character*?!"

"You're welcome," Caesura purred, the same hint of a smile playing on her lips. I began to wonder if stabbing her in the Dream Slip would do any good. It would sure feel good.

"And the princesses? Were you the one responsible for torturing them?"

Her almond-shaped face tilted downward, as if she were… embarrassed? "I have to admit, that was an unfortunate and unforeseen side effect. I was manifesting a great working through the tree, and I didn't realize the ripples it would create in the Apple."

"It was… all of that was a *side effect*?"

"This conversation will take much longer if you insist on restating everything I say."

I quickly calculated whether I was close enough to fling my dagger at her face, but I figured that would be petty at best and self-destructive at worst. "What were you actually trying to do?"

"There was one particular sleeping curse I was trying to break, one that has been in existence since the beginning of the Apple. It has grown obstinate over the years, calcified with the magic of your world overspilling its bounds. But I've determined it's time for it to be broken."

It was all too much, the offhanded way she was talking of centuries-old magic and cosmic curses. "Who were you trying to wake?"

Caesura smiled like a cat with the cream, and a door opened in the bark behind her. "I'll show you."

I was fairly certain she couldn't actually hurt me through my dreams, but, given all the new things I was still learning, I wasn't exactly sure. Her arrogance made it clear that if she intended me any harm, I would be powerless to stop her.

She turned and stepped through the door, and against my better judgment, I followed.

The inside of the tree was darker than I remembered, the book-lined walls just barely visible in the gloom. A golden glow lit the tree's central column, at the base of which a large table was set. Caesura was already standing on the opposite side from me as I walked up.

On the table was set a beautiful, intricate model of the Poisoned Apple and the Afterwoods surrounding it. The level of detail was mind-boggling, from the glittering cobblestones of Looking Glass Lane to the bits of luminescent moss growing on the roof shingles of Grimmour Tower. For a moment, I was awestruck, walking around the table and reveling in seeing my city from a bird's eye view.

"It's beautiful, isn't it? Seeing your world like this, above it like a goddess."

Her black eyes gleamed as I looked up from the model to meet them. Something in her tone felt dangerous, and I waited for her to finish her thought.

"What if you could craft your own world, Briar? What if, instead of living in the world the Fata created those many generations ago, you could have a hand in growing your own Garden of Eden? What would you create? Somewhere free from a cruel, uncaring Nobility with unrivaled control? A world where harsh, avaricious men like Baron Landgreaves got what they deserved?"

Her seductive words wrapped around me like velvet, but I shook my head. "Spare me the sales pitch. What do you want from me?"

"Exactly that. Your assistance in growing a new World Slip from the ground up. You've got power. True power. You're ready now, ready to join me in the pantheon of this incipient universe."

The flowery words, the display of the Apple, it was all too curated, too *perfect*. If twenty-three years in a fairy tale pastiche had taught me anything, it was that the shiniest apples hid the most poisonous cores.

"What's the catch?"

"It shouldn't come as a surprise… for one World Slip to be born, another must die. There is no creation without equivalent destruction."

I hate it when I'm right.

My hands came up in a defensive gesture, and I stepped away from the table. "I'm sorry, you've watched me for years.

What in the name of Snow White's sweet ass would make you think I'd agree to help you destroy my home?"

"Oh, Briar," Caesura said with a condescending smile. "I'm asking for your help with the creation. The destruction has already begun."

My heart stopped for a second and I shook my head, not trusting a word she said. "The spell you were working... who were you trying to wake?"

"Look closer."

The dreamworld around me tunneled into the icy sharp focus of a nightmare, and I stepped forward to the model. My eyes traced the turrets and towers of the Apple, but after a moment, my eyes blurred, seeing patterns and shapes I'd never noticed before. The shape of the hills around Castle Fortnight, the twisting of the streets. I focused on the sharp peak of Drake Mountain, with its twin caves at the base. The ones that exhaled warm air from their depths.

It wasn't a mountain—it was a nose. The entire Apple rested on the sleeping figure of a man, so massive my city took up only a section of his chest. My head spun—the scale was so massive, it was almost impossible to see.

"Who—who is that?"

"The giant at the center of all of this. My intent was to wake him, to empower him with the strength needed to tear off the city that has been festering on him for centuries, leeching the magic from his very heart. I had no idea some of that spell was getting siphoned off to affect the Apple's sleeping beauties."

"And what now? What happens if he wakes?"

Her smile cut like a knife to the stomach. "You'll find out soon enough, dear cousin. And thank you. It took someone truly powerful to break all the sleeping curses in the Apple."

ACKNOWLEDGEMENTS

This book, and the one that preceded it, would not have existed without the help of a fantastic cast of characters, who will, I hope, forgive my oversight in not including any acknowledgements in Book One.

First off, to the amazing team at Bleeding Ink—Sherry, Jon, Ethan, Stephenee, and all my talented & kind fellow authors—thank you so much for believing in this story and working tirelessly to find its audience for its first edition. What I've learned from you about the business of telling stories has been invaluable. And to my champions at Owl Hollow Press—Emma, Hannah, and the rest of the flock—thank you for your incredible enthusiasm and fresh perspective on my work; I'm so excited to continue this journey with you!

To my Honors Thesis Committee at Cornell, Professors Thomas Hill, Michael Koch, and Kathleen Long, thank you for taking the time out of your grading period to read and respond to an overambitious undergraduate's fantasy novel. Also, thank you to Rebecca Gowers, who provided much needed tough love to my first manuscript when it was in its infancy.

A massive thank you to Cristi Marchetti, whose early belief in this world and continued interest ensured its publication. Your dedication has earned you at least a small fiefdom of your choosing in the Poisoned Apple.

To the friends I've had, throughout the years and across the continents, who have contributed to the patchwork of names, dialogue, relationships, and puns that characterizes Briar's funny family of friends, thank you. My words can't capture the magic I've been fortunate enough to experience by your side.

And finally, to my family, Ann, Tom, Danny, and Claire, thank you for being a support system, cheerleading squad, and sounding board throughout all my creative adventures and misadventures. From my first words to my final proofreads, you've always been there for me.

SCOTT MOONEY is a writer, improviser, and director from Ann Arbor, Michigan. Even before he could hold a pencil, he dictated stories to his parents.

He currently lives in Chicago after time in New York, Los Angeles, England, and a dozen fantasy worlds of his own creation.

His debut novel, *Pricked*, was written during his studies at Cornell University and Oxford University.

WWW.SCOTTMOONEYWRITER.COM

#Pricked
#ScreamingBeauty
#TalesfromthePoisonedApple

www.ingramcontent.com/pod-product-compliance
Lightning Source LLC
Chambersburg PA
CBHW060805190726
48285CB00002B/557